THE MISSING ONES

OTHER TITLES BY A. R. TORRE

A Happy Marriage

The Last Party

A Fatal Affair

A Familiar Stranger

The Good Lie

Every Last Secret

The Ghostwriter

The Girl in 6E

Do Not Disturb

If You Dare

PRAISE FOR A. R. TORRE

The Last Party

"Even savvy veterans who predict every twist will keep turning the pages compulsively as the mystery curdles into suspense."

—*Kirkus Reviews*

A Fatal Affair

"Nothing is remotely routine in Torre's heady brew of serial murder spiced with fraud, torture, impersonation, and assorted celebrity hijinks . . . you won't put it down till every last drop of blood has been shed."

—*Kirkus Reviews*

"A thriller with surprises aplenty and a breezy pace that includes well-written characters and the singular challenge of looking for truth 'in a sea of professional liars and seducers,' this novel is sure to have wide appeal."

—*Library Journal*

A Familiar Stranger

"A whiplash suspenser that's a model of its kind."

—*Kirkus Reviews*

"The author skillfully reveals the characters' many lies and secrets. Torre knows how to keep the reader guessing."

—*Publishers Weekly*

The Good Lie

"Ambitious and twisty . . . Great bedtime reading for insomniacs and people willing to act like insomniacs just this once."

—*Kirkus Reviews*

"This kinky tale is compulsively readable."

—*Publishers Weekly*

"A blend of serial-killer story, court cases, and even romance, this is a tricky story that will keep readers going."

—*Parkersburg News and Sentinel*

Every Last Secret

"Deliciously, sublimely nasty: *Mean Girls* for grown-ups."

—*Kirkus Reviews*

"Torre keeps the suspense high . . . Readers will be riveted from page one."

—*Publishers Weekly*

"A glamorous and seductive novel that will suck you in and knock you sideways. I love this story, these characters, and the raw emotion they generated in me. I devoured every word. Exceptional."

—Tarryn Fisher, *New York Times* bestselling author

"Raw and riveting. A clever ride that will make you question everyone and everything."

—Meredith Wild, #1 *New York Times* bestselling author

THE MISSING ONES

A. R. TORRE

This is a work of fiction. Names, characters, organizations, places, events, and incidents are either products of the author's imagination or are used fictitiously. Otherwise, any resemblance to actual persons, living or dead, is purely coincidental.

Published by Thomas & Mercer, Seattle

www.apub.com

EU product safety contact:
Amazon Media EU S. à r.l.
38, avenue John F. Kennedy, L-1855 Luxembourg
amazonpublishing-gpsr@amazon.com

ISBN-13: 9781662534218 (paperback)
ISBN-13: 9781662534201 (digital)

Cover design by Logan Matthews
Cover images: © Sarawoot / Shutterstock; © oak-motion / Unsplash

Printed in the United States of America

To Ana.
If I ever disappear, I'm leaving Donut with you.

In Crestmore, no one spoke of the summer of 2021. It clashed with the crisp white gloves of the doormen, the green lawns cut twice a week, the fresh lilies on polished teak surfaces, the perfect smiles and surgically corrected noses on trophy wives who sported three-carat rings.

That year, three residents of Crestmore disappeared. Here one day, gone the next. For some, like Roxanne Kendal, their disappearance was immediately noticed. Police were called, search parties sent out, investigations conducted. For others, like David Batcher, it started with whispers, followed by questions, suspicions, then outright accusations. Country club memberships were rescinded and friendships broken.

With all three, we never got an answer. Bodies were never found, the crimes unanswered for. That summer was a bloodstain on our perfect community, one that eventually faded, the spot scrubbed clean until it was as if it had never happened at all.

But for the three of us, we didn't forget that stain. We couldn't. That history was a part of our lives, the stench of it heavy in our households, the air tainted with the ghosts of the missing.

We were the spouses, and in 2026, our ghosts came back.

CHAPTER 1

ANDREA KENDAL

"She's a trophy wife. Think plastic Barbie with a head full of nothing."

1442 Kingsmere Drive
Hole 6, Stone Hollow

Andrea Kendal sat in a rocking chair on her wide front porch, a steaming cup of espresso in hand, and watched the parade of masked men swarm the tee box across the street. They were all in blue jumpsuits, waders on, with sticks, cameras, and flashlights in hand, methodically combing the neatly cut golf course fairway and venturing into the neighboring woods.

It was, to put it lightly, out of the norm for Crestmore Estates, a neighborhood that prided itself on perfection without disturbance. Andrea took a sip and pondered what they might be looking for. Was this an environmental inspection? Was there a radiation leak? She had a moment of concern for her own health, then noticed a group of three men, standing by one of the all-white vehicles, all mask-less. One of them strode around the front of the car, and she saw the big block letters across the back of his jacket.

SFPD

San Francisco Police Department.

A chill ran down her spine, and she set her mug on the small adjacent table and stood. She walked slowly and calmly, in case they were watching, down the row of rocking chairs and to the mansion's double front doors. She sneaked a glance over her shoulder, but the men were still focused on the course. Pushing down on the door handle, she quickly stepped inside and closed the door.

"Eric!" she called out to her husband, who was in their formal dining room, with the newspapers and his breakfast. He subscribed to three—*The Wall Street Journal*, *The New York Times*, and the *San Francisco Chronicle*. Dozens of trees killed every year just so he could flip through the stacks while eating three boiled eggs and extra-crispy turkey bacon. In an attempt to manage their carbon footprint, Andrea had a section of the garage dedicated to recycling bins—one for glass, one for paper, and one for plastics. The containers were beside the compost depository and emptied twice weekly. But recycling didn't make up for the waste, which was why a seed of irritation ran through her each morning she collected the newsprint stack from the front porch.

"What?" Eric called, his voice muffled by the thousand-square-foot stretch between them. She hurried to the entrance to the dining room so he could hear her better.

"Something's happening on the golf course. They're looking for something."

"They lose balls all the time, honey." He flipped a page and shook out the newspaper, getting it into place.

"No, this is the police. There's dozens of them."

This got Eric's attention. He set down the paper and looked at her over the top of his reading glasses. "The police are out there?"

She jerked her chin in a stiff nod. "Come look." She moved the curtains on one of the front windows aside and pointed. It was hard to see past the porch furniture, columns, and mature landscaping, but across the road, the men were visible.

Eric rose and journeyed down the long table to join her side. He glanced through the part in the curtains, then continued on to the front stateroom, which was their interior designer's term for the large sunlit area that overlooked the front gardens and tree-lined road. It was one of Andrea's favorite rooms, especially in the mornings. Once Cameron and Ryder were happy and settled into their activities, she loved to open the windows and curl up in one of the big soft chairs by the built-in bookshelves that stretched all the way to the ceiling. During the winter, she liked to light a fire in the small hearth; if there was a more perfect combination of smells than smoky charred wood and the vanilla scent of the sweet box shrubs outside the windows, she didn't know what it was.

It had been Roxanne who had designed the layout of the room and worked with the designer on the feel and utility of the space. Eric's first wife had had a degree in interior design, and there had been no need for Andrea to change anything when she moved in with Cameron on her hip. Some women in the neighborhood had thought it strange, Andrea using another woman's house as is, so over time she'd redone some of the social spaces, just for appearances' sake—but it had never felt right, like the house was wearing clothes that didn't fit. It had been better before. Everything had seemed better before.

"I wonder if someone's on the run. Those dogs are probably following a scent." Eric pointed to a pair of German shepherds who were straining on their leashes, heading toward the woods.

Andrea thought of the news footage from five years ago—the packs of search dogs that had scoured the park for weeks, trying to find Roxanne's body. They hadn't been successful in following her blood trail or scent, though they had unearthed a pile of bones that gave the public a burst of excitement, until it was revealed they were coyote remains.

One of the police turned in their direction, and Andrea immediately stepped back, away from the window. "Do you think they can see us here?"

“They aren’t looking. This isn’t about us. Don’t we have binoculars somewhere?” His nose was almost touching the glass, which fogged from his breath.

Andrea moved to the built-in cabinets underneath the bookshelves, opening the doors and uncovering board games, a few extra throw blankets, and . . . There. She grabbed the binocular case and opened it up. The manual and tags were still on the expensive pair, and she peeled off the protective sticker from the lenses before handing it to Eric. “Maybe someone’s lost. A kid or someone with dementia. There’s that older couple down at the end of the lane. There was an ambulance in their driveway last week.”

A lost individual was more likely than someone being on the run. It wasn’t as if they lived near a prison or a bad area. Just to get in the neighborhood, someone had to go through two gates and a security checkpoint. There wasn’t a house in this neighborhood worth less than $4 million, which was probably why there was this level of response. Wealthy areas rarely had to call the police, but when they did, law enforcement scrambled into action.

So different from the area she’d grown up in. There, they had been taught, from the time they could talk, that a uniform was the one person you never ran to for help. If a cop asked questions, you pinned your lips shut. And the disdain had gone both ways. If anyone called the police for help, it might be an hour before one showed up, assuming they did at all.

Her husband adjusted the scope on the binoculars, his shoulders hunched forward, stance stiff. Eric had attended Stanford, then med school at UCLA. He was a stickler for rules, had been his whole life. Prior to Roxanne, he had never had any interaction with law enforcement other than a pleasant exchange over a minor traffic infraction.

His breakfast wouldn’t get finished today. Not with this far more interesting distraction.

“Look.” Andrea tapped on the window, at a golf cart that was approaching from the left. “More cops.”

"I think those are the neighborhood security—but look over here." He passed her the binoculars and pointed to the edge of the woods. "That's the police chief. He wouldn't be here unless it was something big."

"Is this what it was like at the park? This many people?"

Treveley Park. Blood all over the scene. His first wife: gone.

"No." Eric shook his head. "At least not when I was there. I saw a half dozen officers. But maybe there were more in the woods. They didn't let me go there."

Andrea thought of the woods around the parking lot. The thick trees. The running path that went deep into the park. The lot had been at the north end of the Treveley Park trail and rarely used at that time of day. Not a good place for a woman, alone. The crime scene photos from Roxanne's attack were all over the internet, mostly on sites run by her family, who still hadn't given up the hunt. The photos detailed in high resolution the blood smears on the Audi's door handle and on the monogrammed leather steering wheel.

Too much blood. Overkill.

Andrea lowered the binoculars, suddenly nauseated at the thought. "You should go get changed for work. I'll watch and tell you if anything happens."

He gave one last look out the window and nodded. "Don't worry," he repeated. "This isn't about us."

CHAPTER 2

SARA BATCHER

"Oh, I always knew Sara killed David. Meet her and you'll see that her whole scrawny body is bottled up with the guilt—so much she's, like, vibrating from it. I swear, her head's going to pop off one day from keeping it all in. I'm telling you, it's the women with the to-do lists that you should be the most scared of."

16 Branwyn Hill
Hole 18, Silverwood Preserve

Sara Batcher was power-walking down the neighborhood's main avenue, wrist weights on, music pumping through her headphones, when the crime scene investigation vans passed. An alarm bell chimed in her head at the sight of the white vans with bold green lettering. Not a good sign, and not something that belonged in this neighborhood, where Rolls-Royces were as common as guesthouses. The vans meant that someone would receive a visit from a set of uniforms, the officers' faces grave, their voices somber. Today's date would, for the rest of that person's life, be a painful reminder of what had happened.

May 5. That was her date.

That morning, David had joked with her about her inability to knot a tie. He'd kissed her on the way out, spirits high as his body responded to the pills. There had been no sense of foreboding. No mental warning that that kiss would be the last one she would receive. She hadn't followed him to the door, or called him at lunch, or thought anything strange when he wasn't home by dinner. It wasn't until she'd woken up in the middle of the night, her body tense, her breath short, heart hammering, that she had a hint that anything was wrong. She'd lain there in the dark and tried to understand what the panic was from—what meeting she had forgotten, what email she hadn't responded to, what voicemail she'd left unreturned.

It had taken her forty-five minutes to fall back asleep, and she hadn't, for one moment, considered that David was the source of her anxiety. A wife, alone in a bed, who hadn't heard from her husband in more than eighteen hours . . . she should have at least called him. Looked to see if his location was turned on. Sent him a text just to see if he was up.

Maybe he would have answered. Maybe he would have texted her back. Maybe his location had been visible and she would have been able to give the police something to help them in their search.

Instead, she had rolled onto her side and gone through the fine points of the deposition questionnaire her company's legal department had sent over. She thought about wording and positions and how the deposition could help or hurt the value of the company, until her eyes grew heavy and she fell asleep.

May 5 had never received the proper level of alarm. There had never been a knock on Sara's door or a solemn announcement. There had been no body, no crime scene, no clues—and therefore, no funeral, no tearful memory recaps or condolences offered. She had been cheated of all that and, instead, treated with a general mix of suspicion and pity. According to everyone they knew, Sara had either killed David or run him off. The judgment seemed to be evenly divided, and neither take garnered sympathy.

A police car passed, then another, then a K9 van. Sara paused her playlist and turned to look back, curious if there were more. She had lived in Crestmore for nine years and could count on one hand the number of times she'd seen a law enforcement vehicle inside the gates. The neighborhood's security vehicles were always around. But San Francisco PD? No. Even when David's disappearance had been deemed suspicious, it was a detective's unmarked car that had pulled into the gates, not this level of alarm-inducing presence.

"It's strange, right?" The dark-haired woman in the house with the gaudy red metal roof stood at the end of her drive, one hand to her temple, shielding against the sun. "You have any idea what's going on?"

"No." Sara strode across the cobblestone road toward her. "Some forensic vans passed by just a minute ago, so something must have happened."

"Maybe a murder." The woman's eyes gleamed and she craned her thin neck, trying to see down the road in the direction they had gone. "I gotta tell you, this would be the first exciting thing that's happened in ages. Wouldn't it be something if someone was killed? You know that big house on the hill? The one with the tennis courts? The husband was murdered there a few years ago. The wife cashed in big on the insurance, then started trotting around town with her yoga instructor."

Was that what they were saying? Sara shook her head. "No, that was just a rumor. He disappeared. There wasn't a murder."

"Oh, because no body was found?" The woman scoffed and moved closer, crossing her arms and tucking her hands underneath her biceps, a move that pushed her already enormous breasts farther out the top of her lavender athletic set. "That just means the wife was smart. Trust me, I listen to all of the crime podcasts, and if there's one way to hide a murder, it's to make sure that the body is never found."

It was true. David's missing corpse was likely what had kept the detectives from pursuing a deeper investigation into Sara. "The yoga instructor was gay," Sara said—not that this woman's opinion mattered. No one had listened or cared that Philip liked his sexual companions to be well endowed and bearded. All they cared about was that he was young, gorgeous, and at her home every day. "I mean, he still *is* gay," she corrected. "*Very* gay."

The woman snorted. "Oh, I'm sure."

Sara bit back the urge to underline the point, since arguing with idiots wasn't on her schedule this morning. "Well, I've got to go." She checked the road to make sure no traffic was coming, then headed back across.

"Be careful!" the woman called. "There might be a murderer out there!"

CHAPTER 3

KATIE MORROW

"Katie was an odd choice for a second wife. I mean, not that any man would blame Mark for wanting Katie. She's beautiful and sweet and keeps her house in perfect condition. She's just the polar opposite of Willow, which is why everyone's eyebrows raised a few inches when they started becoming serious."

28 Blackberry Summit Road
Hole 1, Stone Hollow

Katie Morrow stood in the middle of her giant walk-in closet and stared down at the pair of panties she'd just found tucked into the pocket of her husband's suit. For a moment she stopped breathing, then forced herself to suck in a deep gulp of air.

The suit was one of Mark's heavier ones and rarely got any use because of its double lining and wool material. In the three years they'd been together, she'd never seen him wear it. Slowly, she unfurled the bit of lingerie and wondered how her husband would react if he did happen to pick out this suit and discovered this in the pocket.

Would he tell her?

Would he throw it away?

Or would he hide it, as a souvenir from *her*, a reminder of the life he'd once lived, the relationship he'd once had?

It's sad that you can be married to someone for two years and not know the answers to those questions. In some ways, they knew each other intimately. Beyond so. It felt like she could read his thoughts most days, they were so clear. Plus, there were the little things. Take, for instance, the fact that Mark's celebrity crush was Jennifer Garner's character in *Alias*. That his TikTok feed was full of sheepdog-herding videos and landscape remodels, and that if he needed to assemble a piece of furniture or replace the windshield wipers on her Porsche, he'd be helpless. She knew the temperature he liked his swordfish, his top-ten wine vintages, his pant-inseam length, the name of his cigar broker, and his biggest insecurity—his ears.

All that, but she didn't know how he would handle this expensive piece of pale-pink lace.

It was obvious these had been worn. She stumbled backward on the plush white carpet and dropped into the chair beside the room's makeup counter.

When Katie had moved in, this closet was the one place she immediately both loved and hated. It was every woman's dream. A massive space, over a thousand square feet in total, the masculine and feminine sections in quiet harmony, with discreet doors keeping all the messy items hidden and the open lit cubbyholes displaying the finer items like jewels in a case.

It had a counter for Mark, with a sink for him to shave at, a rack of clippers and trimmers, his toothbrush, hair products, and colognes all in perfect rows along a crystal shelf.

The female counter was built for a full glam squad, with every hair-care tool plugged in through the base and nestled in its own precut holder. The lights changed depending on the user's choice, and there were a half dozen machines that were salon grade and ready for an intensive facial experience. When she'd moved in, all the clothes and shoes and purses had been relegated to the basement, but Willow's makeup and beauty items had been left behind, likely forgotten or ignored by the moving crew, their curiosity and oversight not extending to the hidden cabinets and drawers in this section of the room.

Katie was a woman who had always been fairly high maintenance, with a makeup drawer full of Sephora purchases, regular facials, quarterly Botox injections, and a healthy addiction to an evening skincare routine.

This setup took that level of self-care, laughed in its face, and raised it to the nth degree.

Now, with the first scrap of Willow's clothing in hand, Katie wondered if Mark's ex had approached their sex life with the same fastidious level of attention she had devoted to her appearance. She hoped not. Add in any level of sexual gymnastics, and Katie would drop even further behind in this wives' race.

Putting your used panties in your husband's suit pocket was a triple-twisting double back tuck compared to Katie and Mark's own sexual adventures, or lack thereof. The issue wasn't Katie. She was always prepped, shaved and clean. Always willing, though she could be more of an initiator at times. Still, she was always vocal and complimentary. Honestly, if someone stood outside their bedroom door, they'd think Katie was in a cheerleading competition, she was so damn enthusiastic.

But their sessions never felt like Mark's heart was in it. His orgasm was an effort. The erection was never at full attention, and it seemed like the act was often more of an obligatory chore.

Maybe the panties weren't Willow's. The possibility knocked her in the gut, and she put a hand on her stomach, pressing her fist against the sharp pain.

Maybe Mark had been cheating on her and these were his assistant's, or a client's wife's, or some stranger's from a bar.

She should ask Mark. Just confront him with them and see what he said. Katie had always had a good bullshit meter. If she surprised him, she could judge his reaction, his expression, the smoothness or anxiety of his reply. And maybe it was a conversation that would lead to a deeper dive, an uncovering of some of the details of the marriage he used to have.

She straightened up, enthusiastic about the idea, even as the pessimistic side of her psyche laughed at the idea of Mark saying anything about his first wife.

Mark never spoke about Willow.

Ever.

"Mrs. Morrow?" One of the maids stood at the entrance to the closet, her fist raised as if she might knock on the wall.

"Yes?" Katie closed her hand around the thong, hiding it in her fist.

"There's someone here from the police department. They'd like to speak to you."

CHAPTER 4

ANDREA KENDAL

"Andrea's a really good mom, I'll say that about her. And Eric's a good dad. I mean, she really hit the jackpot with him. A rich heart surgeon and he took on a single mom with a bratty infant? Not many men would do that, and he was definitely in demand after Roxanne was murdered. Every single woman in the county pounced on him, and some married ones too."

1442 Kingsmere Drive
Hole 6, Stone Hollow

Andrea called the guard gate, then Tia, then the mom in the mid-century modern on the eighteenth hole. No one answered, so she swung by Ryder's nursery to check on the baby. He was still asleep, on his back, his mouth half open. The seven-month-old slept like he was dead, and she took a moment to watch his little tummy moving up and down in peaceful serenity.

He had no idea how lucky he was. Neither did Cameron. They would never understand how close they came to a life of control and intimidation, of always looking over their shoulder and having to choose between violence or fear.

She gave the baby one final look, then went down the wide vaulted hallway to their bedroom. Inside the two-story suite, Eric had already changed into his surgical scrubs and was in the bathroom, brushing his teeth in front of one of the sinks.

She passed through the large suite and took a moment by the bed to smooth a dent in the neatly made cover. Crossing through the open doors into the bathroom, she rested her weight against the long granite counter. "I made some calls to see if anyone knows what's up, but I didn't get a hold of anyone. Think I should go across the street and ask what's going on?"

"No." Her husband spit into the sink, then filled a glass from the filtered tap and took a sip, rinsing his mouth. "It's none of our business."

"Maybe they're looking for a convict or something. We could be in danger." She opened the closest drawer, anticipating his next move. He stacked the toothpaste and his toothbrush into their appropriate slots in the drawer, then used a monogrammed hand towel to dry his mouth.

"Just turn on the alarms. I've got to get to the hospital." He stepped back from the sink, giving her room to close the drawer.

"What's your schedule like today? Do you want to meet for lunch? Or I could bring you something." She used the hand towel to wipe the water drops from the counter, then picked up his glass and followed him out through the suite.

"Not today. I'll be home in time for dinner, though. Could you do a roast?"

"Sure." A roast would mean a trip to the butcher, then the market. She could stop at the nursery off Park and get some fresh-cut blooms to refresh the house's arrangements. A perfect day, with plenty of time to get everything ready before Eric got home.

He stepped forward and gave her a soft kiss. "Love you."

His mouth was cool, the faint scent of spearmint on his breath. She gripped his scrubs and pulled him tighter to her, stealing another kiss before letting go. "Love you too," she said thickly.

"Don't let Cameron sleep too late," he warned.

"I won't." She glanced at her watch. "I'll get them both up shortly." She returned to the window; the search party had moved farther down the course, almost out of sight. In a little bit, she'd head to the playground with the kids. There, the gossip circle would certainly have some idea of what was going on.

CHAPTER 5

SARA BATCHER

"We went to dinner with them once, and I got to say, I didn't know why David was with her. She spent the entire time typing away on her phone, and stepped away from the table twice to take calls. I mean, yeah, I get that she had her stationery company, but what could be that important on a Friday night? When David disappeared, we knew what happened: He left her. And I don't blame him. I would have done the same."

16 Branwyn Hill
Hole 18, Silverwood Preserve

Sara was standing in the middle of her bathroom, a heated towel wrapped around her body, her hair pinned up away from her face, when the bathroom door banged open, letting in a gust of air-conditioning and her flustered dark-haired house manager.

"I spoke to Flavia," Maggie said with high importance. "They found a *bone*."

Sara turned, her fingers wet with a pale-blue moisturizer, the application forgotten as she stared at the woman, who looked especially pretty under the bathroom chandelier. "Who found a bone?"

"Flavia's dog. You know, that big hairy one that ate through the handle of Melissa's Birkin? It got out through the fence last night and went exploring and came back all wet and dirty and had a human bone in its mouth. She had to wrestle it away from him!" Maggie used both hands to pull out the stool that was tucked under the makeup table, then plopped down on it. Her feet were bare, and she hefted her generous frame to one side and bent her leg, tucking her right foot under her thigh. "Give me a minute. I had to sprint up the stairs." She inhaled deeply, patting her chest.

"Here." Sara quickly smeared the moisturizer on her cheekbones and then opened the lower cabinet door, exposing the hidden fridge, and withdrew a bottle of spring water. "Is that why the cops are all over the place?"

"Flavia said she called 9-1-1 right away but it was dark, so they came last night and looked at the bone but said—" She paused to take a sip of the water. "They said they'd have to start the search in the morning, and they did—they started in at six a.m. Flavia said they closed the entire Stone Hollow course. Canceled everyone's tee times, even the pros'."

That couldn't have gone over well. If there was one thing this wealthy neighborhood cared about, it was the ability to hit a tiny white ball with a stick. Damn any dead bodies that were in the way.

A human bone. Sara's stomach twisted and she felt a moment of genuine nausea as the room tilted to one side, then righted itself. She carefully moved toward Maggie, pulling out the second stool and gingerly taking the seat. "What kind of bone was it?"

"Human," Maggie repeated.

"Yes, I know that." She pressed her fingertips to her temples, massaging the delicate cluster of nerves and trying to clear the knot that was beginning to form. A migraine was the last thing she needed right now. "But what bone was it?"

"Oh, I don't know. Flavia said it was a big one."

"Does she have a picture of it?"

"A *picture* of the bone?" Maggie stared at her in bewilderment. "I doubt it. I think the police took it away when they came last night."

"Did it seem old?" Dots were beginning to form in Sara's vision, and she forced herself to breathe in short, shallow huffs of air. She should lie down and put up her feet before she fainted. "Help me to the bed."

Maggie stood and used both hands to raise Sara's small frame, supporting her as they took the long journey through the decadent bathroom, past the sitting area and morning nook, and up the three steps to the bed. The California King was already made, the sheets changed while she was on her walk. David had always thought it wasteful that she had the sheets changed daily, but what was the point of having money if you couldn't spend it the way you wanted to? Sara donated large sums to a clean-water charity as penance, and who was to say that wasn't ample compensation for what might amount to a thousand gallons or so of excess?

Maggie positioned her on the bed. "You want pillows under your feet?"

"Yes, please." Sara tried to help, raising her feet when Maggie brought the body pillows, the action lifting her towel almost to her waist. "Please cover me up with the blanket if you can."

"You're white as these sheets," Maggie remarked, and gave her a mischievous look. "I know what happened. I was about to collapse from sprinting up those stairs, and your body got all concerned that I was going to get all of the attention. It couldn't have that."

Sara laughed despite herself. "That's exactly what happened. You know me so well."

The divorced mother of three, who lived in the guesthouse at the back of the property and was the primary recipient of Sara's will, pulled a thick blanket over Sara's body. "It's not David. You know that, right?"

"It might be. We don't know." She met the woman's eyes; there were no innocents in this room.

"Flavia said the bone was very clean. No hair or fat or anything on it."

"Right, probably because it's old. Five years old." Sara stared up at the vaulted ceiling, which was a mosaic of glass tiles. It'd taken the workers two weeks to lay all the tiny tiles in the intricate pattern.

"Maybe it's Willow Morrow. Or Roxanne what's-her-face. Her husband could have moved her body from Treveley Park to the neighborhood."

It was true. It could be either one of those women, but Sara knew that it wasn't. Any moment, the police would ring the security call button at her gate and come to arrest her.

CHAPTER 6

KATIE MORROW

"I had lunch with Willow—that's Mark's first wife—three days before she supposedly left him. We were practically best friends, and she didn't say a word to me about leaving. We're just supposed to believe she left town and no one ever heard from her again? It's bullshit. And then, three years later, he started bringing Katie around the club. I gotta tell you, as a Willow loyalist, I refused to be Katie's friend. Most of the women at the club did. I mean, we all liked Willow. She was just . . . so fun. Effortlessly chill. If there was a queen bee of the Crestmore circle, it was her. We all wanted to be her friend, but I was probably the one she liked the best."

28 Blackberry Summit Road
Hole 1, Stone Hollow

Katie slowly took the stairs down to the first level, her nerves tightening at the thought of speaking to the authorities. She adjusted the neck of her baby-blue romper, a silk blend that elongated her legs and cinched at the waist, the neckline hinting at her cleavage without being ostentatious about it. Her personal shopper had sworn over the outfit, purchasing it in three colors and promising that this was an ensemble Katie could put on without thought—no way to screw it up. Nude sandals and a chunky stone necklace were the only accessories, the items placed in clear bags and attached to the hangers so no guesswork was needed.

Clothing had always been a concern of hers. When she'd started at Mark's agency—and chanced a run-in with a celebrity athlete at each day of the job—she had been almost paralyzed with indecision each morning over her outfit. When she'd begun dating Mark, and confessed the insecurity over a candlelit dinner in Palo Alto, he'd immediately placed a call to Saks. Within five minutes, she'd been assigned a stylist and given an unlimited budget, billed to him.

Such a large source of anxiety, suddenly gone. Her student debt had been the next problem—resolved. Mark had been like a magician, removing one obstacle, then another, and then she was suddenly in an evening gown, surrounded by hundreds of candles, him on one knee, a four-carat diamond ring in one hand.

And Willow hadn't even been a thought. Not that night, and not during the wedding, and not until she had moved into this house and was suddenly surrounded by the ghost of a woman whom everyone seemed to love.

The housekeeper stood in the foyer with an apologetic look, and Katie smiled tightly, as if everything was okay.

And it was. There was nothing to be nervous about. This was probably something trivial and had nothing to do with the red light she'd run last week, the one at the giant intersection that most definitely had a red-light camera, and was a home visit really necessary for that infraction? She had assumed she would get a ticket in the mail with a hefty fine or, at the very worst, a notice to appear.

As she approached, the housekeeper opened the door. On the front mat, their shoulders side by side, as if they were blocking her exit, were two men in the standard black police uniforms of the San Francisco Police Department. "Mrs. Morrow?" one asked.

"Yes?" Katie smoothed a hand over the top of her hair, and for once the blond strands seemed to be behaving. Idiot-proof, the expensive hairdresser had promised her. Just do this, this, this, and nine more other things, all in the right order, and then it'll look perfect! You know, there *had* been a sound when she had zoomed through the intersection. A horn, or maybe the squeal of brakes. What if she'd caused an accident?

They introduced themselves, the left one and then the right, and she tried to capture and remember their names but promptly forgot. "Do you have a card?" she asked. "My husband will want to see it."

Maybe someone had been in the crosswalk. Someone she hadn't seen. She had felt a bump but thought it was the reflective markers in the crossing path, the ones that helped to guide the visually impaired.

The officers didn't hesitate, digging in their pockets and coming up with twin white cards, the seal of the San Francisco Police Department on the left side of each. She studied each one and repeated the names three times in her head.

Antonio Bridges. Antonio Bridges. Antonio was the one with the clipboard.

Terry Reyes. Terry Reyes. Terry was the bald one.

"Maybe I should call my attorney," she said, and the words came out just right. Confident, like someone who was well protected and shouldn't be messed with, especially not over a minor traffic infraction.

They exchanged a look, and the one on the right—Terry—coughed out a laugh. "Uh, Mrs. Morrow, we're just stopping to ask if we can search the pond on the back of your property. You're free to consult with an attorney if you like. But we aren't here on suspicion of any crime."

The other one frowned at her, and if they hadn't been here on suspicion, now they kind of looked like they were.

She shifted her weight to one leg and hoped they didn't look down at her feet. She had missed her weekly pedicure due to an overbooking at the spa. Inconvenient, since there was a chip on her left big toe. "You want to search the lake?" That made no sense. The small pond was behind their firepit area, to the left of the pool. It wrapped around the back guesthouse and second garage, and provided a nice buffer between them and the golfers, who sometimes got loud and obnoxious. Once, one hit a ball into the pond and waded up to his knees in an attempt to get it. "Why?"

"Something was found on the course last night, and we're trying to find the source of it. It appeared to be from a body of water, so we're searching all of the course lakes and private ponds."

"Something?" Katie pressed, her toe forgotten. "Like what?"

Antonio shifted his stance. "We're keeping the details private at this time, but we'll let you know if we find anything."

"I'll have to ask my husband." Keeping the details private. That was interesting. Almost juicy. This was something she could share at the Chinese checkers game Thursday at the country club. Finally, she had something to contribute. She always felt like a stump, taking up one of the chairs, with nothing worthwhile to say.

"Sure. Would you like us to speak to him?" Terry asked.

"Time is of the essence," Antonio added, as if whatever it was might crawl out of the pool and slither up the bank.

"Um, maybe." She twisted around, and the maid was right there, hovering. "Oh, Jackie. Can you please get me the house phone?"

The woman jumped into action; she had definitely been listening to their conversation. Katie was beginning to understand why Mark's first wife had insisted on not having help. She had started to hide in her bedroom in the hope of avoiding them. She turned back to the officers. "Can you give me a few minutes?"

"How long have you been married to Mr. Morrow?" Antonio asked, his head cocked to one side.

"Uh, two years." She adjusted the neck of the romper and patted the chunky necklace, making sure it hadn't twisted out of place.

Terry spoke up. "How long did you date before that?" This wasn't a good feeling, being a ping-pong ball between the two of them.

"Six months. But I worked at his agency for at least twice that, so we knew each other well. Mark's a sports agent. Represents a lot of really big athletes."

"So . . . did you know the prior Mrs. Morrow?" Antonio glanced at the clipboard in his hand. "Mrs. Willow Morrow?"

Willow Morrow. It sounded like the name of a gated neighborhood. "No." Katie shook her head. "She left a year or so before Mark and I met."

"'Left'?" Terry smiled as if she'd said something funny. It was annoying, when people did that, and everyone seemed to have an annoying opinion where Willow was concerned.

The maid returned with the cordless handset, and Katie took it and pressed the digits of Mark's cell phone quickly, then held up a finger to the officers and stepped back into the privacy of the small library just off the foyer.

"Yep," Mark answered on the third ring, and from the shouts in the background, she could tell he was at the office. There were only eight agents in the firm; it wasn't like it was the stock market trading floor. But yelling at each other and on the phone seemed to be how they landed the big names and fat deals. Whatever the equation, she didn't question it, not with the size of the commission paychecks he brought home.

"It's me. There are some police officers here. They're asking if they can search the pond."

"What?" The background noise softened. Mark must have closed the door to his office. "What do you mean?"

"They said they found something and are searching the lakes and ponds in the neighborhood. They want to search ours."

He was silent for a long moment—rare for a man who loved to hear himself talk. "They're searching all of the lakes and ponds in the neighborhood?"

"That's what they said." She glanced back at the front door, where both of the men were staring at her, their faces fixed in a scowl. She must be taking too long. She wiggled in place and willed Mark to hurry up.

"Do they have a warrant?"

"A warrant?" Katie repeated, surprised at the question. "No. They're going door-to-door. They said this is urgent. Or of the essence, or something."

"And everyone is letting them do it?"

"I don't know," she huffed out. "Do you want to talk to them? Because right now they are just staring at me." She gave the officers an apologetic frown.

"Tell them I'm fine with them searching the pond, but I want to be there when they do it. I have a call I need to reschedule, then I'll head there. Are they searching the golf course also?"

"I can ask them." She turned back to the door, grateful for an answer.

"Don't," he interrupted. "Just tell them what I said, and don't let them touch anything until I get there."

"Okay, okay." She ended the call without waiting for him to respond and gave her best smile to the officers. "He said that's fine, but he wants to be here when you do it. He can be here in, like, twenty minutes."

"Great." Antonio held out the clipboard. "If you can sign here, giving your permission for a search and seizure, we'll be back then."

A search and seizure. That sounded intense. Katie scrawled her signature on the line. "Everyone's giving permission for this?"

"Well, the innocent ones." He smiled at her as if it was a joke, but it didn't sound like a joke. "Thank you, Mrs. Morrow." He stepped back but the Terry guy stayed in place, his hands resting on his belt.

"So, you've never spoken to or met Willow Morrow?" Terry repeated, as if he hadn't believed her the first time.

"No?" Katie repeated, but it sounded almost like a question. She cleared her throat. "Like I said, she had been gone for a couple of years before I met Mark." She stepped back and wondered if slowly closing the door in his face would be rude. Probably. Rude *and* suspicious.

She opened it a little bit wider, just to be sure. There. Nothing suspicious here.

"You know, I worked her missing persons case. We swept this whole house and property back then. We didn't search the pond, though."

"Well, why would you?" She smiled again, as brightly as an idiot, as if she already knew the details of Willow's absence. That's what Mark called it, an *absence*. Not a disappearance. Willow had left him—that was what Mark had told her, and that was the nondramatic truth of the matter. Willow wanted a divorce, wanted out of their marriage, so she'd signed divorce papers, packed up a bag, and left. The neighborhood liked to make it sound scandalous, but that was because they were always looking for something to gossip over.

It was Willow's nail tech who had called the police and asked them to check on her. Willow had no-showed to their weekly appointment. Calls to her cell had gone unanswered, so the nail tech called the house and left a few messages. Mark had finally returned one of her calls and informed her that Willow had left him and he didn't have any future contact info. The nail tech hadn't been happy with that answer, and tried to reach her via social media, but all Willow's accounts were closed. Eventually, she had called the cops and they had done a cursory investigation.

Katie hadn't been here for that, but that was how Mark had described it. Cursory. A few questions, and then they were satisfied. Mark had told her the history on their first date, over sushi and edamame. His explanation had made sense, and Katie dismissed Willow as a non-factor in their future or in any evaluation of Mark as a romantic prospect.

Then Katie had moved into his home, and Willow's ghost seemed to be everywhere. She'd heard the whispers at the country club and seen the suspicious looks cast Mark's way. Right after Katie had moved in, she'd gone to the next-door neighbor's home with a loaf of sourdough bread, wanting to introduce herself, and gotten the entire story from Monica, a stick-thin wife who had flung open the door, stared at the plastic-wrapped loaf in Katie's hands, and shrieked at her that she was off carbs! Had been for two years! She had then seized the sourdough with both hands and sniffed it as if she were a Dalmatian. Within two minutes, she'd invited Katie in, had the sourdough cut into quarters, and begun a twenty-minute monologue about Willow and Mark's relationship and Willow's disappearance.

"You know," Monica had said while slathering butter onto one of the wedges of bread. "I called the cops on them once. I heard her *scream* in the middle of the night."

"Scream?" Katie had repeated. "Like, she was scared?"

"No." Monica had stuffed the wedge of bread into her mouth and closed her eyes in bliss, chewing the large bite slowly. "Not scared," she'd said through a mouthful of bread. She finally swallowed and paused. "In pain. She was screaming in pain. Tomas wanted me to mind my own business, but I couldn't go back to sleep after hearing that." She'd lifted one of her bony shoulders in a shrug. "So I called the police. Just to be safe, you know." She had leaned forward across the kitchen's marble island. "You should have heard the scream, Katie. I mean, anyone would have called the cops. It was terrible."

Terrible.

Katie had never asked Mark about that night, but now she wondered if either of the cops on her doorstep had responded to Monica's 9-1-1 call, and if that was the reason for this suspicion.

"If you ever need anything, you have our cards." The taller one stared in her eyes as if trying to send her a telepathic message. "Anything."

"I can't imagine what we'd need," she said brightly. "Thank you both."

She tried to shut the door as politely as possible, but it was awkward since he was still stubbornly on the mat, his feet planted like he had something else to say. She slowly pushed the handle until it clicked into place. This was why she'd tried to convince Mark to move, for them to start over somewhere fresh, somewhere no one would ever think to ask about her husband's first marriage.

But he'd refused and now they were here, dealing with this. Some imaginary excuse to try to search their pond. *We found something.* What did that even mean? What could they have possibly found that would cause them to search the whole neighborhood? She flipped the dead bolt and passed the phone to the maid. "Please hang that back up."

She should call Viv, who lived three holes over. Her house backed up to a pond. Katie could ask her if the cops were searching that pond. But what if they weren't? It'd give Viv a juicy bit of gossip. She'd call every wife in Crestmore. Probably make a post on social media about it.

No. She couldn't call Viv. Katie headed up the staircase two steps at a time. On their third floor, there was a widow's walk balcony. From there, she should be able to see whether there was any truth to the detectives' assertion, or if their property was the only one being searched.

CHAPTER 7

ANDREA KENDAL

"You know, they act like that boy is a Kendal, but Andrea was a single mom when she met Eric. An NFL player is the real father—that's what I heard. Knocked her up and paid her off."

1442 Kingsmere Drive
Hole 6, Stone Hollow

In Crestmore, the pavered streets had two periods of activity. Between 5:00 and 6:00 a.m., you had the executives. They sprinted through the dark with an almost-constant eye on their watches, their earpieces in, strides quick, the run completed in time for them to make it to the office or a conference call with Singapore. Around ten, the moms and nannies arrived, convening on the lakeside path that journeyed between the children's park and the playground. There, the nannies and any employers separated, two clusters of socialization as the children ran between them and among each other.

It was traditional, once Eric left for the hospital, for Andrea to head to the park, where Cameron loved the ropes and rock-climbing course. He was now able to make it to the second level, a height that terrified Andrea, despite the large pool of cushioned cubes below the structure. While she had spent months recovering from her painful plastic surgery procedures, Cameron had never had more than a skinned knee. Andrea's biggest fear each playground session was that he'd break a bone, which wasn't the worst fear in the world. She'd certainly grown up with a lot worse.

They were either late this morning, or the group was early. Andrea checked her watch and confirmed that it was the latter. The gossip, it seemed, couldn't wait, not with all the excitement. As she took the path toward the park, two police vans passed on the main road. Was it her imagination or did they slow down to study her?

Definitely her imagination. She lifted a hand to wave to them, but the occupants weren't even looking in her direction, their attention fixed forward, their mouths moving in conversation.

"Mom." Cameron pulled on her hand. "I'm going to run ahead."

Andrea released her grip and the four-year-old sprinted forward, his Velcro-fastened sneakers loud on the sidewalk.

Ryder cried out from his place in the stroller and she walked faster, trying to keep up with his brother, who was now careening around the bend in the sidewalk and beelining for the gate to the playground.

Andrea passed a small cluster of nannies first and smiled at the blonde in the pink sweater, whom they'd hired when Ryder was first born. Andrea had been bedridden for two weeks after the emergency C-section, and Claire had been an enormous help in getting Ryder settled in the nursery and helping Andrea's nurse with her daily care. Andrea had been fairly drugged up and struggling to get as much time with Ryder as possible, but she remembered that the girl was studying to be an aesthetician and had a father who worked at an auto plant. She called out a hello and continued on, curious about the tight cluster of moms by the duck-feeding station at the right side of the playground entrance.

The ring of women was complete, three of their backs to Andrea, and she saw the visual impact that occurred when one of the women at the opposite end of the circle saw her. It was an immediate explosion of the ring, one where backs straightened, heads whipped toward her, and conversations ceased. She paused, uncertain.

There was a moment of standoff, a line of carbon-copy wives faced off against her. Five different flavors of the same mold. The younger women all favored slicked-back ponytails, big sunglasses, and matching skintight athletic-wear sets. The older women—God, that included her—were in varying shades of neutrals, their hair impossibly full and glossy, lips plumped and the jewelry layered. Here, at least, Andrea's excessive plastic surgery was in good company, though the women would never expect how much work she'd really had done. She stepped forward, ignoring their stares. "Good morning. What's going on?"

The tall, skinny one, who used to be a professional volleyball player, spoke up. "Well, it's a body that they're looking for. A *female*, from a few years ago."

A female. More knowing looks, as if it were obvious the body belonged to Eric's first wife. Andrea flipped up the cap of her protein shake and took a sip, then shrugged. "What do you mean, they're looking for a body? They think it wandered off?"

A wave of giggles went through the group and they advanced, like velociraptors around their prey, surrounding her. Ryder let out a nervous shriek and she shushed him gently, rocking the stroller in an attempt to calm him from the intrusion.

"No," Tina Faith said importantly, as if she had all the information, and given that her brother-in-law was the district attorney for San Francisco County, she probably did. "A dog dug up some human *remains* and carried them home. They're trying to find the rest of the corpse now."

Corpse. It was a word that was so out of place in the sunny morning, a butterfly lazily flying by on its way to the bright-orange poppies along the path. Andrea had seen plenty of dead bodies in her time. Once, she had come home from a study group and there had been one sitting at their dining room table, his head sideways in a pile of her mother's meat loaf, his eyes wide open and staring in the direction of their framed family photo.

Never, in her upbringing, had the word *corpse* been used.

From the splash pool, a kid started screaming, and the group turned to see whose child it was, their attention momentarily off Andrea. She understood why they assumed the body was Roxanne. If it was a female from this neighborhood, and from a few years back, that left only two possibilities: Willow Morrow or Roxanne.

The group of women twisted back to face her, and the same suspicious condescension was on all of their faces—as if Andrea were married to a monster, one who would have killed his first wife and then buried her somewhere in their neighborhood.

"You know, we're here for you." The newest arrival to the group, a giant-breasted yoga instructor with fake eyelashes, touched Andrea's arm, and she somehow managed not to flinch at the contact.

"I appreciate that, but I'm fine. It's probably Willow Morrow. Has anyone reached out to Mark's new wife? Her name's Katie, right?"

Their gazes darted away, and you could taste their pity on the air.

"Well, we haven't done anything yet," someone said.

Nothing except gossip about Eric. Hell, they should know better. They'd trusted him with their bodies, their surgeries, their children—yet believed him capable of murder? Look at Mark Morrow if you wanted a killer. The sports agent had rubbed Andrea wrong from the first moment they met. All white teeth and designer clothes, he always parked his sports car along the curb at the country club, and had a habit of winking at Andrea, as if they shared some secret.

Maybe she should reach out to Katie herself and offer some support. The blonde had to be freaking out. If not now, she would be once the body was identified as Willow.

Andrea glanced at her watch. "We've got to run. Cameron has a swimming lesson at eleven." She called out for the boy, who was climbing up the rope ladder, a big smile on his face. The news hadn't yet infected the children. Two boys ran around the climbing rock, screaming. Unlike her and Eric, the Morrows didn't have any children. Thank God. She couldn't imagine trying to hide that news, that subsequent investigation, from Cameron and Ryder. Katie and Mark would be able to handle it on their own, though their marriage probably wouldn't survive the event.

Brittny, who never missed a chance to mention her husband, stepped forward, her threaded eyebrows pinched together in faux concern. "If you need an attorney, Tom would be happy to—"

"We won't," Andrea snapped, then forced a smile. It didn't matter what the women thought. In a day or so, the cops would identify the body, and given that it wasn't Roxanne's, everything would go back to normal. One odd bubble, popped.

But the suspicion still hurt. While husbands were always the first suspect in a wife's abduction, it was unfathomable to Andrea that anyone who knew Eric would suspect that he would do anything to Roxanne. The man was a saint.

As a doctor, he was a god, with more successful surgeries than any other cardiac surgeon in the county.

As a father, everyone praised him for welcoming Cameron in as his own and mastering diapers and bottle-feeding and bedtime regimens.

And as a husband, he was doting, caring, and an excellent provider. Perfect, if you could overlook the fact that he was still in love with his first wife.

Her phone rang, a chime of bells, from inside the pocket of her cashmere jacket, and she fumbled for it, getting the device out just in time. It was Eric, and she looked for Cameron, verifying his location before wheeling Ryder's stroller away from the group. "Hey."

"They found the remains of a body somewhere on the golf course," Eric said, and she could hear the chaotic sounds of the hospital in the background.

"Yes, that's what I just heard. I have the kids down at the playground. All the wives are talking about it. They think—well, you know the gossip. There's a lot of insinuation that it's Roxanne."

"Yeah, that was my first concern," he said flatly. "We have to be very careful how we handle this, to avoid raising red flags."

"I told the wives it was probably Willow."

He sighed. "Try not to talk to anyone else. Let's think through this. As much as I hate to say it, it may be an opportunity."

In what twisted world would a dead body be an opportunity?

But he was right. As much as she wanted to defend him to the hilt, that wasn't the smart play here.

"Oh." She inhaled. "I'll head home now. Just—be careful."

It was a waste of a warning. Eric was, above all other things, always careful.

CHAPTER 8

SARA BATCHER

"Everyone in the neighborhood knew Sara as David's wife. It was like everyone ignored the fact that she started InkRose while an undergrad at Harvard, built it into a massive stationery brand, and then sold it for mid–nine figures. They all acted like she married David for his money, but she was the breadwinner in that relationship. He did well in pharmaceutical sales, but nothing close to her."

16 Branwyn Hill
Hole 18, Silverwood Preserve

Sara stood in warrior position in the yoga room, one leg extended out in the air, her weight precariously balanced on the other, her arms stuck out as if she were flying. Sweat ran down the center line of her back, and she gripped the rubber mat with her toes. She'd built the studio around an average temperature of 92 degrees but had turned it up to 95 this morning. Letting out a controlled exhale, she attempted to relax, but despite the sound of crashing waves coming through the speakers and the row of candles that flickered in the dark room, every muscle in her body was on high alert.

When they had built the house, David had originally allocated the large adjourning space as a weight room, which it was, for about six months. Then her husband had a short-lived obsession with P90X, then CrossFit, then gave up all aspirations of cardio and turned it into a golf-simulator theater.

In the five years since David had disappeared, Sara had toyed with doing something else with the space, but in a house of twelve thousand square feet, it hadn't been a top priority.

And now . . . the mystery of her missing husband was finally solved. After all the rumors, the whispers, the theories . . . David was dead and right here in the neighborhood.

Asshole.

Of all the times for his body to pop up, it would make sense for her narcissistic husband to choose this moment out of them all. After all, Sara had finally adjusted to an empty house, a clear schedule, no drop-ins by detectives or pesky questions from the insurance companies. Everyone had finally stopped thinking of Sara as a widow and started to think of her as all the other things that she encompassed. She was, as her therapist loved to preach, so much *more* than just the former Mrs. David Batcher, and that's what she should embrace!

The problem was that Sara had spent seventeen years as a wife, and that identity was hard to shake off, especially when that connection didn't get a clean ending. Instead, with David just dropping off the face of the planet, it had left everyone in limbo, not sure what to think, who to support, who to suspect, or who to blame.

Of course, everyone had blamed her. His mother had been horrific about it, but then again Nora had always been a bitch about everything regarding Sara. No one was good enough for her baby, especially not a Jewish girl from Brooklyn with a nose ring. Let it be known for the record that Sara had removed the nose ring prior to meeting Nora, had covered up the tiny hole with concealer and powder, yet the woman had still managed to spot the jeweled stud in a photo of her and David and had never gotten over it. The decision, as she had told David over and over again, just went to show what kind of judgment Sara had. The type of mother she would be. The sort of reckless decision-making he would have to live with for the rest of his life, should he make the unfortunate decision to marry her.

They say that mothers know best, and maybe she did. After all, David *had* regretted the marriage. He'd never said that, but he'd shown it, over and over again, in tiny ways. The disappointed sighs. The lack of invitations to group events. The long business trips. Rushing her through dinner without allowing for dessert. The repeated wearing of his favorite cologne even though she was allergic to it.

Nora's concerns over Sara's suitability as a mother had also been a nonfactor, because they'd never conceived a child. Another strike against Sara; it would have been better, in Nora's book, to be an unfit mother rather than a barren one. The retired science teacher couldn't visit without tsking her tongue over the empty bedrooms on the third floor. "No children?" she had wailed. "You want me to die without any grandchildren, is that it?"

They hadn't, but she did. They'd buried her three months before David's disappearance in a huge mausoleum with a long list of achievements underneath her name. *Philanthropist. Teacher. Mother. Aunt. Grandmother* had not been on the list. Sara had noticed the absence but hadn't felt any regret. She'd taken the vitamins, the hormone injections, the tests. She'd gotten in the proper positions, timed her ovulation cycles, and always been willing, sexually instigative, and enthusiastic on the days that promised maximum potential.

Leaning forward, she reached down to the mat as her back leg lifted higher into the air, transitioning into standing splits. It was for the best that they hadn't gotten pregnant. By now, the kid would have been five or six. Instead of doing yoga, Sara would be chasing them around a playground, a cell phone in the crook of her neck, trying to keep them entertained while juggling the rest of her life.

She'd be miserable, and maybe that was what Nora had seen. Not so much that Sara couldn't have a child, but that she didn't really want one.

Maybe David had sensed that as well.

Maybe all this could have been avoided and he'd still be here, they'd still be married, there would be no investigation at all, if she'd done a better job of hiding her feelings.

CHAPTER 9

KATIE MORROW

"Well now, they've been married two years, because our son had just been born when Katie moved in. I remember when I first saw the moving truck, I thought that maybe Mark was finally leaving, which made sense given that's an awfully big house for one person. But then tiny little Katie hopped out, with a rock on her finger I could see from my house. And later that day she came over and introduced herself and brought me a beautiful purple orchid plant. She's a sweet girl. Naive, but sweet."

28 Blackberry Summit Road
Hole 1, Stone Hollow

Once the police left, Katie hid the mystery woman's thong and then completed her morning routine. She hesitated, glancing at the date on her phone, then grabbed a pregnancy test from the bottom drawer.

Crouching over the toilet, she counted out loud as she peed on the small white stick. Her urine stream was strong, a result of three empty glass bottles that were now on the drying rack in the kitchen. Hopefully, the sample wouldn't be diluted. In high school, she and her friends had chugged water for two hours before a drug test, frantic to hide the presence of marijuana in their results. It had worked then, so what if the similar process hid the hCG hormone that indicated a little baby, one with Mark's cute nose and her blue eyes?

The doctor had assured her it wouldn't, but she still worried over the pale-yellow color of the toilet water. Placing the stick on top of the toilet stand, she pulled up her underwear and the romper, putting it back into place. After entering the bathroom, she washed her hands with the black currant hand soap Mark loved, then set the timer on her phone for two and a half minutes.

She decided, as she opened the middle drawer beside her sink and withdrew the boar-bristle brush, that no matter what the test said, she wouldn't tell Mark. There was too much uncertainty prior to three months. That was what the ob-gyn had said last time, and look—he had been right. No point in letting Mark down, not before knowing for sure.

She bent over and ran the brush through her hair, from back to front, her movements brisk. After a dozen strokes, she straightened, flipping her head over and giving the strands a quick pat down. The hairdresser had outdone herself with this last session. Katie's hair was the perfect shade between blond and white, with enough seemingly natural variation to add depth. She turned her head to the left and the right, critically examining her makeup. Glancing down at the timer—fifty-seven seconds left—she opened the second drawer, revealing the neat rows of powders, glosses, and brushes. She removed a powder and brush and spent the final minute doing a quick touch-up. She was applying a fresh coat of clear gloss on her lips when the timer went off. It took two tries to get the applicator back in the tube. Damn her shaking hands.

Turning off the timer, she methodically returned everything to its place. It didn't really matter if the pregnancy test was negative; there would be another month, then another. All they had was time. After all, Katie was only twenty-six. It wasn't like Willow. Willow had been thirty-one and uninterested in kids. Mark liked to joke that it would have taken him ten more years to talk her into kids, and she would have yielded only when it would have been conveniently too late.

Underneath the sink was the cleaning spray, and she gave the white marble a few quick squirts and wiped down the area. Glancing over the long expanse, she decided to clean it all the way down to Mark's sink. It wasn't until that task was finished that she returned to the water closet.

Her mother had found the concept of a tiny closet for a toilet to be ridiculous, but that was what life was like in this tax bracket. Excess upon excess. This bathroom had two—one for Mark and one for Katie. How else would an architect fill up six thousand square feet with only four bedrooms?

She picked up the test quickly, before she found another reason not to do it. Taking a deep breath, she looked at the small display screen.

CHAPTER 10

ANDREA KENDAL

"Roxanne, that was Eric's first wife. She was an absolute sweetheart but always looked a little shell-shocked, like she was anticipating a reason to run out of the room. But that wasn't a huge surprise, given her background. Who knew what kind of things she saw growing up. You wouldn't have known it to look at her—I mean, she married a surgeon—but her family was all trash. Gangsters and such. And that's what I think really happened to her. I think someone from her family, or from some other crime family, whacked her. That's what they say over there, by the way. Whacked. Honestly, they do. It's not just a thing from the movies."

1442 Kingsmere Drive
Hole 6, Stone Hollow

Andrea sat on the floor of the kids' playroom and eavesdropped on her husband's interview with the police. Her legs were spread apart, a large coloring page before her, a big marker in hand, the *r* in Cameron's name half filled in. Across from her, the boy attempted to color in the flames on a race car illustration, his efforts going out of the lines as much as in.

"Come on, Tony. We've been over this." Eric sounded calm, but Andrea knew every octave of his voice by heart. She could hear the tightness, could feel the pause before he answered, the thought that was going into each sentence. "Roxanne was taken ten miles from here. I was six hours away. You, more than anyone, know how much this was looked into."

Tony. Roxanne's uncle. When she'd disappeared, he was a thirteen-year veteran on the force. Now he must be close to retirement. Andrea had heard from Eric how he had all but moved in after Roxanne disappeared, watching Eric like a hawk. Tapping his phones. Following him. It had taken months for Tony to back off, and that happened only after the police chief had piled more cases onto his workload.

She reached over and turned up the volume on the baby monitor, one she had put in the library before the cops arrived, just in case they wanted to question Eric. He'd suggested she stay out of sight, advice she readily agreed with. The last thing she wanted was any scrutiny, especially from Tony. He had shown up once, right after she had moved in. She had seen him through the security system and almost fainted at the outline of his large build, his shield and ID held up in front of the camera.

She had double-checked her appearance in the mirror before cracking open the door and had kept her back stiff, voice breathy when she said hello. She knew what he would see and what he would think. A woman almost a decade younger than his niece, with breasts and lips three times bigger, the assets showed off in a low-cut top and bright-red lipstick. His gaze had gone right to her cleavage and stayed there, but his message still hit its mark.

"You're in danger, Mrs. Kendal. Your husband is a bad man. Don't believe me? Look up Roxanne Kendal. Her story didn't turn out too good."

After he'd left, Andrea went straight to the liquor closet and poured a double shot of vodka and chased it with two Valium. She had called Eric at the hospital and reported the event, and he swore to her that she'd never have to see Tony again. A promise that, like many he'd made, he had no way to keep.

Cameron held up his artwork, beaming at her. "Look! It's good!"

She smiled back and a wave of affection hit at his cherubic face. "It's perfect. Just like you."

She reached for the little boy and pulled him onto her lap, inhaling his infectious smell of applesauce and the tear-free shampoo she used on his thick curls.

"I would kill to protect you," she whispered. Quietly, so the little boy wouldn't hear.

CHAPTER 11

SARA BATCHER

"We lived next door to David and Sara, so we were one of the first to know when he went missing. I remember seeing a detective's car coming through their gate, and I asked Sara about it the next day and she said that she didn't know where David was. As if he was a dog or a purse she'd misplaced. I mean, how do you lose your husband? I asked her if she thought he ran off, but she said he definitely didn't. And he was in pharmaceutical sales, so it wasn't like he had engineered a Ponzi scheme or something like that, something he might run away over. We always thought he would show back up, but as time passed, that seemed to be less and less likely."

16 Branwyn Hill
Hole 18, Silverwood Preserve

The maids were done with the main-floor clean and were polishing the staircase banister when the police buzzed in at the gate. Maggie welcomed them in and led them to the front sitting room, where Sara was waiting. The two officers took the chairs in front of the three-story fireplace, and Maggie brought them sodas and a sparkling water for Sara.

"I heard that you found a body," Sara said, cutting to the chase. "Is it David?"

The taller one, who had given a low whistle when he'd come into the room, winced. "Well, that's not exactly true. A dog in the neighborhood found some human remains. We're trying to locate the rest of them now."

The rest of them. Like they were puzzle pieces that had fallen off the table and were lost. Was it a head that had been found? A jawbone? A femur? How decayed or intact had it been? She swallowed the urge to ask all the questions and settled on one. "So how much do you have?" Again, the wrong choice of words.

The two men exchanged a look. There was a long pause, and finally, the shorter one spoke. "At the moment, one bone."

"That's it?" All this hubbub over one bone. Maybe it wasn't even human. The tight knot of anxiety in Sara's abdomen eased slightly.

"Well, that's not a minor thing, Mrs. Batcher. Human bones don't just fall out of the air—especially not in areas like this." He smiled as if she were a child.

"But you've been looking for hours. I saw crime scene vans pass by at eight thirty." In her peripheral vision, she saw movement, and turned her head to catch Maggie passing through the large arched opening to the north foyer. Maggie would want to know every detail once they left. The woman was a fiend for information and coveted it like a prize.

"Well . . ." The shorter one shifted in his seat. Neither one of them had taken a sip of their sodas. "There are over forty-seven lakes in the neighborhood. Three golf courses."

"Six nature preserves," the other one jumped in. "It's a lot of ground to cover."

Yes, there was. Sara had walked every street, path, and course in the neighborhood and could have told them—anyone—where the most logical place to hide a body was, if that was your goal. Would they have started their search with the duck pond behind Stone Hollow's eighth hole? Or maybe the thick forest on the edge of Ramsey Lane?

It probably depended on where the bone had been found. She'd never considered a dog *unearthing* part of David. Ironic, that of all the things she had envisioned, obsessed over . . . it was the unimagined that had actually happened. She cleared her throat and refocused on the conversation. "Okay, so . . . why are you here?"

"We wanted to update our records. After all, it's been a while since we spoke with you. Given that the age of the bone puts it in a time frame that correlates with your husband's disappearance, we thought it best to touch base." The tall one set his glass down on a coaster on the table and reached into the front chest pocket of his white button-down shirt, withdrawing a thin notepad and pen. The pen didn't have a cap, and she could see a small blue ink stain in the bottom of his pocket.

That wouldn't come out. Ink was like bloodstains: It was better to just throw something out than try to remove the evidence.

"This is your only home, Mrs. Batcher?" the one with the notepad asked.

"Yes—and don't worry. I won't leave town." She smiled, hoping they would laugh off the thought.

They didn't.

"It looks like you had David declared as deceased two years ago and collected his life insurance at that time, is that correct?"

"Yes." She could have elaborated. Waiting three years for a man to show up was long enough, especially for a man who was on time for everything. She gave David a new watch each Christmas as a running joke on his punctuality. Upstairs, still in its box, was the one she purchased the December after he disappeared. A waste of $8,000, but you never knew who was watching or what might later make her look guilty. A woman was expected to hope for and expect her missing husband to reappear, even if it wasn't logical or likely.

Sara was as logical as David was dead.

"So you haven't heard from him in five and a half years? Not since the date you reported him missing?" the short one asked.

"That's correct. May fifth was the last time anyone saw him, as far as I know. There's been no credit activity, no sightings . . . They found his car downtown. We have a condo there—or we did. I sold it a few years ago. His car was in that garage. He was supposed to be here that night. I expected him home, which is why I called the police the next morning, once I didn't hear from him." They should have this information. She had told it so many times the information was branded on her brain. "At first, the police didn't find it suspicious. It wasn't until it had been a few days that they started to really look for him."

The tall one lifted his drink and took a sip. His beard was clipped short down his neck, and she could see the glug of his Adam's apple as he finished off almost half of it before lowering the glass. David had drunk the same way. Two chugs and it would be gone. It was one of the reasons why she had decided to hide the crushed pills in his drink. He was always done with the glass before he had a chance to consider that the taste might be off.

"Whatever you found, it's not David," she said. "I mean, he was last seen downtown. He didn't walk seven miles to Crestmore and then die in the woods somewhere, all without being seen."

"What do you think happened to your husband, Mrs. Batcher?" The detective set the glass down, and his wet lips glistened in the light from the overhead chandelier. She'd ordered the light from a Native American ranch in Colorado, and they'd brought it in on an 18-wheeler, it was so large.

What do I think happened to David? What a great question.

"Honestly? I have no idea."

Among the various lies, this bit of truth was the easiest to say.

CHAPTER 12

KATIE MORROW

"Well now, let's see. After Willow left, there was a time when Mark was the most eligible bachelor in Crestmore. Forget the whispers about him killing Willow—women will overlook pesky little things like that when it comes to a handsome, rich man. And he's both of those things. I think he's possibly the best-looking man in Crestmore. And his job gives him a bit of star power, especially with the men in the neighborhood. My husband was at the club when Mark scrolled through his cell phone contacts and said it was like the call sheet at the ESPYs. I'm telling you, the man's a god inside these neighborhood gates—at least to the husbands."

28 Blackberry Summit Road
Hole 1, Stone Hollow

Pregnant.

Katie's knees gave out a little at the word on the white stick. She carefully lowered herself to the toilet and stared at it, her vision blurring a bit. She placed it on the top of her thighs and unrolled a length of toilet paper and dabbed at her eyes, careful not to smudge her mascara.

That would be just what she needed with the cops hovering around—to look like she'd been crying. They wouldn't know that they were tears of joy, and would be suspicious if she was beaming.

Choking back a sob, she carefully wrapped the stick in tissue paper and then carried it into the bathroom. Opening up one of the lower cabinets, she stowed it away in a pull-out drawer that was filled with face wipes. Tomorrow, she'd take another. Just to double-check. And maybe on Monday, a third.

Facing the mirror again, she checked her makeup and allowed herself one secret smile. Another chance. This time, she wouldn't take any risks. No rigorous exercise. Only clean eating. Extra bed rest. Yoga and meditation sessions every day. This time, everything would work in her body and they would have a healthy, beautiful baby.

Her phone chimed with a text from Mark.

Make sure the cops don't go into the backyard. I'm almost there.

She texted back a thumbs-up and moved through the bedroom and out onto the second-floor landing, taking the steps two at a time as she headed for the downstairs, her excitement painting everything in a new hue. Would he be able to tell from looking at her? It felt like her entire face was flushed—*the pregnancy glow*, they called it. She had been too afraid, up until now, to celebrate the possible symptoms, but they were all there. Tender breasts. A slightly queasy stomach. Headaches. All beautiful, wonderful parts of the process.

She pulled open the front door and stepped out onto their front porch, verifying that the police officers were still waiting by their cars. It was a gorgeous day. A little windy. She should probably go inside and grab a pullover, something to stop the chill. But the sun was bright, the planters on either side of the front entry steps in full bloom, the red zinnias bold and happy. The home was a Mission Revival–style, according to Katie's mother, who watched home-remodeling shows each afternoon with a fresh bottle of merlot. It had rounded bell gables, a red-tiled roof, tan stucco walls, and cobblestone flooring. The estate had been built in the 1920s and had a front porch that was deep enough to park a car. They had never used the couch or seating clusters underneath the front eaves, preferring to sit on the back deck overlooking the golf course, but now Katie settled into the couch and tucked her bare feet underneath her butt, crossing her arms against the chill.

Any minute, Mark would pull through the gates and into the drive. Last time Katie had gotten pregnant, she told him immediately, hiding the test in the liquor cabinet, next to his favorite brand of scotch. As soon as he'd walked in the door, he went straight for a drink and then froze, his back to her, and stared at the item for a full ten seconds before he spun around, his features crumpled in hope and happiness. "Are you sure?" he'd whispered.

She should have said no. She should have told him that 40 percent of first-time pregnancies fail, that they could hope but not get too excited. Instead, she had jumped into his arms and pressed her lips against his, and they had spent the entire evening interrupting each other to discuss crib placement, their stances on nannies, baby names, and birthing methods. Mark was an only child, as was Katie, and they had agreed that two children, minimum, were in their future.

This time, as difficult as it would be, she'd keep the news a secret. Just until she got further along and passed the danger zone.

At the end of their drive, the nose of Mark's two-door BMW convertible eased through the gates, and she stood, joy pumping through her at the sight of the red car. They would have to trade it in, of course. The first time she'd gotten pregnant, he ordered the big Range Rover, a reservation they canceled after the miscarriage. They could order another one, and also keep her Porsche SUV, though she'd overheard one of the moms in the neighborhood complaining that the back seat on hers was too tight for getting a car seat in and out.

Mark parked by the fountains, beside the police cruiser. When he stepped out, the wind rustled his thick hair. He was so gorgeous. With his black designer sunglasses, his cashmere pullover, the collar of his button-down shirt visible, the confident stride of his long legs as he closed the distance to the officers . . . you couldn't see any of the stress that had coated his voice when she had spoken to him on the phone. That must have been related to something at the office, because his steps were smooth, his smile wide, and he said something and the three of them laughed.

Any iota of worry she'd been carrying about the search dissipated, and it felt silly that she had even been concerned. It had been the mention of Willow that had unnerved her. She knew that nothing nefarious had happened to Willow; Mark had been clear on that. Willow had wanted a divorce and she left. Had packed several bags and gone. Women leave marriages all the time. It didn't mean that she was dead, certainly didn't mean that whatever they were looking for had anything to do with her. Willow was just an ex-wife, one who had never come back to Crestmore or been seen or heard from again. One who'd abandoned her business, her friends and family, her social media accounts, and her credit cards, and started a new life somewhere else, off the grid.

A little odd, yes. But Willow had been a free spirit, according to Mark.

Katie was a little grateful, actually, that Willow had disappeared. Other than the whispers in the neighborhood and her mother's nosy concern—it was refreshing not having an ex they continually bumped into or who wanted alimony. This neighborhood was full of stories of ex-wives who were nightmares, both to their ex-husbands and to the replacement wives. One had started sleeping with the husband, and they ended up getting back together and he divorced his second wife!

Mark turned and spotted her on the front porch. He looked surprised, which was reasonable, considering that Katie never waited on the porch for him. She waved and he lifted his hand in response, then gestured for the officers to follow him around to the side of the garage.

Maybe she should go out to the pond with them. Even though there wouldn't be anything there, it still felt like something she should see.

CHAPTER 13

ANDREA KENDAL

"I think she's too young for Eric, personally. I mean, Roxanne was his age. Maybe four or five years younger. But Andrea? She's, like, late twenties, tops. He's in his fifties. It's ridiculous."

1442 Kingsmere Drive
Hole 6, Stone Hollow

At 2:30 p.m., Andrea gathered up Cameron and Ryder and headed for the garage. She was loading Ryder's stroller into the back of her SUV when her phone dinged.

It was the app for the front-door camera, and she tapped on the notification to view the video.

On the front porch was a heavyset woman, her dark hair pulled back in a severe bun. Even through the small video, Andrea could see the bright-red smear of her lips, the crook of her large nose. Andrea's fingers slipped and the sleek phone dropped, skittering off her knee and underneath the vehicle. She swore, her eyes pinching shut against the pain in her kneecap. Hissing out a breath, she slowly straightened her leg, the joint smarting in protest.

From inside the SUV, Ryder shrieked and kicked his legs, anxious to get to the frozen yogurt place. He would want Superman flavor, and Cameron would want chocolate. Their verbal contract was signed, the yogurt restaurant the first stop on their itinerary, a reward for them behaving during the forty-five-minute-long book club discussion that Andrea had attended via Zoom. But she couldn't pull out of the garage right now, not with Patrizia on the front porch. Her car was probably in their driveway, which was ridiculous. What was the point of having a security gate and paying an ungodly amount each month for them to guard the entrance if they were then going to let someone through?

But she knew the answer to that. They let Patrizia through because she was on the list. Her driver's license was on file, her name and phone number in the database, their address beside it. Each home was allowed six permanent guest passes, and Roxanne had completed the paperwork for Patrizia. Paperwork that Andrea had never considered revising. The deletion felt like a cruel move to a woman who had lost a daughter. Even now, with the mistake darkening their front porch, the thought was too taboo.

She crouched and felt along the floor, trying to reach the phone. It was too far, and she had to lie on her stomach and inch underneath the car before she could reach it. Her fingers nudged the phone, then closed on it, and when she rolled upright and looked at the display, she froze.

The drop had answered the doorbell, Andrea's microphone recording, their connection live. She held her breath, hoping Ryder's babbles from inside the car weren't audible.

Cameron opened the car door and stuck his head out. Andrea held up her hand in warning, then put a finger to her lips in the *be quiet* gesture. The boy obeyed, his eyes widening at the expression on Andrea's face. So smart, that little one. He suspected, even at his age, how terrible the world could be.

Her forefinger shaking, Andrea reached out and pressed the end button on the connection. The video disappeared, but if anything, her anxiety spiked further with the woman out of sight. Who knew what she was doing on their property. What window she was looking in. What door she was trying.

Tony must have called her and had her drive up from San Diego. An infection spread quickly, and that was what this police investigation was. A fresh infection that would dominate their lives for a period of time. Maybe Andrea should take the kids and go to their home in Florida. Ride out the investigation there, let Eric handle it all, and come back once the dust had settled.

Eric had done it before. He'd dodged a murder investigation and emerged unscathed, ready for love and with an engagement ring in hand, one that was three times bigger than the one he had given Roxanne.

This was ridiculous. Andrea shouldn't have to hide in her driveway, on the verge of a panic attack, her heart hammering in her chest, all because of a woman who was over sixty years old. Patrizia may have ruled Roxanne's and Eric's lives, but she was no threat to Andrea. Intimidating, yes. Dangerous, no.

Still, Andrea waited in the garage, slipping quietly into the SUV and sitting with Cameron and Ryder for almost ten minutes before she felt brave enough to open the garage and start the car.

The driveway was empty, with no sign of Patrizia's car. Andrea gripped the steering wheel tightly and drove slowly down their drive and through the front gates.

That was close. She stopped at the end of the drive and looked to the left, waiting as a Mercedes convertible eased by. Letting off the pedal, she rolled forward, then slammed on her brakes at the sight of the woman standing in front of her car, blocking her exit.

Patrizia.

Patrizia hadn't changed since the last time Andrea saw her, three years ago. She had Roxanne's heavy build and a bitch face that was permanently in place. Holding her palm up like a traffic cop, she stared

Andrea down and circled around to the driver's-side window, rapping on the glass with her knuckles, then making the universal *roll down* sign with her hand.

Andrea considered, for the briefest of moments, *not* rolling down the window. She could, in theory, just drive off. Patrizia was on the side of her car, wouldn't be able to do anything to stop her if Andrea just stomped on the pedal and zoomed forward. The woman already hated her, so it wasn't as if she needed to preserve their relationship.

Andrea lowered her sunglasses and pressed the button on her door. The window hummed downward. "Hello," she said as sweetly as possible.

"You know that it's her they found, right? My daughter?" Patrizia gripped the window frame with both hands and leaned in, her breath smelling of cigarettes. "That's who they've found. I told them. I've told them for five years that he's a killer. You're *married* to a killer."

"Hi, Patrizia." Andrea pressed her lips together, a move that accentuated the lip injections she received every six months. "I'm sorry, I'm late to an appointment and can't talk."

"Listen here, sweetie. Tell Eric that he can't ignore me and Tony. We both know that story about his business trip is bullshit, and he's going to pay for what he did to her."

The words sent a chord of unease through Andrea and she hesitated, unsure of how to respond. *He's going to pay for what he did. We both know that story is bullshit.* Everyone seemed so sure of Eric's culpability, but his timelines were watertight. He had been six hours away, at an event with dozens of witnesses. It was impossible for him to be Roxanne's killer. Plus, there was no motive.

Patrizia's eyes roamed over the car's red interior. "She had a car just like this one, you know."

Not just like this. Roxanne had driven an Audi SUV, which was why Andrea had chosen a Volvo. She pushed aside the thought of the Audi, the blood splatters and smears well documented in the crime scene photos. The police had said that she had likely been stabbed once or twice before she tried to return to the car, and possibly a third time after she was pulled out, according to the blood pool on the ground. They'd said she'd likely fought off her attacker with her hands and gotten them cut up in the process, hence the blood on the steering wheel, gearshift, and center console.

"I'm very sorry about Roxanne," Andrea said carefully, letting her Jersey accent slip a little. "But I promise that Eric doesn't have anything to do with it."

"She was going to leave him," Patrizia hissed. "You know that, right? I've told you that?"

Yes, Patrizia had told her that. Andrea had received all the letters Roxanne's mother had sent and had listened to all the voicemails. She understood Patrizia and Tony's stance on the matter, but she knew the truth. Patrizia and Tony had been leeches, two members of a family who had sucked the life out of Roxanne.

Patrizia's gaze roamed to the back seat, and her expression soured a little at the sight of the two boys.

Andrea took her foot off the brake pedal and the car rolled forward a little, pulling Patrizia off-balance. "I'm sorry, I'm late to an appointment," she repeated.

The woman said nothing, and Andrea pressed the gas and left her behind, standing in the middle of their street, her face pinched in anger.

CHAPTER 14

SARA BATCHER

"I was Sara's executive assistant for three years. During that time, I never once saw David in the office. We knew she had a husband, we just never saw him. I think they were both workaholics. She definitely was. She ate, slept, and breathed InkRose, all the way up to the day she sold it."

16 Branwyn Hill
Hole 18, Silverwood Preserve

Sara considered canceling her evening plans but didn't. She stepped into the garage, surveyed the options, then opened the door to the Bentley coupe. Settling in behind the wheel, she raised the left bay door and started the engine.

It wasn't like she'd even needed David's life insurance. The $5 million had been a nice deposit in her account, but she was already wealthy, and from her own efforts. Sara's bespoke stationery company generated millions of dollars each year. At the time David had disappeared, she had just signed a contract with one of the superstore companies, guaranteeing that InkRose desk sets would be stocked in all their North

American stores. A week before he left, they had celebrated the deal over dinner at Swanti, at one of the oceanfront tables they reserved for VIPs.

David had been quiet that night, his smile slow to come, his distraction evident as he half-heartedly participated in the conversation. Her irritation had grown as the meal went on, and she considered, in the long pause between the third course and dessert, excusing herself to the restroom and leaving him there.

The David she had met, the pharmaceutical sales rep who had wooed her, the man she had fallen in love with . . . it had been so long since she had seen him. The night they'd met, she was twenty-six, at a sales conference in Laguna Beach. He was a handsome and charismatic stranger who'd had their entire table in hysterics over a story involving him, two strippers in Reno, and a semi full of rotten fish. She hadn't been able to take her eyes off him, and she wasn't the only one. Every woman at that table—and half of the men—had been in awe of him.

Later that night, the conference had hosted a meet and greet on the upper-level deck. Waiters passed by with stems of champagne and tiny strawberry-topped brownie bites, and David had gently pulled on her elbow, steering her away from the women she'd been talking to, and they all gaped in jealousy as he maneuvered her to the side and put a glass of champagne in her hand and said, "Sara, what would I have to say to close the deal with you?"

All he'd had to say was her name. She hadn't even realized he knew who she was, or had any interest in her at all, and there he was, staring deep into her eyes, his mouth crooked in a smile.

That version of David, she'd fallen head over heels for. She'd married that David. Had planned to have a family with that David. And then had lost him twelve years later to Vicodin.

That was what she had wanted to say to the detectives. David hadn't disappeared on May 5.

He had been gone long before that.

CHAPTER 15

KATIE MORROW

"Everybody thought that Mark and Willow were the perfect couple, but I always knew there was something off about them. It was like they hated each other and loved each other, all at the same time. I think he killed her. I think she pissed him off one day and he snapped."

28 Blackberry Summit Road
Hole 1, Stone Hollow

The pond behind Mark and Katie's house was large and stocked with fish, the bluegills purchased online and delivered from an aquarium company on a Tuesday in April while Mark had been at work. Katie hadn't understood the reason, given that they never went near the pond and it only served as a buffer between them and the golfers, who liked to stare at her in her bikini on the days it was warm enough to lay out poolside. The pond was Mark's baby, a good part of his weekends dedicated to balancing the PH level of the water, planting starwort and waterweeds, and installing a UV filtration system and underwater lights. Katie could have put on her skimpiest two-piece, but unless she posed with a fish in her teeth, he preferred to focus on the pond.

There were many amazing things about her husband and their relationship, but his attraction to her had always been, at least in her mind, in question.

It had been that way from the very beginning. Katie had been on shift at the coffee shop, pulling a double, the place packed with its normal lineup of oat-milk-latte-drinking Silicon Valley tech heads. She had been hungry and irritated, the former triggering the latter, and when the hot man in the thousand-dollar suit had ordered a mocha latte, she accidentally rang it in as a matcha latte instead.

When he had hesitated, raising his eyebrows at the green liquid in the cup, she had realized her mistake. "Drink it," she'd snapped. "It's what you really wanted."

"I really wanted *that*?" he'd asked, looking at the color with skepticism. "I don't think—"

"Drink it," she'd interrupted, with a confidence she didn't feel, her anxiety rising at the heat of her supervisor's stare, the woman easing closer, ready to jump in and assist. Exactly what she didn't need, given that she'd been written up three times already for similar mental snags. Staring in Mark's eyes, she willed him to understand.

He had taken the cup from her and pulled the straw cover off while holding eye contact with Katie. It was a good stare, a sort of tractor beam that made everything else in the crowded room disappear for a moment.

He'd paused, his mouth an inch from the tip of the straw. He had nice lips. A clean-shaven jaw. A little bit of a butt-crack chin, but the rest of his face made up for it. Good eyes—blue, with the kind of thick lashes a girl would kill for.

"You should work for me," he'd said, right there in front of Becca. "I'll pay triple whatever you're earning here."

"You want to try the drink first?" She'd broken their eye contact to glance at the line, which was beginning to wrap around the end of the muffin display, a cardinal sin in the world of Loop & Bean.

"You want me to try the drink first?" he'd repeated, his mouth still hovering above the straw.

"Yeah," she had shot back. It had felt like a game, and that, combined with the job offer, filled her with a giddy joy that cut right through her black mood. Triple what she was earning? He could definitely afford it. That was a black Centurion Card he'd tapped on their register. According to Tig, who worked the afternoon shift, someone could purchase a condo on that card; that was how big the limit was.

He'd closed his lips around the straw and sucked. There was a pause while he swallowed, and then he frowned. "It's disgusting."

She had laughed. She hadn't meant to. It was an involuntary vomit of a reaction, one born from stress and anticipation and the agreement that matcha really was gross, but surely he could have pretended, especially with Becca right here, staring at them both.

He had smiled, and she reached up and untied the neck of her apron. "I'd like to accept your offer of employment if it still stands."

His grin had widened. "It does."

And they had left together, right then, riding up the elevator to his sports agency on the forty-eighth floor, where he introduced her to the contracts' manager, who gave her a desk right next to Mark's assistant's. Her new role was to organize and execute the mountain of paperwork involved with each new client or contract that Mark secured. The manager had shown her the ropes and advised her to expect long hours. Mark was, as the woman had put it, the busiest sports agent in California.

The accolade had been accurate. The office phone rang constantly, and it was exhilarating, hearing the names his assistant would mention. Mark represented the biggest stars in basketball, football, and golf. Katie had mentioned a few of them to her father, and he'd made her repeat them, on speakerphone, so that his coworkers could hear them.

Her life, within a week, had changed completely. She started to visit Loop & Bean as a customer, not an employee, wearing designer suits and heels and with hair fresh from salon appointments, courtesy of her new boss's charge account. She regularly attended lunches with sports celebrities, in restaurants where the lunch bill hit four figures, and could get skybox tickets to the Giants or courtside seats at the Warrior games with just a snap of her newly manicured fingers.

And Mark had been a complete gentleman as her boss. For a while, she had wondered whether he was gay. Granted, she'd known about Willow, of course. Her photo had been in a frame on his desk, her birthday and their anniversary in his calendar, and there'd been a folder on the work drive where his assistant had saved any receipt, travel itinerary, or document associated with her. The office gossip mill loved to speculate over what had happened to her. Everyone had an opinion and a theory, ones they shared with Katie in the break room, the copy room, the conference room, and the coffee line.

Willow was everyone's favorite topic of debate. Whether she was nice or a bitch. A deserter or a victim. Alive or dead.

After a year as his contracts coordinator, Katie had worked up the nerve to ask his assistant about their relationship. "What were Willow and Mark like together?"

Miriam, who had been a hospital administrator before she moved into the corporate world, took a bite from her energy bar before answering. "Them two? Oh, like rabbits in heat. They couldn't keep their hands off each other."

They couldn't keep their hands off each other. That response had given her hope. So Mark *wasn't* gay. Probably just mourning the loss of his wife. After all, it had been almost two years at that point. Still relatively fresh, in the world of divorces.

Of course, if Mark was straight, his strict adherence to professional boundaries likely meant that he simply wasn't attracted to Katie. And that was fine. For most men, she was ideal. Blond, with giant blue eyes and a petite build. The combination had typically opened the door to romantic relationships, but some men preferred a different look. And Willow had been very different from Katie, with wild dark hair, a deep tan, and a big smile. She'd been almost as tall as Mark, but with a softer, curvy shape.

Katie had shelved the idea of a relationship with her boss and accepted a date with one of the investment bankers in the building. They had been two months into a half-hearted fling when Mark finally asked her out.

Katie hadn't hesitated to accept, and on that date—and each subsequent one—she played every card she knew, hoping one would pay off. And they finally had. She was now Mrs. Katie Morrow, with Mark's ring on her hand, his baby in her belly, and her desk at the office now manned by a different woman, one her husband had no romantic interest in.

They can't keep their hands off each other.

Would anyone say that about Katie and Mark?

No, but it didn't matter. She wasn't competing with a ghost, and her husband would be ecstatic once he found out about the baby.

Mark strode toward her. "They're going to start diving, but it'll take a few hours," he said. "We should order food in, something to feed them." Stopping in front of her, he placed his hands on the sides of her arms and bent forward, pressing his lips against hers for a short, perfunctory moment. Withdrawing, he fished his cell phone out of his pants pocket. "I have to make a call. Can you handle the food?"

"Of course." Katie glanced past him, at the men. Two divers were starting to wade into the pool, clad in all black, with tanks and face masks on. "Did they say what it was that they found?"

He threw the bomb as if it were nothing. "They're looking for a body."

"A body? What do you mean? A *dead* body?" She felt unsteady and grabbed hold of his shirt, clinging to it.

"Yes. Don't answer any questions if they try and ask you anything. Just let Andrew take care of that."

Maybe it was Willow. The thoughts she never allowed herself to consider wormed their way inside her head and shouted for attention.

Kalessa in Accounting had been convinced that Willow had been killed, had said that the brunette would *never* leave like that without stopping by the office and telling everyone goodbye. Kalessa had had a long list of suspects, and hadn't mentioned Mark by name but made the possibility clear. And the accountant hadn't been alone in her suspicions; she'd just been one of the only employees bold enough to voice them.

"Katie." Mark disentangled her hands from his shirt. "I have to make a call. You'll get everyone dinner? I want it here before it gets dark."

I'm pregnant. It was a horrible time to share the news, especially given her vow to wait until the second trimester, but the statement almost fell out. She swallowed the urge and nodded. "Sure. Fausto's?"

Her husband nodded and looked down at his phone, scrolling through the contacts as he backed away. "Don't talk to them," he repeated as he turned to head toward the house. "Let Andrew handle it."

She glanced back at the police officers. The two detectives she'd spoken to earlier were standing side by side, facing her, on the other side of the pond. *"You've never spoken to or met Willow Morrow?"*

"They're looking for a body."

It wasn't Willow. It couldn't be.

CHAPTER 16

ANDREA KENDAL

"The problem with Andrea is that she's too pretty. I mean, obviously she's had work done, who hasn't in this neighborhood? Don't tell anyone, but I've had a facelift and cheek implants. You can't tell, right? Spend enough on a surgeon and it's like invisible magic. Ugly one day, a supermodel the next. But anyways, I'm getting distracted. Andrea is probably the prettiest woman in Crestmore, and that's part of the reason why she doesn't have any friends. It's annoying, that sort of physical perfection."

1442 Kingsmere Drive
Hole 6, Stone Hollow

Andrea dropped Cameron off at the Montessori center for his weekly sensorial lesson, then headed up the interstate and into Richmond's Iron Triangle suburb. She made the turns without consulting the GPS, the streets familiar, the rough area one she felt comfortable in. The nail salon was in a strip mall, between a shuttered-up Best Buy and a discount beauty supply. Andrea pulled Ryder out of his car seat and carried him inside, locking and arming the Volvo's security system before pulling open the salon's glass door.

There was only one other client in the shop, an older Black woman in a chair at the end of the row, her bare feet already in the water, a gossip magazine open on her lap. Andrea conversed briefly with the technician, then placed Ryder in the chair next to the woman.

"Hey." She leaned over and gave her a hug. It lasted for a long moment, neither woman wanting to let go, and Andrea closed her eyes, inhaling the familiar scent of Kisi's perfume.

"Hey, you." Kisi kissed her on her cheek, then released her. "Now, let me see this beautiful boy."

"Careful, he'll steal your heart." Andrea laughed and picked up Ryder, transferring the pudgy boy to Kisi's open arms.

"Oh, that's a battle I won't win," she cooed, bringing her face close to the toddler. "Look at those fat cheeks. He's got Eric's nose, doesn't he? And your eyes."

"Sounds about right." Andrea settled into the chair and reached down, unlacing her sneakers. "Definitely has Eric's appetite and stubbornness."

"Aw, you've got a streak of stubbornness yourself. And hey, maybe he'll follow in Daddy's footsteps and become a doctor and save lives." She blew softly into the boy's face, and he giggled. Ryder may be strong-willed, but he was also, by all accounts, a happy baby. Not a fear in the world. He'd never have to go to bed at night to the sound of his wife sobbing, or wondering whether today was the day he would be killed. His entire life would be one easy walk in the park, thanks to the sacrifices she and Eric had made.

"I miss you." Kisi reached out and gripped Andrea's hand tightly. "You should come and see me more."

"I know." Andrea looked down at their hands. "It's just . . ."

"I know, I know it's risky. I follow you on social media so I can see the pictures of the kids—but it's not the same as this."

No, it wasn't the same. Andrea lowered her bare feet into the swirling hot water and accepted a ring with different polish swatches hanging from it. In a perfect world, Ryder and Cameron would grow up knowing Kisi. She'd be an honorary aunt to them both, and the first person Andrea would call when they needed a babysitter, or to extend an invite for a birthday party or school event.

But it wasn't a perfect world, and Eric would be furious at just the thought of her talking to Kisi. Which was why he would never find out about this meeting, or any of the times she had sneaked away to see her best friend.

Andrea selected a pale nude color and passed the ring back to the technician. "You know . . . they found a body in our neighborhood. The detectives say it's from about five years ago."

Kisi looked away from Ryder. "A body? You mean a dead body? Male or female?"

"The rumor mill says female, but who knows. Right now, it's just partial remains. They're looking for the rest of it."

"The police think it might be Roxanne?"

"Well, Tony does. And a few other detectives came by the house, asking questions. I don't think it makes sense. I mean, our neighborhood is twenty miles from the park, but . . ." Andrea shrugged. "I don't like Tony being around. And Patrizia showed up today, being all . . ." She blew out a breath. "Aggressive."

"Well, they'll identify the body and Patrizia will go back home and Tony will find something else to focus on." Kisi shrugged, as if it were easy and within a few days, everything would return to normal.

And maybe it would. But what if it didn't? Statistically, it was much more likely that this was the first spark of a match that would start a forest fire. She pressed the massage-function button on her chair and tried to relax against the leather.

"Trust me," Kisi commanded. "Look at you. You're obsessing over this."

Which was a perfectly normal thing to do, Andrea reasoned. Right now, every woman in Crestmore was thinking about this development. It only made sense for her to be among those ranks, especially with everyone assuming the body might be Roxanne's. "It might take years for the body to be identified, especially if it's been in the water for this long."

The former obstetrician clicked her tongue. "Identified, yes. But you don't need an ID. They just need to eliminate Roxanne as the victim. Why does it matter who it is? As far as you're concerned, it only matters who it isn't. They have Roxanne's dental records, don't they? So there. Tony and Patrizia will go away, and you'll be fine."

She was right. In addition to dental records, they also had Roxanne's DNA. It should be quick and easy to prove that the body wasn't hers. Maybe this whole thing *would* easily blow over. Ryder laughed and she looked over to see him tugging on a curl of Kisi's hair. She had gorgeous hair. It was an extension of her personality—all wild beauty. Andrea got a sudden lump in her throat at the painful awareness that she was, over time, losing her best friend. You couldn't maintain a connection with stolen meetups once or twice a year. She blinked and her vision blurred. Swearing, she reached for her purse and the small package of tissues that she kept there.

"Hey now." Kisi patted her arm. "It's okay."

But it wasn't okay. It hadn't been for years.

CHAPTER 17

SARA BATCHER

"Sara was a pain in the ass when it came to law enforcement. She would call every day when David was first missing, trying to get someone to take the case seriously. But guys run off, you know? Especially when married to a type-A woman like her. Hell, I was exhausted just from ten minutes of listening to her. I couldn't imagine being in a relationship with that. She was lucky the chief liked her. He catered to her demands and made us dig into a case that was pretty much dead. So we dug. But there wasn't anything there. The husband ran off to the Cayman Islands or wherever it is that rich people go to escape their problems."

16 Branwyn Hill
Hole 18, Silverwood Preserve

Sara and Chief of Police Joel Stanton had sex first, as they normally did. No dinner, no conversation—just a quick strip and screw. Tonight's session was unusually unsatisfying, and Sara analyzed the reasons while on her forearms, her knees digging into the worn-out mattress, the fan above them rattling.

It could be David. The potential for his body to turn up after all these years was of concern. Maybe not a *concern*, because it was kind of a good thing, having closure. Finally, everyone would have all their questions answered. No more speculating. No more suspicions. It would be like ripping off a Band-Aid. Painful for a moment, then over.

Of course, Sara might have to move out of Crestmore. Maybe not. It would depend on what the police determined.

"You like that?" he grunted from behind her, his breaths getting louder, and she gave an encouraging sound in response. It normally didn't take Joel this long. Maybe he was waiting for her to come. Had she? Probably not. She began to rock against him, giving her own grunts of pleasure, and then she let out a long wail that sounded very convincing. She stretched it a little longer than normal, then swore with a string of compliments about his enormous size. All false, but it did the trick. He completed his own celebration of pleasure and then collapsed on the mattress beside her, his hairy chest heaving, eyes closed.

Joel needed to work on his cardio. That would be her luck, him having a heart attack while they were screwing. She could just imagine how that would go over at the station, the sort of questions they would ask.

No, if Joel were going to die, it needed to be somewhere far, far away from her, and right after he'd wiped his cell phone.

She pulled a pillow over her head in an attempt to muffle the overhead fan's rattle. Joel always asked why she never stayed the night, yet she had mentioned this stupid fan four or five times and he hadn't fixed it. "Do you have any updates on the search?"

"No. They'll call me when they find something. And then I'll tell you."

"Like you told me this morning?" She turned her head and shot him a glare.

He chuckled and raised his hands in innocence. "Hey, it was just a bone. By the time we got forensics out there and verified it was human, I still didn't know what was what until past noon. It wasn't until we nailed down an age of decay that David's name started getting brought up."

She rolled toward him and he lifted his arm, putting it under her head like a pillow. It was an unusual pose for them, but she completed the position, snuggling into the crook of his arm and appreciating, for just a moment, the warmth of a human body. Joel had a good body. Just soft enough, but still strong. She shifted closer and wrapped her leg around his. "But there are a couple of people it could be, right?"

"Kind of. He's the top of the list. You should touch base with your attorney."

She already had, and they'd gone back over her detailed alibi for the twenty-four hours before and after David's disappearance. It was easy—everything was time-stamped and documented. Back when he'd vanished, she had pulled and filed the three months prior and post of credit card statements and phone records, plus the exterior security camera footage of her home, ready for sharing. Ian had worked with a psychiatrist to build psychological reports on both her and David's state of mind. They'd created a list of character witnesses, and Sara was trained on how to defeat lie detector tests and skirt questions. Five years was a long time, and she had spent it waiting and preparing for every possible outcome.

She ran her hand across the soft hair of Joel's chest, then farther down his stomach. His penis was flaccid and wet, and she gently ran her fingers over the top of it. "What's going to happen if it's him?"

"You'll be a prime suspect. We'll reopen the case and look at his last twenty-four hours. It doesn't help that you sold the condo."

Well, it wasn't her job to help their case. "So, you're thinking foul play?"

"Well, he didn't bury himself in the neighborhood." He chuckled. "So, yeah."

No, Sara thought. *He definitely didn't.*

CHAPTER 18

KATIE MORROW

"Rumor was, Mark and Willow were swingers. I don't know if I believe it, but that's what my wife says. I guess I could see it. Willow was really sexy. Not like that stiff prude he's married to now. She's the type of woman who tells you she's married within ten seconds, when you were just asking her some innocent question."

28 Blackberry Summit Road
Hole 1, Stone Hollow

Katie Morrow watched her husband pace the length of their upper deck. Mark's whiskey was gone, the empty glass still in hand, his navy bathrobe fluttering in the wake of his strides. Anxiety was a new look on her husband, one she didn't like.

"Please, just sit." She patted the seat next to her. "I'll get you another drink."

"I don't want another drink." He stopped and glanced down at the glass, then placed it on the railing. He rested his forearms on the wide concrete surface and stared out into the night. Normally, the course was dark, their view only lit by the moon. Tonight, there were clusters of light in the distance as the search teams moved. Katie had expected them to stop at dusk, but apparently, they were going to go all night. She had mentioned as much to Mark, and he had practically sprinted upstairs to see what she was referring to.

"Is it Willow you're worried about?" Katie asked the question carefully, well aware that his ex-wife was a subject that was off limits. Early on in their relationship, she had asked a few questions and seen how quickly he shut down. Tiptoeing around topics was a skill she was well versed in, so if Mark didn't want to talk about his first wife, that was fine with her.

Except that now they kind of needed to, especially if these were her bones the police were searching for. And there didn't really seem to be a delicate way to bring that subject up.

"Is it *Willow* I'm worried about?" Mark repeated, and she hated his slow and deliberate tone, as if she'd asked a dumb question, which she hadn't. It was a perfectly reasonable question, one she had turned over in her head a dozen times before she voiced it. She'd been careful with both the words and the tone, had mastered both, and yet here he was, mocking her.

"No, Katie. I'm not worried about Willow. Wherever she is, Willow is fine. Willow is fine, while I'm stuck here, having to deal with this . . . mess." He gestured to the backyard in frustration.

Stuck here didn't really seem like a fair descriptor. And what mess? So far, this had barely been an inconvenience. A search of their pond? Which had, of course, turned up nothing. A few questions from the cops? They had just been doing their job, and they already seemed to be done with that. As long as it wasn't Willow's body out there, Katie doubted they would even get asked any more questions.

As long as it wasn't Willow's body.

Was he worried that maybe it was?

She pushed the question away before it grew legs and ran over her heart.

CHAPTER 19

ANDREA KENDAL

"Their house is stunning. It's at the end of Kingsmere, overlooks the tee box on hole six. I look at the back of it a lot when I golf, but I don't ever see the husband there. Guess the heart-surgeon shtick keeps him busy. His new wife, she's just like the old one. They both liked to lay out by the pool on a nice day, and I gotta say, it's one of the best parts of the round, seeing a beautiful woman in a bikini. And the new wife, she's a ten. Last one . . . about a six."

1442 Kingsmere Drive
Hole 6, Stone Hollow

Eric didn't notice Andrea's new nails, not that she had expected him to. Her husband was a rarity of the male species—uncommonly generous, protective, and thoughtful—but not one who observed the little things. Especially not on evenings such as tonight, after days such as this.

Their meal was almost silent, the long gaps in speech only interrupted for functional reasons.

Please pass the corn.

The lamb is delicious.

Would you like more wine?

Eric rarely drank, but tonight he finished off two bottles of Kistler, then poured a brandy and took it up to the widow's walk to see if they were still searching for the body.

Kisi was right: The sooner they found the body, the better. Roxanne would be eliminated, and everything could just return to normal.

Andrea had stopped at the guard gate on the way back in and asked for the paperwork to update their list of trusted contacts. Patrizia needed to be off the list immediately. She couldn't take another interaction like today. It wasn't safe, especially not if Ryder and Cameron were with her.

She stood at the kitchen counter and rinsed their plates, stacking them and the pots in the sink for the housekeeper to take care of in the morning. After finishing the task, she wiped down the counters, then picked up Ryder and carried him into his big brother's room.

The little boy was on a stool in his bathroom, staring into the mirror while he brushed his teeth. He had already changed into his pajamas, a matching yellow set that had green aliens all over it. Aliens, right now, were Cameron's favorite thing. Last year it had been race cars; prior to that, bats. Thank God the bats phase was over. Cameron had campaigned hard for a pet bat, and had pitched a mini–temper tantrum every time he was told no. Eric had started to say *maybe*, and had even reached out to the homeowners association to ask about the rules regarding unorthodox pets. Before they could respond, Cameron had discovered model sets, and Andrea breathed a huge sigh of relief.

Now aliens were everywhere. As soon as he finished his bedtime routine, he'd watch an episode of *Ancient Aliens*—a show Andrea thought was too old for him, but that Eric considered educational—then go to bed. Cameron had already seen every episode in existence, most of them two or three times, but that didn't dampen his love for the docuseries. If anything, he had started repeating some of the lines along with the narrator, deepening his voice to match the serious pitch.

Eric found it charming, and Andrea couldn't help but agree.

She placed Ryder in the center of Cameron's bed, then flipped on the night-light and closed his closet door. From inside the bathroom, he rinsed, then loudly gargled and leaned forward to spit in the sink.

"Why are your boobs so big?"

Andrea paused, then leaned against the doorframe and met her son's eyes in the mirror. "Cameron. It's rude to ask about someone's body. Where did you even learn that word?"

He fisted the hand towel and pressed it to his mouth, then shoved it onto the counter. "Mason said that you have the biggest boobs in the country." He stepped carefully down from his stool, and Andrea reached forward to help.

"In the country?" She laughed. "I'm not sure mine are the biggest on this street, sweetie. But you shouldn't talk about people's boobs. They are private."

"Dad shows his boobs all the time." He lifted his own T-shirt, examining his nipples in the mirror and swiveling to the left and then the right, admiring them.

"Well, it's different for daddies and little boys." Andrea swung the door open farther and gestured toward the room with her head. "Come on, let's get you in bed."

"They *are* really big." He dropped his own shirt and spun around so he was facing Andrea and stared at her chest. The worn T-shirt Andrea was wearing didn't do a great job of hiding her double E's, which she thought were too big but Eric had asserted were the right size. All he had cared about was that they would attract attention, and they certainly did that. No one looked at her face, not with the best implants money could buy.

"Yeah, well, you have big elbows." She ushered him out of the bathroom and flipped off the light.

"I do not!" he said indignantly, then examined his left one to be sure.

"You do. They're enormous. I was telling Daddy that we might need to expand your bedroom into Ryder's just to make room for them."

From the bed, Ryder giggled at the sound of his name, and Cameron sprinted over and gave him a messy kiss on the top of the head.

"If we expand my room, I want to add an RC track inside of it. With a monster-truck jump for my Bigfoot crawler." He pantomimed his truck soaring over Ryder and then crashing, the fake explosion loud and dramatic.

And just like that, Andrea's surgically enhanced breasts were forgotten, at least until his friends brought them up again. Hopefully, that wouldn't happen for another decade or so, and by then the internet would have taken over their sexual education to the point where Andrea's then-saggy breasts would be uninteresting. She picked up the remote on his bedside table and pressed the top button, raising the television out of the base frame of the bed. "Now, I'm going to put Ryder down. One episode, then go to sleep, okay?"

"Which episode is it?" He crawled under the gray-striped blanket and kicked his feet, giving them room under the cover.

"Let's see . . . 'The Mystery of Puma Punku.' Are you good with that?"

"Yep."

"Okay. I'm setting the sleep timer for thirty minutes." Andrea kissed his forehead, and he wiggled away from the affection. "Sleep tight."

He didn't respond, his focus already on the opening credits.

She scooped up Ryder and hugged the baby to her chest, backing slowly out of Cameron's room and closing the door.

In the dark, less than a hundred yards behind their house, a shovel hit another human bone.

CHAPTER 20

SARA BATCHER

"I was part of the takeover team that came in with the InkRose purchase, and while Sara looks sweet and meek, she's not. We spent over thirty hours in negotiation calls with her, and she was ruthless. Drained every last dollar out of the deal. I think she would have thrown her own mother into the asset list if she thought it would have sealed the deal at a higher margin."

16 Branwyn Hill
Hole 18, Silverwood Preserve

Sara was asleep, one leg flung over Joel's thigh, when his phone rang. She jerked to life and rolled to the side, propping herself up on her forearm as she watched him fumble for his glasses and then his phone.

"Chief Stanton here." He coughed.

"Okay." He glanced over his shoulder at her, and she tried to read his expression in the dark. "Have you called the ME?"

The medical examiner. That meant they had found something. Sara looked through the sheets, searching for her shirt. She should get home in case someone showed up.

"I'll be there in fifteen. Everything by the book, you get me? Tell forensics to be on point."

He ended the call and turned on the lamp, flooding the room in soft light.

"They found more?" Sara asked.

"Almost a full skeleton." He twisted toward her. "Sara, it's male. Likely between five eight and five ten in height."

She pulled on her shirt and digested the news. "So it's David."

"Could be."

She rubbed her face with both hands. She needed to be very smart from this point forward, with every single thing she did. "Okay. I should go home."

"We shouldn't follow each other through the guard gate. You go ahead. I'll leave five minutes after you."

She nodded and pushed to her feet. Her jeans were on the ground near the window, and she hopped on one foot, pulling them on. She grabbed her sneakers and ran a hand through her hair. "We probably shouldn't see each other again, until this blows over."

"Agreed." He sounded grim. Maybe tonight wasn't the best night for her to have come over. At least, not for him. She'd been desperate for information and learned more in the last six hours than she had known in the last two years. Plus, if she hadn't pushed to stay the night, she wouldn't have gotten this news—not this quick. Now she would be prepared when the officers come tomorrow. She'd know what to expect and would have time to game-plan how to act. That advantage was worth the lackluster shag and blow job.

She didn't waste time putting on her shoes. She grabbed her purse and keys and jogged across his front lawn and to her car. Climbing in, she tossed her shoes in the passenger seat and started up the powerful engine.

So, after five years, David had finally shown up.

CHAPTER 21

KATIE MORROW

"Last Christmas, Mrs. Morrow gave all the trash guys a tin of homemade cookies and a $100 Costco gift card. Most of the people in this neighborhood treat us like shit, but she sees us as real people. Knows my name, always asks about my son. She's my favorite wife in the neighborhood. One of the prettiest too."

28 Blackberry Summit Road
Hole 1, Stone Hollow

Katie woke up in the middle of the night and reached for Mark. His side of the bed was empty, and she sat upright and listened. Their bathroom was dark, no light coming from underneath his toilet stall. She called his name and waited.

Twisting to the side, she looked at the clock on the bedside table: 3:02 a.m. Mark typically took a sleeping pill, one that left him snoring and half dead until seven, when his alarm went off. He didn't even wake up to pee, much less to wander the house. She pulled back the covers and swung her feet over the side.

One side of their bedroom was all floor-to-ceiling windows that overlooked the backyard. The blackout curtains in front of them were all closed, keeping the bedroom dark, save for the pale-blue light from the fish tank inset in the far left wall. The tank had been an anniversary present from Willow and was over seven hundred gallons. It stretched over fourteen feet across and five feet deep, and was a rainbow of exotic corals and structures, including a sunken ship and various treasure chests. During their marriage, Willow had supplemented the tank on every holiday and birthday, her gifts ranging from a rare eel to a monitor system that measured pH, salinity, temperature, and nitrate levels. That beauty of a gift meant that his phone chimed at inopportune times with alerts from the system's app.

Katie hated that stupid app almost as much as she hated the fucking aquarium. For one, it required its own technician to come three times a week to care for the fish and clean the tank. Mark insisted that she be home to supervise the activity, which meant that three days a week, her entire schedule revolved around babysitting the human equivalent of a Siamese algae eater. The second source of her ire was Mark's obvious love for it. In the unlikely case of a random predicament where Mark could rescue only one item from their home, she wasn't entirely sure that he would pick her over the tank. A woman—a wife—should never have to question her husband's fondness for her over an aquatic money pit.

She checked the bathroom, just to make sure, but he wasn't there. She checked the bedroom's small living room—nothing—and the balcony—empty.

Maybe he'd gone down to the theater. Sometimes, if he didn't take a sleeping pill, he would stay up late watching MMA fights or sports recaps. She'd found him there before, asleep in one of the recliners, his hand still on the remote, a few empty beers beside him. She took the back stairs off their bedroom down two flights to the basement to check.

The basement was original to the house, the sort of California feature that had surprised her when she moved here from Florida. There, everything was built up to avoid flooding, so the first basement she'd entered had blown her mind. It was like an entire extra house, hidden underground. Mark's was built to excess and one of the few parts of the home that didn't have Willow's touch. It had been an empty shell when Katie moved in, and Mark had given her an unlimited budget and the freedom to build it out however she saw fit.

The door to the basement was ajar, and she pushed it open, comforted by the signs of life. The wall sconces were on in the clubroom, bathing the pool table and leather couches in warm light. The carved-wood walls had various art pieces hung and the spotlights to each were on, bringing the paintings to life.

There was a sound from down the hall, and relief flooded her. He was in the theater. Probably asleep in front of the giant screen. She moved quietly down the hall and stopped outside the room.

Mark wasn't asleep. He was talking. She put her ear to the door, trying to hear what he was saying. He was agitated, his voice fast—so much for thoughts of him being zonked out at 3:00 a.m. She caught the words *plane* and *cops*. Placing her hand on the door, she pressed gently, but it creaked and she stopped.

Willow. Was that what he had just said? Her gut, already twisted into a knot, dropped to her feet, and she thought of the body. The search. The police.

So, you didn't know the prior Mrs. Morrow? She had seen the look in their eyes. Pity. Suspicion. It was the same combination she'd seen from their neighbors, the other wives, their so-called friends.

No one believed Mark. No one trusted him. And now look at her. Hovering outside the door, her ears straining to eavesdrop on his conversation.

Did she really believe that her husband, the love of her life, the father of her baby . . . did she really believe that he might have killed his wife?

The question should have been easy to answer, but it wasn't.

CHAPTER 22

ANDREA KENDAL

"It wasn't right, Eric marrying so quickly after Roxanne died. That right there shows his culpability. There should be a mourning period after a murder. Four, five years, at least. He started parading around that tart just a year after what happened."

1442 Kingsmere Drive
Hole 6, Stone Hollow

Eric was in the kitchen feeding Ryder when Andrea trudged through the wide, arched opening. Her bathrobe was on, her face scrubbed and pink, her hair not yet brushed. She yawned and kissed Ryder on the head, then wrapped her arms around Eric's waist and looked up at him, accepting a kiss on the lips.

He was in surgical scrubs and had likely been up since five. He and Ryder were on the same schedule; for every middle-of-the night feeding he'd missed out on with Cameron, he'd more than made up for it with Ryder. She was the only wife she knew who was able to sleep in and wake up knowing her husband had already fed and dressed the kids.

She returned to Ryder, who was happily babbling to himself while he smeared applesauce over his high chair, and dropped into the chair beside him. "What's your schedule today?" She rolled his high chair closer to her.

"First surgery at nine. I'll be done around seven, maybe a little earlier if everything goes smoothly."

Or maybe later if it didn't. She was used to the life of a surgeon's wife. Cardiac surgery didn't take second fiddle to dinnertimes, date nights, or lunch meetups. There had been countless times when Eric had gotten a call in the middle of the night, or gotten up mid-meal for a VIP or difficult case. That was the side effect of being the best, and from the moment he'd decided to go into medicine, being the best was the only standard he was happy with. Perfection, for her husband, was the minimum.

She caught her reflection in the window and turned her chin slightly, examining the smooth line and absence of a double chin. She had never been fat, not in the slightest. But she'd always had a small pocket of fat under her chin that, at certain angles, showed itself. Eric had worked with the surgeon to suck out the fat and shave down the jawbone to create a more feminine line. Heart shaped—that was her face now.

His standard of perfection had extended to all parts of his life except in the area of Roxanne. Roxanne had been a mess. A natural beauty, if you didn't mind a misshapen nose and slightly hooded eyes. A flat chest and a pear-shaped physique. She'd had slightly crooked teeth and a smile that showed too much of her gums.

And Eric had loved every inch of her. Worshipped her. He thought Andrea didn't know about the photos, but she'd found the folder that was hidden in the bottom drawer of his desk. Candid shots of Roxanne laughing, her eyes pinched shut, her crooked teeth on full display. Personal shots of them in bed, her dark hair everywhere, her lipstick smeared, her eyes soft as she looked into the camera.

Andrea understood why she was different. Eric had approached her desire to change her appearance with the same rigorous attention to detail he applied to a surgical ventricular restoration. He'd asked what she wanted, and she said to be beautiful. What woman didn't want that? What woman didn't yearn for the opportunity to look into a mirror and see perfection?

But maybe seventeen surgeries hadn't been necessary. Maybe she should have spoken up before he'd gone too far. Because it had been years and she still saw a stranger every time she looked at her reflection.

A perfect, beautiful stranger who was the complete opposite of Eric's first wife.

Could he really love them both?

CHAPTER 23

SARA BATCHER

"I used to work at a pharmacy in the Mission District, and David Batcher came in and tried to fill a script for Vicodin outside of insurance, but it was a dupe and the system flagged it. He was not happy about me denying him, and got pretty hostile, which is why I remember it. When I left work a few hours later, I saw him outside the store, talking to one of the customers, and I swear I think he was trying to buy their pickup prescriptions off of them. Trust me, in this business, you see it all, and the suits in the health-care industry are the worst. More money they make, the more screwed up they are."

16 Branwyn Hill
Hole 18, Silverwood Preserve

Sara walked up the largest hill in Crestmore, a set of five-pound weights in hand, stride brisk. In her ears, a decades-old Britney Spears song pumped. She had been through the entire north end of the neighborhood and, so far, hadn't seen any sign of the police. Joel hadn't told her where the body was found, but she knew the likely culprits, and she was running out of them.

She should have used the two-pound weights instead. Her arms were burning, and if she was going to cover Laurelmeade to Fernlight, they were going to give out. She spotted a trash can at one of the golfing refreshment huts and detoured off the road, cutting across the grass as she headed toward it.

"Morning, Sara." The retired COO of Whole Foods waved as she passed in a golf cart, her tennis outfit on, giant sunglasses obscuring most of her face.

Sara grunted, lifting one of the weights in a wave. The woman didn't slow—thank God—and Sara hopped over the curb and onto the cart path, skirting around a foursome of golfers and their clubs. She made it to the shade of the hut and undid the Velcro enclosure of the weights, freeing her hands and dropping the items into the trash. She'd have to get more, but that was what money was for. Right now, the relief on her arms was more valuable. She lifted one elbow above her head and stretched her obliques, almost moaning at how good the stretch felt.

". . . closed the entire back nine." Two men came out of the restroom. One was wiping his hands on a paper towel, which he dropped into the trash can next to Sara. "So I'm going to call Beau and see if he can get us a tee time at Silverwood."

"Excuse me." Sara dropped her arms by her side. "They closed the back nine of which course?"

The second man spoke. "Stone Hollow. No word on how long." He lifted the visor from his head and smoothed over the scant bit of hair that he had, then repositioned it in place.

"Did they say why?"

"Something's going on with the cops. That's what the starter said." The man's gaze drifted down the length of her body. If he thought she was interested, he was wrong.

Sara skipped the water cooler and changed directions, cutting across the fairway and heading toward her house. Stone Hollow was on the opposite side of the neighborhood. Within walking distance, sure, but she'd be exhausted by the time she got there, and she'd still have to get back home afterward. Better to fortify herself first.

She turned left at Whippoorwill and moved onto the bike path, weaving around a mother with a stroller. The kiddie park was ahead, and there was already a crowd gathered.

She looked away from the reminder of her childless state and refocused on her current situation. A checklist, that was what would make this more manageable. Back in the InkRose days, she had lived by checklists. David had once joked that she should add *pay attention to your husband* to her daily check-off routine. Little had he known that he was on dozens, if not hundreds, of lists. He had thought that she was emotionally absent from her marriage, never acknowledging the herculean attempts she had made to check in with him, ask about his work projects, reorder his favorite supplements, schedule his dentist appointments, and more.

Yes, a checklist was exactly what she needed. First item of business: Have another meeting with her attorney. It was important to keep Ian abreast of this development, whatever this development was. Evidence of a murder? Maybe. Maybe not. Maybe David got drunk, wandered around the golf course, tripped, hit his head, and died. It was possible, if not plausible. A prosecutor could punch a million holes in it. Like his car, which had been left at the condo. Of all places for his body to turn up, why Stone Hollow? Talk about the shittiest course in the gates. He couldn't be at Red Palms or the Brintmore?

This was *just* like David. The man was meticulous about some things and a complete airhead about others. He'd once scheduled a pickup of every single nice suit in his closet by a dry cleaner, then forgotten which dry cleaner it was. Sara had had to call twenty-three cleaners in the area before she found the one he had used. She smiled at the memory, which had been a funny moment, once he had taken a Vicodin and refound his high. He'd had to do a heart-valve sales pitch wearing khakis and a golf shirt, but had told the story and gotten a big laugh, plus the account. And later, he'd been so grateful he'd taken Sara to that French restaurant in Marin County, and they binged on lobster and champagne, and when they got back home he'd made love to her, and it had been messy and drunken and perfect.

They hadn't had enough sex, her and David. Maybe that had been the issue in their marriage. It was hard to tell what had caused the disconnect, because the Vicodin had ruined his life, but also his erections.

Back when he'd disappeared, she didn't mention his drug use to the cops. It had seemed like a detail she should hold close to the vest, but maybe now was the time to share it. Depending on what the cause of death was—if they could even determine it after all this time.

Her anxiety spiked as she rounded Tetterran Drive and headed up the boulevard, toward her street. There were just too many unknowns. She'd go crazy waiting to find out everything. She wasn't a big drinker, but maybe this was the kind of occasion that warranted a stiff drink or two. Maybe three. Maybe she'd just take that bottle of Van Winkle from the back of the liquor cabinet and chug it like it was water.

She turned onto her street and slowed at the sight of three police cars, parked at odd angles, in front of her gate.

So, no time to get wasted.

CHAPTER 24

KATIE MORROW

"I always wondered how Mark got two women like that. Some guys, you know. They're like catnip. Plus, of course, the money. That's probably what it was. Make him a taxi driver and neither one of them would have looked twice at him."

28 Blackberry Summit Road
Hole 1, Stone Hollow

Katie was in the second-floor yoga studio when she heard the chime of the front door. She was in a low lunge with a backbend, one knee down, her chest lifted high, her fingertips reaching up toward the high ceiling's exposed wood beams. She carefully pushed to both feet and tucked a stray hair behind her ear. "Hello?" she called out.

Grabbing her water bottle, she opened the studio's door and peeked into the hall. The house was quiet and still. The morning staff had left two hours ago, and Mark wasn't due back until five or six. She walked out on the landing and peered over the railing, looking at the first-floor entranceway. The door was closed, the landing empty.

She frowned, trying to think if she had an appointment or service call she had forgotten about. Nothing came to mind, and if she did, they certainly would have knocked on the door, not opened it and walked right in. Had she left it unlocked?

Katie never left doors unlocked. If anything, she double-checked locks three or four times, then convinced herself she had just unlocked the doors instead of locking them. And that must have been what happened here. When she'd walked down to the street this morning to get the newspaper, she must have flipped the dead bolt the wrong number of times and left it unlocked.

Which meant that someone was in their house. Someone who hadn't answered her call. Why wouldn't they?

There was no good reason not to answer. Not unless they didn't hear her, and maybe they hadn't.

She was unprotected, armed with nothing but a sore set of abs and an inflated yoga ball. Useless. She performed a slow swivel, considering her resources on the second floor. Mark's office. Three guest suites. A bunch of bathrooms and the elevator car. Mark's office potentially held a letter opener, but not much else, unless she was going to hit the perp over the head with a printer cartridge.

But she did have her phone. She carefully unplugged it from the wall and considered what to do. Dial 9-1-1 and go downstairs, her finger poised and ready? Have the phone in hand while researching the sound and, if she saw anyone, press the call button?

Or maybe she should call Mark now and have him on the line while she looked. And then *he* could call 9-1-1 if she screamed or suddenly went silent.

She didn't love either option. Mark would likely be annoyed and call her paranoid, and Katie was already second-guessing whether she had heard the door chime at all. Maybe she hadn't. And she did always lock the door. Certainly no one had broken it down. That, she would have definitely heard.

To double-check, she bent back over the railing and got a better look at the front door. It was closed. No sign of damage. Straining forward, she focused her eyes on the dead bolt.

Locked.

So, see? No one could come in. She had locked it behind her, and must have imagined the sound. That was what she got for spending a half hour hanging upside down in various positions. All the blood had probably rushed to her head and busted a capillary.

She checked her watch: It was time to stop yoga anyway. It was almost four, and she should start the pork marinade. She returned to the studio and placed her blocks and medicine ball in their appropriate cubbyholes, then blew out the candle and flipped off the light. She was heading down the entryway stairs when she heard the fridge door close.

She froze at the sound, one she definitely had not imagined. Her grip grew clammy, and she quickly unlocked her phone, pressing 9-1-1 into the keypad and creeping down the final steps. Maybe it was one of the housekeepers, who had forgotten something and come back. Maybe Mark's assistant was picking up his weekly set of lunches, though she had been by yesterday and had no need to be back.

Footsteps sounded—the intruder was walking toward her, their steps confident, passing through the eating nook. Any moment they would step into view.

Katie raised the phone, her finger hovering over the call button, ready to press it depending on who came into view.

The person rounded the corner and came to a sudden stop at the sight of her.

Katie's phone fell from her hand and hit the tile with a loud crack.

"Hi, Katie," Willow said calmly. "It's nice to meet you."

CHAPTER 25

WILLOW MORROW

"We were called out to the Morrow house twice with reports of a domestic disturbance. Both times, they said everything was fine and sent us back home. I spoke to the wife myself, in both instances. When she ran off, that was the first thing I went back and checked. I just wanted to see the paperwork, see if I missed something there. And maybe I did. Or maybe she just did a really good job acting like everything was okay."

28 Blackberry Summit Road
Hole 1, Stone Hollow

It wasn't Willow's first look at Mark's new wife, but seeing her in Willow's old house was still jarring. She was pleased to see that the woman did use filters in her online photos—her skin wasn't as smooth, her browline as perfect, her lips as full. But still, Katie was beautiful. More than Willow.

"Willow," Katie breathed. The look on her face was really satisfying. Willow had imagined for so many years how this exchange would occur, and while this one wasn't the ideal—she had envisioned walking up during their anniversary dinner at Luciano's and sitting down at their table, then reaching over and giving Mark a kiss on the lips—this was pretty good.

From the shock on Katie's face, she'd believed that Willow was dead, and that filled Willow with a particular kind of perverse pleasure.

"What are you doing here?" Katie asked, gripping the banister tightly. It looked like the blonde might faint, and Willow stepped forward, unsure whether she should take the steps up to her and help her down the rest of the way. "I mean . . . I thought . . . I didn't know what to think." She slowly sank down until her butt was on the step, and stared at Willow with wide eyes.

"Mark called me, so I thought I'd pop in. Stay a few weeks, just to make sure everyone knew that those weren't my bones strewn all over the course." Willow smiled, and maybe Katie didn't get her brand of humor, because she only looked more stricken.

Or maybe that look was over the length of Willow's visit. She didn't really need to stay for a few weeks, but who knew what the next few days would bring. Mark couldn't handle this police investigation on his own. He could tell them Willow was alive until he was blue in the face, but if people didn't see her in person, they wouldn't believe it.

"Mark called you?" Katie whispered. "Mark has your phone number?"

Oh, if this sweet doe only knew what Mark had of hers. Interesting that this innocent thing was what Mark had chosen as a second wife. Willow thought of the bruises, the hidden cuts, the black eye that had taken a week to heal, and wondered if he had ever done any of those things with Katie. Not likely. Not if Katie was cracking at the seams at just the sight of Willow and the knowledge that he had her contact info.

"Would you like a drink?" Willow gestured over her shoulder, to the kitchen. "I was just about to fix a cocktail. You look like you could use one."

"Ummm . . . a water, yes." Katie was still clinging to the banister column, so Willow headed back to the kitchen. They'd replaced the countertops since she'd left. White granite, which was an interesting choice—one that clashed with the walnut cabinets, but hey, she didn't have to look at them every day.

She opened the fridge, and it was like looking through a kaleidoscope. Some triangles recognizable, but a different perspective entirely.

There were the protein shakes that Mark loved, the Babybel cheeses he snacked on, his vials of medicine in the door. But everything else was different. For one, the organization. Everything—and truly *everything*—was in clear plastic or glass containers. The grapes and strawberries. The sliced meats. The cheeses, the eggs, the yogurts. There was a row of glass carafes labeled as milk, orange juice, cranberry juice, and creamer, and another row with all the condiments.

It was psychotic and pleasing, all at the same time. Willow withdrew a water bottle, then a mini glass bottle of Diet Pepsi, and placed them both on the counter. Crouching, she examined the produce containers and withdrew a container of limes. Presliced. How fancy. After closing the fridge, she opened the double doors to the liquor cabinet.

Ah, home sweet home. Here, everything was chaotically the same. She pulled out the Boss Hog, sighing in appreciation for the expensive whiskey. It had been years since she'd had anything but Bacardi, save a few rare moments in bars when someone offered to buy her a drink.

Katie appeared, her steps slow and unsteady as she made her way over to the counter and pulled herself onto a stool. "Where have you . . . been?"

"All over. I'm a house and pet sitter, so I go where the jobs are. I got lucky this time. I just finished a job in Las Vegas, so I was close by. Got here in less than eight hours." Willow grabbed a glass from the cabinet by the fridge, then opened the ice maker. Nugget ice. Another luxury she had sorely missed. She filled the glass and pushed the bottled water toward Katie. "You sure you don't want a whiskey soda?"

"No, thank you." Katie checked her watch, and the gesture didn't go unnoticed by Willow. Yes, it was ten in the morning. And yes, she deserved this. Honestly, a stiff drink would help Katie with processing this whole thing.

Willow studied her replacement while she mixed the drink. "So, how is Mark?" she asked in a singsong way.

"Uh, fine. I should call him and let him know you're here." Katie looked around, then started to rise. Willow waved her back down.

"Oh, I called him when I was coming in the neighborhood. He's on his way."

Katie looked alarmed. "What? He had a client-onboarding meeting this morning with the new Jets quarterback."

"Well, he'll reschedule it." Willow shrugged and raised the glass to her lips. "This is more important. I mean, how often do his two wives meet?" She grinned. "We should totally fuck with him. Like, when he pulls in, I'll be straddling you and we'll pretend like we're in the middle of a fight. He'd love that."

If it was possible, even more blood left the blonde's face. "Where are you staying?" Katie managed. "Maybe you could get settled and we could pick you up for lunch? There's a great place that just opened in the town square. It has really good acai bowls."

"Oh, I'm staying here." Willow rolled her eyes as if this was obvious, and it should have been to Katie. "I'll take the green guest suite. I'm *dying* for a soak in that tub. You know Mark wanted to put a claw-foot in there? I told him if he ever touched that Jacuzzi, I'd kill him." She picked up the whiskey and topped off her glass.

"We did put a claw-foot in there. Last summer," Katie said faintly.

"Fuck off, you didn't." Willow slammed the bottle down on the counter.

"Yes, we did." The blonde pushed away from the counter. "I'm sorry, I'm feeling a little nauseous. It's not you, I promise. I just need to lay down for a moment. This is a lot to process."

"Sure, lay down." Willow waved off her apology. "I'll get my bags and bring them in."

She considered bringing her drink but instead tilted back the glass and finished it off. The whiskey was tart, and she shuddered as it went down, then let out a small belch. After putting the glass in the sink, she put away the liquor and cleaned up the fixings. When she looked up, the kitchen was empty and Mark's delicate new wife was in the living room, as stiff as a dead body, lying on the couch.

CHAPTER 26

ANDREA KENDAL

"Roxanne Kendal was thirty-four when she was attacked. It happened at Treveley Park around 7:45 p.m. The amount of blood at the scene indicated a fatal stabbing, but she was taken from the scene, so finding foreign DNA or enough to prove a murder was tough. The husband had a strong alibi, but we've always suspected a murder for hire. Hard to prove anything without a body, though."

1442 Kingsmere Drive
Hole 6, Stone Hollow

The knock on the door sounded official, a battering ram of authority that was rapid enough that Andrea set Ryder down on his play mat.

"What is *that*?" Cameron asked, his eyes wide.

"There's someone at the door. Watch Ryder for a moment?"

The boy nodded, taking Andrea's place and picking up Ryder's favorite toy—a fire truck with a big crane on top. Andrea straightened her cream lounge suit into place. The set was linen, a designer brand that cost way too much and wrinkled way too easily. It had been picked out by her stylist, along with the rest of her neutrals-focused closet.

Sometimes when she was drinking, she would go into the basement and go through the boxes of Roxanne's clothes. They were an explosion of color, and items with history—a threadbare pair of coveralls with paint splatters on them and a faded 49ers sweatshirt with a mustard stain on the front. She had tried to pull on a sparkly blue evening gown and almost burst into tears when her breasts were too big to zip the back shut. She'd penguin-walked over to the couch and collapsed there, hugging a bottle of wine like a life preserver. That was how Eric had found her, the gown bunched around her waist.

He hadn't understood. He'd offered to buy her a new dress in a size that fit her enhanced build, but he didn't understood the intense jealousy that Andrea had for Roxanne. Not that Andrea had called it that, but all the words she'd tried to use hadn't fit. Eric didn't understand the complicated mess of emotions she had for a dead woman. A woman whose life she lived in but wasn't a part of. How could she tell her husband that he didn't look at her the way he'd looked at Roxanne? That he didn't love her that way?

Of course, he said he did. A few times, he'd even said that he loved Andrea more.

But that was a lie. She knew it, even if he didn't.

She checked the peephole, and her stomach dropped at the sight of a police officer standing there. Would it ever feel like it wasn't about her? Would her fear of the cops ever subside, her guilt and culpability fade away?

She was worried it wouldn't. That forty years from now, she'd still lose her breath every time a uniform looked at her for a moment too long.

After taking a moment to compose herself, she opened the door with a reserved smile. "Good morning?"

"Hello, Mrs. Kendal. Detective Ted Palentick. Is your husband home? We need to speak to the two of you."

The two of them. Not a good sign. "Oh, no—he's at the hospital in surgery. I mean, performing the surgery. He won't be home for hours."

"Well, there's been a development." Palentick hitched up his belt and stared at the ground, as if deciding what information to share.

"About the body?" Andrea asked. They must have identified it. Or at least, ruled out Roxanne.

"Yes. That's what we need to talk to you about. Do you think you could come down to the station?"

Andrea stared at him, confused. "What? Why?"

"Well, we need to ask a few questions. Really, we're interested in speaking with your husband, given that you didn't live here at the time of the incident. Is that correct, that you moved in . . . Well, when did you move in?" He tilted his head. It may have sounded like an innocent question, but she could see the gleam in his eye.

"About three years ago." The lie fell out smoothly; she'd said it so often she almost believed it herself.

"And when did you meet Dr. Kendal?" He glanced toward the front yard as if he didn't really care about the results.

"I'm sorry, do you need me to come to the station or not? Because it sounds like you don't," Andrea snapped.

"Maybe better for you to, just to be safe." He smiled like he was doing her a favor.

"I need to call our attorney and leave a message for my husband. Why don't you leave me your card, and I'll call you when I have had a chance to coordinate childcare and will be able to come? I'd like my attorney to be present. I'm sure you understand that." She smiled like she was returning the favor, and he seemed to appreciate the gesture as little as she had.

"Mom!" Cameron called from the living room. "Ryder pooped!"

"I really have to go. Do you have a card?" Andrea half closed the door, hoping the man would take the hint. He sighed, then unbuttoned the front pocket of his shirt and pulled out a small clip of cards. He removed one and held it out to her.

Ted Palentick, Senior Investigator: Homicide.

She gripped the doorframe and tried to stay upright. "Okay, Ted. Thank you. I'll call you in a bit. Might be a few hours."

"You can't avoid this, Mrs. Kendal. This needs to happen today. Same with your husband. His work schedule is not an excuse."

It wasn't a *work schedule*—Eric was saving lives. If this man ever had his heart fail, he wouldn't want his surgeon skipping out the hospital door to answer some stupid questions about something he wasn't involved in.

Unless he was involved. The little voice she often drowned with pills and alcohol piped up before she could smother it.

They could hope and pretend this wasn't about the past, but maybe the police department's questions were about Roxanne and what happened five years ago.

CHAPTER 27

SARA BATCHER

"Sara was sleeping with her yoga instructor. Everyone in the neighborhood knew it. Have you seen the guy? I don't blame her; I'd kill someone for a chance with him."

16 Branwyn Hill
Hole 18, Silverwood Preserve

The detectives introduced themselves to Sara in the driveway and formally invited her to the police station for questioning. *Invited.* That was how they worded it.

Even with all the madness surrounding David's disappearance, even with the insurance company's rigorous investigation, Sara had never been officially questioned as a suspect. Apparently, a dead body changed that. Now David wasn't just a missing person—he was a homicide victim, a distinction that seemed to infect every single aspect of this situation.

She drove herself to the station. On the way, she called Ian McKenna, her attorney of over fifteen years, and her father's best friend. Ian—who was retired, save a few favors for old friends—was on the pickleball court and gasped into the phone that he would meet her at the station in twenty minutes, and to not say a word until he arrived.

She had been to the station before. When David had disappeared, her initial calls to the police had barely raised an eyebrow, so she had come in person and filed a report. Back then, it had been a quiet afternoon with a sleepy receptionist, who passed her off to an officer, who all but rolled his eyes as he filled out the form.

It wasn't until David's assistant also called the cops, concerned because he hadn't shown up all week, and then they found his car at the condo and no activity on his bank accounts . . .

Three weeks—that was how long it had taken before the police stopped treating Sara like she was a hysterical housewife and started to actually look into her husband's disappearance.

Three weeks, and by then, it was too late. Most CCTV footage was overwritten, eyewitness memories were fuzzy, dates askew.

They say the first forty-eight hours are the most important. Sara had barely gotten in within the first forty-eight days.

This time, when she walked into the station, it was packed and humming with activity. There was a full waiting room, the previously bored receptionist replaced with a haggard-looking one. Sara signed in at the front and took a seat in between a homeless veteran and a bearded man reading a sci-fi book. She had barely settled in, her phone in hand, on level three of a shelf-organizing game, when her name was called.

Apparently, suspects get pushed to the front of the line.

She followed another officer down a hall and into a small room that looked straight out of every detective movie. Overhead fluorescent. Empty table, chairs on either side.

There were two detectives seated, and they rose at her entrance.

She smiled and they smiled, and if there were fangs present, it wasn't clear who was hiding them.

CHAPTER 28

KATIE MORROW

"I married Katie because she was easy. Easy and calm. Being married to Willow was like being in a tornado. You didn't know when you were heading up in the air or when you were crashing to the ground. It wasn't all bad. To be honest, I miss the unpredictability and the stress. Stress is a good distraction, and I need that sometimes."

28 Blackberry Summit Road
Hole 1, Stone Hollow

This is not happening. Katie lay on the bigger couch in the living room and tried to breathe in through her nose and out of her mouth. The risk of a panic attack, which had been welling in her chest in the kitchen, had receded slightly but didn't go away completely.

In the kitchen, Mark's first wife happily shut cabinet doors, clinked glasses, and ran the sink.

This is not happening. Willow had been gone for five years. Presumed dead—at least, that was what almost everyone thought. Katie had laughed off the rumors, but even she had suspected that outcome. No one just dropped off the grid overnight. Why would you? If Willow had wanted a divorce—and according to everyone (including her divorce petition), she had—why hadn't she gone the normal route? Move out and stay cordial, or at least in contact, while the attorneys did their thing? Instead, she had disappeared in the middle of the night, never to be seen again. Hell, Mark had been investigated! He'd lost clients as a result of the rumors.

And apparently, all the while, Willow had been just fine. Traveling the country and house-sitting. Healthy as could be, not a scratch on her.

It was bullshit. Almost as much bullshit as the idea that Willow was going to stay with them. That was ludicrous. Ex-wives didn't stay in the houses of their ex-husbands. Especially not when there was a new wife in play. It was . . . disrespectful. Very disrespectful.

And it was worse because she'd just assumed. If she had asked, then maybe Katie would have said yes. It would have been rude not to say yes, and then at least it would have been, sort of, Katie's decision. Instead, Willow had dictated that she was staying here and also which room she was staying in. She was helping herself to their kitchen, acting like she still owned the place, and giving Katie that knowing look like she had all the answers and Katie was still catching up.

Mark was going to have some serious explaining to do. With all the speculation about Willow, not just in the neighborhood but also in Katie's mind, he had never—*never*—bothered to mention that he could just call Willow up whenever he wanted to and see how she was.

Her breath hitched at the awareness that he probably *had* called her. Maybe often. Maybe her husband talked to Willow every Thursday night, when Katie was with her meditation group. Maybe Willow called him on his birthday, and he on hers, and they giggled about their day and their dreams and memories of the past.

Maybe he complained about her to Willow. Had he told her about the miscarriage? About their fight in Fiji? About how, on the night before their wedding, he had called it off, only for her to beg him into staying?

Tears pricked the edges of her eyes, and she wiped them away as she heard the clatter of ice in one of their crystal glasses.

Willow swept in the room and sank into the chair beside the fireplace. "God, I love this room. You know, when we bought it, you couldn't even see the course? I had them trim down all of those bushes so you could see the green." She drummed her hands on the arms of the chair. "And I like this chair . . . I would have gone with leather, though. You know Marky has an issue with any kind of animal hair. He'd break out in hives if he sat in this thing."

Marky. That nickname definitely didn't fit Mark, or sit well with Katie. "He's fine with it. Doesn't bother him." He wasn't fine with it. He'd sat in it just once, and his forearms popped a red rash all over. He'd had to take Benadryl for a week and apply a steroid cream.

"Oh-kay," Willow said in a singsong voice that indicated that it definitely wasn't okay and that she had some sort of crystal ball that showed exactly what he'd gone through. Maybe they'd discussed that in their phone calls, which Katie's paranoia had now decided were monthly at best and daily at worst. The rash had probably had its own dedicated place on his work calendar, the chat scheduled by Miriam, his assistant, who had always gushed over Willow and "what a woman" she had been. Willow this and Willow that. It had been excusable only because Katie had thought that Willow was dead, and everyone spoke kindly of the dead.

But now Willow wasn't dead, and Miriam had probably known that this entire time. Maybe she sent money to Willow, the same way that she paid off Katie's credit cards each month, or paid their property taxes and wired funds for the new car Katie had bought last year. It had always been glorious, having ready access to what seemed to be an unlimited amount of cash. But maybe Katie hadn't been the only one making dips into the coffers. Maybe this bitch, who was currently snuggling into the mohair armchair like she was preparing for a nap, had been financing her new life with their future retirement funds. The baby's college fund. The renovation to the outdoor kitchen, which Mark had suggested they postpone till next year . . . Katie closed her eyes and willed the nausea to subside.

Mark would be home soon, and then he could answer all these questions. She was being paranoid. Her teachers had always said she had an overactive imagination, and this was it, going crazy. That's all this was. Maybe.

She thought of the thong, tucked in his jacket pocket, and a new, horrible thought occurred to her.

Maybe it hadn't just been phone calls since Willow disappeared.

Maybe it had been more.

CHAPTER 29

WILLOW MORROW

"Willow house-sat for me when we were in Toronto for the summer. She did a good job with the house. She definitely isn't the cleanest person in the world. I don't think she cleaned the ceiling fans or a baseboard the whole three months."

28 Blackberry Summit Road
Hole 1, Stone Hollow

The new wife wasn't handling this well. Willow watched her carefully and wondered whether she should call someone for help. The woman was still lying stiff-straight on the couch, her hands laced together on her stomach, eyes pinched shut, in a very similar pose to when Willow used to brace for Botox.

"Are you sure you don't want a drink?" Willow asked, finishing off her cocktail and rattling the ice in the glass. "I make a mean Irish coffee if you prefer something that falls into the breakfast category."

"No, thank you," Katie said tightly. "I just . . . I just want Mark to get home."

"Well, traffic's a bitch on the 101 this morning. Can you believe it took me an hour to get from East Palo to Redwood?"

Katie didn't respond. If she thought things would be better with Mark here, she was in for an awkward surprise. This entire situation was going to be bad before it got good, at least as far as Willow was concerned. For her, this wasn't about making the situation easier.

This was about making sure no one found out the truth.

"So . . . I heard they found a dead body." Willow broached the subject, curious at Katie's thoughts. "Who do you think it is?"

"I have no idea," Katie said weakly and pressed a hand to the top of her forehead as if she were checking her own temperature.

"Did you think it was me?" Willow dug into her glass and pulled out a chunk of ice pellets, transferring them to her mouth and crunching on them.

"No, of course not." Katie said it too quickly and too emphatically, like she was trying to convince herself of the fact. Willow didn't blame her. No one, if given the choice, would pick a murderer as their husband.

Willow hunched forward in the chair. "But you were told about me, right? You knew that Mark had a runaway wife?"

Katie knotted her hands together, and the tendons in her forearms flexed. "No one ever called you that—at least not to me."

Interesting. Willow sat back in the chair. "So what did they say? Did Sophia call me a bitch? You know, she's had a wet spot for Mark for years."

"Who's Sophia?"

"John Kincaid's wife. The redhead with the Southern accent."

"I haven't met her. I only saw John once, at the annual awards night."

"Oh." This piece of information stunned Willow, and she took a moment to chew over the fact that Mark's best friend was no longer in his life, at least not in a social sense. She and Sophia had been friends by forced approximation, and she hadn't even considered staying in touch with the former beauty queen. Willow had assumed, all this time, that Sophia had taken full advantage of their prior association and centered herself in any and all gossip concerning Willow.

Or maybe she and John had gotten a divorce. That possibility filled Willow with a jolt of glee, and she made a note to ask Mark about it. She rose from the chair. "So, if they don't think I was a runaway wife, what was the general assumption?"

"I don't know," Katie snapped.

"Oh, come on." Willow wandered around the coffee table, which she and Mark had picked up at an Amish festival. There used to be a bunch of junk littering the surface, but now it was bare, save for a giant crystal on top of a few large books. It looked like the top had been refinished, and she considered setting her glass on it, just to see Katie's reaction, but didn't.

"People don't talk to me about you. They probably think it'd be rude."

Meh, since when did that ever stop anyone in Crestmore? "The house looks beautiful," Willow said, moving toward the small fireplace that divided this area from the second sitting area that opened up onto the porch. On the mantel was a collection of frames, and she picked up one of the photos and studied it. It was Mark and Katie on a ship, a glacier in the background. "Is this Alaska?"

Katie grunted in response.

"We loved Alaska," Willow cooed. "Did he take you to that romantic bed-and-breakfast with the private Jacuzzis?" She pretended to swoon. "So romantic, especially in the middle of a blizzard." She laughed. "Though, I gotta say, sex in a Jacuzzi . . . not as great as I had imagined, you know?" She glanced over her shoulder at Katie to see if the arrow had hit its mark.

It had. The woman's face had warmed from its shell-shocked white to a more appropriate shade of red. Willow and Mark had never been to Alaska, and Mark would die before staying in a bed-and-breakfast, so she could only imagine what was currently running through Katie Morrow's sweet little head.

Any anger or hurt was good. Cruel, yes. But necessary. Willow had only one job here.

Misdirection.

CHAPTER 30

ANDREA KENDAL

"Everyone says that Andrea and Roxanne are polar opposites, but I'm not surprised that they both appealed to Eric. Even though they have a completely different look, they both have a sort of even temperament, and I think that's what he likes. I'm not sure I'd call it subservient, but that's kind of what it is. Andrea lets him take the lead, from what little I've seen of her. And Roxanne was definitely like that."

1442 Kingsmere Drive
Hole 6, Stone Hollow

CALL ME AS SOON AS YOU HAVE A BREAK. URGENT BUT NOT LIFE-THREATENING.

Andrea sent the text and watched as it delivered. She placed the cell phone on the counter and double-checked that the ringer was turned on. Depending on the surgery and how long ago it had started, Eric might be busy for another three to eight hours.

She'd go mad before then. She wasn't sure she'd even be able to last fifteen minutes. She opened cabinets, looking through the different medications, scanning the bottles for something—anything—that might calm her nerves. There was a bottle of anti-nausea medicine left over from one of her surgeries, and she unscrewed the lid and shook out a pill.

She stared at it for a long moment, the white round pill in the middle of her palm. It'd take the edge off. More than that, it would put her in a deep sleep that would last three or four hours, easy.

She returned the pill to the bottle and went to the fridge instead. Opening the double doors, she stared at the contents, then began pulling out items.

She might not have control over her past, the police, her husband's availability, or her anxiety—but she could cook, and everyone in this house would, at some point, need to eat.

She put a block of cheddar cheese and a stick of butter to the side, aware that Cameron would want a snack as soon as he started to smell the food. A grilled cheese sandwich would keep him happy, at least until the soup was ready.

Ryder rattled by, his socked feet giving him freedom to explore the kitchen in his roller chair. The wheels were loud on the tile floor, but she liked the sound. More so, she liked how happy the activity made him. Leaning to the far right, she put eyes on Cameron, who was lying on the couch, his favorite cartoon on the TV.

Andrea pulled open the linen drawer and chose a jute apron. After looping the strap over her head, she wrapped the red ties around her waist and knotted them in the back.

While she normally didn't allow Cameron to watch TV during the day, she was in desperate need of some peace right now . . . some peace to think. And her husband. While she would never begrudge Eric for his job . . . her heart was currently pounding in alarm, and her heart was as important as anyone's, right? Maybe more so, given the ring on her finger.

She opened the meat drawer and withdrew the paper parcel labeled Beef Short Ribs. Unrolling the package on the cutting board, she grabbed a butcher knife out of the block and started slicing the ribs at their seams, separating them into two-inch sections.

She'd make a Taiwanese-style French onion beef-noodle soup. It was one of Eric's favorite dishes, one that she'd had in mind when picking out the short ribs from the butcher. She pulled out the red Dutch oven and drizzled a little oil in the bottom, then set it to heat. Brushing a strand of hair away from her face, she opened the spice drawer and started to stack the appropriate bottles on the counter.

Her phone rang and she dropped the salt grinder and spun toward her phone, wiping her hands on the apron before answering it. "Hello?"

"Andrea, it's Walter." Their attorney's brusque New York accent was like salve to her open stress wound, and she closed her eyes in appreciation at the sound of his voice.

"Hi. Thanks for calling me back." She leaned against the cabinet and watched as Ryder grabbed hold of the corner of the cabinet and used it to pull himself forward. She broke a piece of cheddar cheese off the block and held it out to him, beckoning him to come to it.

"Of course. What's going on?"

She recapped the police's visit, and when she finished, there was a long moment of silence. "They told you to come also?" he asked. "For questioning?"

"Yes. Well, um. He said I might as well come also. Just to be safe."

"He didn't read you your Miranda rights?"

"No," she said, her alarm rising at the tight tone of his voice. "Is that what they're going to do at the station? I mean . . ." She lowered her voice and stepped around the corner to shield the conversation from Cameron. Behind her, Ryder shrieked in annoyance, his journey to her almost complete. "Am I—are *we* suspects? Is that what you're saying?" She stepped back and handed Ryder the piece of cheese. They could not be suspects, not after so many years had passed. She'd thought they were in the clear after all this time. She had already relaxed, begun to enjoy life, and now, just as everything was fine, it was crashing down.

Unacceptable. Eric had promised her that this wouldn't happen. He had sworn it, and now he wasn't even available to help her through this conversation. She pinched the bridge of her nose. At the stove, the oil popped and began to smoke.

"I'm not saying that you're suspects, but you need to know that the police are *not* your friends. No one is your friend, even those that you think are. No one owes you confidence or loyalty except for me. Not even Eric, though I certainly think you two are in the same corner on this."

Andrea reached out and turned the burner off. "I can't get a hold of him. He's in surgery. The cop said that isn't an excuse, that he needs to come in as soon as possible."

"I'll deal with that, and with getting in touch with Eric. And you—hold off on going anywhere until you hear from me. Stay at home and keep your mouth shut. Don't call or talk to anyone."

Andrea thought of yesterday, her time with Kisi. Not that she had been planning to call her, but now the only thing she wanted was to tell Kisi what was going on and to get her take on it. She nodded, then wet her lips and spoke. "Okay. Don't call anyone or talk to anyone."

"I'll call you back," he promised, and she knew he would. Walter always kept his promises. He might not be able to keep them out of jail, but he would call her back.

She thought of the promise he had made to her five years ago, when he promised both her and Eric that no one would ever find out what they had done. That promise, above all others, was what she needed him, right now, to keep.

CHAPTER 31

SARA BATCHER

"The only people that win in these kinds of situations are the attorneys. Everyone else either gets locked up or spends their last cent to try and get away with murder. Look at O. J. Got off for it, but was broke as a two-dick dog at the end."

16 Branwyn Hill
Hole 18, Silverwood Preserve

Sara's attorney showed up in thin red shorts that clung to his thighs and a baggy white T-shirt with Harvard Law in giant letters across his chest, should someone from across the parking lot not be able to see. His hair was damp from his pickleball excursion, and Sara was careful with her hug, concerned about sweat.

"Thank you for coming," she said.

"Are you kidding me? You're family. I would have left even if I'd been losing, and if you and my pride ever met over a cocktail, you'd understand what a big sacrifice that would be." Ian let out a hearty laugh, then sobered immediately. "I'm really sorry about David, Sara. I'd always kept out a little hope that he'd run off to Tahiti with some blond dimwit. Not that I wouldn't hunt him down and strangle him for that—but dead? No one wants that."

Well . . . there had been moments in their seventeen-year union where Sara had wished exactly this sort of future for David, but dwelling on a few low moments wouldn't accomplish anything, and especially wouldn't help right now, given the circumstances of their situation.

"So, what do we know?" He pulled his seat up closer to the table and withdrew a small legal pad from the gym bag at his feet.

"Not really anything. I guess a dog found a bone somewhere on the course, and so they searched the neighborhood and found the rest of the remains and they identified them as male."

"Do we know for sure that it's even David?"

"I don't know. I mean, when I originally filed the report for him, I provided DNA evidence back then. And dental records? I'm sure they have those." She tried to think back five years, and what she had been asked and provided. She'd gone out of her way back then to be overly helpful. Whatever they'd wanted, no matter how personal or time consuming it had been. Ian had been the one to step in when they had wanted access to financial documents, stating that it was overreach. At the time, she had thought him to be overcautious. But now, sitting in this freezing-cold, tiny room, police officers passing in the hall every few minutes, it didn't feel overcautious. It felt like they were at war.

You weren't polite during war. You were ruthless and self-serving. Ian had tried to teach her that five years ago, and she hadn't listened.

She would now.

"Let's assume that it is him. They're going to ask you a lot of questions about back then, Sara, and I want you to remember three very important words. Are you ready?"

She nodded.

"I don't recall." He stared at her, making sure that the words resonated. "Got that? Repeat it for me."

"I don't recall," she repeated, and of course she had that phrase tattooed in her brain. While it had been years since she'd undergone the training for interrogation, some things were still fresh.

"If they ask something that gives you pause, say that you don't recall. It's natural that you will feel guilty at moments in this questioning. We all have things about our marriage or life that we aren't proud of, or that we feel might be misconstrued if put under a microscope. So if you start getting into the weeds, that's your lifeline. 'I don't recall.' Okay?"

She nodded.

"And if I tap your leg under the table, stop talking. Whatever the hell you're saying, just end it, right away. Or if he asks you a question and I tap your leg, don't answer it. Either let me speak up, or say that you don't remember. Even if it seems like an innocent thing. It's the most innocent things that sink ships. Remember that."

"Okay."

He grinned. "You're a woman of few words, Sara-Bear. You have no idea how happy that makes me. Don't ramble. Keep it short and succinct. Remember that."

"I remember it from the last time you drilled it into me," she said dryly, and he barked out a laugh.

"Oh, that's right. You're a steel trap. Remember when you were twelve or thirteen, and we went to the racetrack down in Palo Alto and you memorized the entire stats card on the ride down?"

She didn't, but it sounded exactly like something she would have done. Numbers had always been a foreign language that she understood. Rules for staying out of jail were a different animal, but one that she should be able to handle. "Ian, I didn't do this. I don't know anything about what happened to David or how he ended up on the course."

"Let's worry about all of that later," he said. "Right now, what's about to happen is that we're going to be in a pickleball match of sorts, except instead of wanting points, each side wants information. We want information on what they have, and they have things they want to know from you. We'll have to give them some things, and they'll have to give us some things. As long as we both walk off the court separately, this will have been a success. Got it?"

"Yes."

As if he'd been waiting in the wings, Detective Ted Palentick swung open the door. "You ready?"

She nodded and he stepped in, followed closely by a second suit whom Sara immediately recognized: Joel. The chief of police.

CHAPTER 32

KATIE MORROW

"We didn't find anything in the pond behind the Morrow home, but still had our eye on Mark Morrow, given his first wife's disappearance and the fact that he acted really odd when we did the search. I have instincts about these things, and I don't know what that guy is guilty of, but it's something."

28 Blackberry Summit Road
Hole 1, Stone Hollow

Katie had always had a complicated bank of emotions when it came to Mark's first wife, but hatred had never been in the mix. Willow had always appeared to be a lovely woman. Intimidating, sure. In every photo Katie had found, she'd always seemed so confident, her giant smile wide, eyes on the camera, her arms possessively around Mark. *Fun* was the adjective everyone used for Willow when Katie had been bold enough to ask about Mark's first wife. She'd been "the life of the party" and they'd apparently had big parties, on a regular basis, in the house.

Katie had never hosted a party in her life. Just the idea of the invitations, a bunch of strangers in her space, the endless small talk . . . it made her throat close. Mark had broached the idea once, when his fortieth birthday was on the horizon, and she'd just looked at him blankly. He'd quickly switched horses and suggested a group dinner at La Torte with a few of their closest friends.

His closest friends. Katie didn't really have any friends, at least not in this circle. Her friends were all from back home, women she could count on for a supportive phone call or for dinner if they ended up in the same city, but none who could fill out a dinner party at a Michelin-starred restaurant.

Mark's birthday dinner had been okay, though it stretched on entirely too long and was ridiculously expensive. For the price of the seven-course meal, they could have all flown to Vegas and each bet $500 on black.

Their drive home had been quiet, Mark tipsy on wine, Katie still wired from the traumatic experience of signing the check.

"Did I ever tell you about the Halloween party that Willow threw?" Mark had said, his fingers caressing the top of Katie's knee.

"Yes," Katie had lied, because right now was not the time for Mark to go down memory lane. Especially when he hadn't even thanked her for putting together this dinner.

"She dressed like Catwoman in this skintight suit and these thigh-high boots. It was . . ." He grinned. "It was hot."

"That's great, Mark. I'm so happy that your ex-wife was hotter than me."

"Aw, come on." He'd pulled her toward him on the bench seat of the limo. "No, I was just thinking about the parties we used to have. You know, our house is a *great* house for parties."

Yes, he had mentioned that several times. He loved to mention it. When they had redone the basement, when he had added the pool cabana—hell, when they had re-pavered the driveway. She got it. Lots of people could fit in their house, and she didn't want a single one in there.

Especially not the brunette who was now picking up their wedding photo, which had been taken on the beach. Watch her ruin that memory for Katie also. *Oh, you wore white? I wore white. Did you ride his penis on the way back from the church? Because I did that, and he loved it so much. Blah blah blah.* Katie pushed herself upright, needing to leave before she heard another word from her.

She had expected Willow to be fun. Kind. She hadn't expected . . . whatever this thing in her living room was. This was a virus, one that was infecting every surface that she touched. Mohair chair—ruined. Alaskan vacation—tainted. Katie stood up. "I need to go to the bathroom."

She didn't wait for a response; she wove quickly between the couch and the column and headed for the stairs, taking them two at a time until she reached the top. The bathroom was a safe space, and she could hide there until Mark got home.

She entered the primary suite and locked the door behind her.

Two years of wanting answers about Willow, and now all she wanted was for the woman to go away.

CHAPTER 33

WILLOW MORROW

"The Morrows have always had their accounts with First Hope Bank, and while I can't disclose any confidential details about their finances, I can tell you that Willow Morrow had a meeting with me a few days before her so-called 'disappearance,' and I never had any doubt that she left on her own accord, without any foul play, and with plenty of financial resources. I would have told the cops that, if anyone had ever asked me. But they didn't."

28 Blackberry Summit Road
Hole 1, Stone Hollow

As soon as Katie disappeared upstairs, Willow moved. After setting down the wedding photo, she took a rapid tour of the downstairs, checking the rooms and refamiliarizing herself with the space.

Some things had changed, some hadn't. There was a new vanity in the powder room and a new hanging chandelier in the dining hall. There was also a complete lack of clutter. Every room looked magazine ready, and she kept opening drawers and closets, looking for the mountain of stuff that was surely hidden somewhere.

It wasn't—at least not in any of the hiding places on the first floor. Even the garage, which now had motion-activated lights that illuminated when you entered the seven-car bay, was perfectly kept, with a pegboard on the wall, each of Mark's tools outlined in paint so you could immediately see what, if anything, was missing.

Did Katie just clean all day, every day? Was that what Mark liked about this woman? Because Willow had to say, so far nothing stood out about the blonde. Yes, she was pretty. And skinny. Too skinny, if you asked Willow, not that anyone was asking Willow about Mark's new wife. But she was a little scrawny, and Mark . . . Willow tried not to think about what Mark had liked best about her body. Definitely not a gap between her thighs or a tiny waist.

She checked the laundry room—a new giant blue washer-dryer set and the same dry-cleaning machine from before.

Next, the junk room.

Willow blinked at the big space, which had previously housed every item that didn't have a logical place. The last time she'd seen the room, the door barely opened and you had to squeeze in sideways. It had held an inversion table, their Christmas tree, two perfectly good lamps that Willow had picked up from the side of the road and intended to donate to Goodwill, boxes of Halloween decorations, some extra luggage sets, a collection of cabinet-door samples from a kitchen remodel they'd abandoned, and about forty-nine hundred other things they had left in the room to die.

Now it was a wrapping room, and it pained her to admit that she both knew what that was and recognized it so quickly. Willow had a photo of a room just like this one on her Pinterest board labeled *Dream House*, only this was better. Forty or fifty rolls of wrapping paper; a folding table; cubbies with gift bows, bags, ribbon, and tissue paper. Built-in cabinets with potential gifts all organized by occasion and price point. She hovered in front of the selection, tempted to grab one of the Cire Trudon candles or maybe a small box of ornate stationery. Speaking of which . . . Willow opened a few drawers and revealed dozens of cards, all organized by occasion, with stamps, pens, and monogrammed letterhead handy. There was an address book and a calendar, and she scanned both, recognizing most of the names, though she'd never had any idea, nor had she given a damn, that Bethany and Trent's anniversary was on March 16, or that Mark's aunt's birthday was on June 23.

Reluctantly, she flipped off the light and left the room, then stared at the door to the basement.

The basement had become Mark's playground—where he had moved their evening activities after a neighbor called 9-1-1 after hearing screams in the middle of the night.

Down there, insulated by the ground, no one could hear anything.

Willow left that door closed and returned to the kitchen, anxious for another drink. She was uncapping the bottle of rum when she heard the sound of the garage-door alarm chime.

Mark was home.

CHAPTER 34

ANDREA KENDAL

"So, the story I heard is that Andrea and Eric met at a cancer charity event in Pasadena. Now, what was a single mother with no job doing at a charity event? You tell me. Fishing for a rich husband, that's my take. She must have gotten a big settlement from her first husband—that's her oldest boy's father—because I've never seen her work. Not when they were dating, and certainly not after they got married."

1442 Kingsmere Drive
Hole 6, Stone Hollow

Three rooms down from Sara Batcher, Andrea Kendal sat in a small police station lobby, waiting on her husband. Beside her, Walter Amos sat in a suit, his ankles crossed and tucked underneath him, his attention on his phone. Andrea's cell was almost dead; she had forgotten to charge the battery last night, and she was now down to 2 percent of life, a level that was giving her increasing anxiety every time she looked at it. She had asked the receptionist if they had a charger—they supposedly didn't—and now warred between dashing out to her car to give it a few minutes to charge or sitting in place and waiting.

Surely Eric was almost here. He had texted her fifteen minutes ago that he was leaving the hospital, which meant that any moment, the automatic doors to the room would open and he would stride in.

As if on command, the doors opened. Her head snapped up, but it was a woman in a dark suit who walked in. She wore no makeup, her hair in a severe bun. She paused, spotted them in the corner, and approached.

"Walter." She extended her hand. "Where's Dr. Kendal?"

Walter rose and tucked his phone in his pocket, taking her outstretched hand and giving it a firm shake. "He's en route. Is it necessary for Mrs. Kendal to be here?" He gestured to Andrea. "She has kids at home waiting for her."

"Not really our problem," the woman said crisply, but smiled at Andrea as if to soften the blow. "We'll let her go as soon as we can, but we'll be questioning Dr. Kendal first, so she'll be after that. Hi, Mrs. Kendal. I'm Bridget, with the San Francisco detective's office."

She shook the woman's hand and tried not to panic. They must have found a loose thread, something that Andrea and Eric had forgotten to close up. Maybe Roxanne's bank account at her old credit union, or that clinic visit three weeks before her attack. Or maybe they'd been digging into Andrea's past. Walter had assured them that he had bulletproofed her timeline, but maybe he hadn't. They were the police, after all. Their job was to find the holes in a story, and she was afraid theirs was more riddled than Swiss cheese.

"I can show you to a room where you can wait."

Walter nudged Andrea, and she realized that the woman was speaking to her.

"Okay. Will it be a while? I need to go out to my car and charge my phone for a bit."

"It might be. Someone can loan you a charger. It'd be better if you stayed in the building; that way we don't have to hunt you down." The phrase was meant in jest, but Andrea's blood chilled at the words. *Hunt you down.* That had always been her biggest fear. Not the catching—not exactly. It was the slow anticipation, the dread of what might happen when the cat caught the mouse.

And she'd always been a mouse. Both before and after marrying Eric.

The sliding doors opened, and this time it was Eric in the opening, his green scrubs on, his face mask hanging from around his neck. His gaze connected with hers, and she stood and they hugged, right there in the middle of the waiting room, in front of the woman and Walter.

He kissed her neck and his stubble scraped her jaw, and his mouth moved close to her ear and he whispered, barely loud enough for her to hear, "We got this. Be smart."

CHAPTER 35

SARA BATCHER

"To be honest, finding the body gave us a victim, but not much else. We knew it was David Batcher, and we knew someone dumped his body. Hopefully when he was already dead, because we found weights at the bottom of the lake, so it looks like his body was weighted down. If they'd dumped him while he was alive, well . . . that'd be a rough way to go."

16 Branwyn Hill
Hole 18, Silverwood Preserve

The detective pushed a photo toward Sara. "This is a photo of the remains. Please note the clothing."

It was a cruel introduction to David's dead body, delivered without warning or cushion. She leaned forward and tried to look at the image under the lens of a product review. *Here is a thing. Study and find what is right or wrong about it.*

Bones. Held together by what looked like string. No, not string. Body matter. Dried and decaying body matter. Sara's stomach, which revolted at something as simple as rotten watermelon, flipped with unease.

The backdrop, a black surface. The skeleton had been assembled in the shape of a body, with bits of disintegrated clothing like patches around the bones. The head was turned to one side, as if it—David—were looking to the left. The position disturbed Sara, and she tried not to obsess over it, but her gaze kept twitching toward it, sticking to it.

David's skull was an item she had never expected to see, his eyeholes large and gaping, the indents on the side disproportionate to how big his ears had been.

She blinked, her vision blurring. She had loved his ears. Mostly because he was so self-conscious of them. David had had so few moments of vanity that this one area had been like a giant target, so easy to touch that it was almost impossible not to poke it on a regular basis.

And she had. She had cultivated that insecurity for no good reason other than the fact that her own shortcomings needed company.

Now she wished she could take back every moment she had grimaced when he tried on a hat, or suggested a different haircut, or told him to turn his head a little to the left so his ears wouldn't stick out so much in a photo.

Ian cleared his throat. "Sara?"

She looked up to find them all staring at her. Joel's face, at least, had some compassion. The detective's look was more of a glare. "I'm sorry, what was the question?"

"We're trying to create a timeline. Do you know if these were the clothes from the day that David disappeared?"

She leaned forward, studying the photo. It looked like he was wearing a pair of charcoal slacks. The leather belt was one he'd worn often. The shirt was mostly gone, but it looked like one of his casual knit-blend shirts that he'd liked to pair with dress pants for dinner or drinks.

"It could be," she said. "I can't remember what he wore to the office that day. If I saw him that morning, it was just briefly. His secretary would probably know."

His secretary, Keely. Sitting naked on his desk, her legs open, his tie loosely knotted, hanging between her small, perky breasts. He'd been on his knees in front of her, his attention where his mouth was, and hadn't even heard her come in. Keely had. Keely had gasped—a sound David likely mistook for pleasure—and frozen in place, her eyes locked on Sara.

Sara pushed the image away and tried to focus on her answer. "If he went out for drinks afterward, he might have changed at the condo. Especially if his car was there." The condo had had several suits in the hamper, waiting to be dry-cleaned. When she'd packed up everything, it was hard to know how long they'd been there or if they were from the day he disappeared. She'd originally put them all in trash bags and held on to them, in case the police wanted to do any tests or analyses on them. After a year of no interest, she'd donated them, along with the rest of his clothes.

"Is this definitely him?" she asked, her voice cracking on the question.

"The dental records match. There's also evidence of a healed broken collarbone."

She swallowed. So it *was* him. Her gut had known it since yesterday, but it was still a lot to take in. She closed her eyes, the room spinning, and held on to the edge of the table, willing her anxiety to leave. She thought of the last summer stationery collection she'd designed. Sun-bleached, acid-free cotton stock with a generous 500 gsm weight. They'd dip-dyed the edges in hibiscus pink and pressed delicate gold-foil palm fronds into the corners. The envelopes were lined with banana-leaf artwork, printed on translucent—

"Where was this found?" Ian asked. *This.* It seemed a crude way to refer to David's remains, but Sara held back from saying anything. She opened her eyes, and Joel was watching her, his brow knitted with concern.

"About a half mile from the Batcher residence. We're trying to do what we can with reconstructing the scene, but we believe the body was dumped and weighed down to prevent being found," Detective Palentick said.

Sara looked up. "So there's no chance this was an accident? He drank a lot. Maybe he got drunk and got lost. He could have tripped and maybe—" She stopped talking when Ian's hand closed on her knee.

"It's highly unlikely," Joel said. "But of course, we're exploring all possibilities."

"Including me," Sara said, looking to the detective. It was dangerous for Joel to even be there, but she wouldn't be the one to give away their history.

"Spouses are always a suspect, especially when large life insurance payouts are involved. I hope you don't take it personally." Palentick gave her an apologetic grimace.

Sara didn't say anything, even though she could have given a twenty-four-point presentation on why she wouldn't have dumped David's body in the neighborhood. For one, she wasn't strong enough. He had weighed a hundred and eighty pounds. He'd once passed out in the car on the way home from dinner, and she had to leave him in the passenger seat, out in the garage, all night.

There was no conceivable way that a jury would believe she'd managed to hide his body in that manner. Not by herself—which would mean they'd have to find a possible accomplice.

She didn't need them to look for accomplices. She needed to nip this in the bud as quickly as possible. If she had to solve this murder for them, she would.

The good thing was, she wasn't the only one who had wanted David dead.

CHAPTER 36

KATIE MORROW

"I never thought Mark was good enough for my sister. Take away his money and he was just a self-centered asshole with a bunch of athletes on speed dial."

28 Blackberry Summit Road
Hole 1, Stone Hollow

Mark came through the garage door like he was late. The door banged against the wall with the force of his entrance, and Katie made it to the bottom of the stairs just in time to see his face when he spotted Willow.

She'd known Mark for four years, and yet this was a new look, one that seared a hot brand of betrayal in the middle of her heart. Mark halted in the hallway and grabbed the wall as if to brace himself. "Willow," he whispered.

From behind Katie, Willow spoke. "Hi, love."

Hi, love. It felt like Katie was eavesdropping on an extremely personal moment—and that wasn't right because this was *her* husband. If anything, Willow should be the one feeling her heart rip in two, because this was Katie's house. Katie's marriage. Katie's life. Willow had chosen to leave Mark. She hadn't wanted this relationship, hadn't wanted him, and she couldn't just waltz in five years later and say those two words with the level of emotion that kingdoms could be built on and lost over.

Katie looked from Mark to Willow and back again. They both stood there, and it was as if neither of them were even aware of her presence. The silence stretched on, and she was helpless to stop it, helpless to say anything to cut the cord between them.

Mark eased forward one step and then another, his hand dragging along the wall as he moved, like he needed its strength to hold him upright. "You're here," he said slowly, as if he didn't believe it, as if he hadn't called her and told her to come.

"Of course I am. You need me." Willow smiled, and this was quite possibly the worst moment of Katie's life—the moment when she saw the facade of her life crumble. *Of course I am. You need me.* She turned back to Mark, half expecting him to protest, half knowing that he wouldn't.

And he didn't. Instead, her husband dropped to his knees, reached out toward Willow, and started to cry.

CHAPTER 37

WILLOW MORROW

"I never wanted my son to marry that woman. She was a vulture. The new girl—that's more what he needs. But Mark always went for the bad girls. You know, he slept with one of his teachers his senior year of high school. I had her fired, and she's lucky I didn't get her ass thrown in jail."

28 Blackberry Summit Road
Hole 1, Stone Hollow

Willow didn't hesitate, closing the distance to Mark and kneeling in front of him. She kissed him on the mouth, then let him wrap his arms around her and pull her tightly to him. They stayed in that position for a long moment, until his labored breathing calmed and he gained control. He rested his forehead against hers and sighed.

"Shit, Willow," he swore. "I missed you."

"Well, I'm back for a bit." She kissed him on the cheek. He smelled exactly the same. God, what a mental road trip that took her on. So many memories with this man. Mini building blocks of a life interrupted. She pulled away before she fell down that hole.

He wiped his eyes, and the last five years hung on him, the evidence everywhere. So much more silver in his stubble and throughout his hair. The crow's-feet in the corners of his eyes. The deeper lines on either side of his nose. It didn't look bad. Rather, he was more distinguished. Damn men and their ability to age well. She was overdue for a facelift and eye job while he was still fuck-worthy seven days a week. Not that she would be doing that. That was the new wife's job. She stood up and turned, wondering where the blonde had gone.

Willow was surprised to find Katie sitting on the couch, her arms stiffly by her sides, her mouth gaping open as she glared at them both. The kiss had probably been a bad idea.

"Where are your bags? Do you need me to bring them in?" Mark stood and gripped her shoulder, squeezing it as if to verify that she was still there. She didn't like the tight hold, didn't like the memories it brought back. *The handcuffs, locking into place with a loud click.* They'd been on for more than twelve hours, no concessions made for a bathroom break. No, a bucket had been brought in for that. For months afterward, she had thought of that night every time she entered their laundry room and saw the red pail hanging in place by the mops.

"No, I can get them." She turned toward Katie, twisting out of his hold. The woman looked shell-shocked, and while she probably hadn't seen her husband embrace another woman before, the blonde didn't have anything to worry about. "Katie will help me." She headed for the entrance and grabbed Katie's wrist on the way, pulling her toward the front door. *Come with me,* she mouthed, and Katie stared at her blankly, then seemed to understand, stumbling after Willow and out the front door.

Mark started to follow them, and Willow spun around, holding up her palm like she was conducting a traffic stop. "Stay here," she commanded. "Let me talk to Katie for a moment."

He stayed, but his eyes narrowed slightly, and in the dark warning she saw a peek at the man she'd left behind. She backed through the door and pulled it closed, cutting off the connection.

Turning to Katie, she flinched at the woman's pale, almost gray complexion. Willow looped her arm through Katie's and pulled the woman toward her ten-year-old Jeep Cherokee, which she'd bought with cash through a shell corporation three weeks before she left Mark. He'd never found out about it, best she was aware, and she'd almost rented a car to come here—not yet ready to reveal that piece of the puzzle. She hadn't, and now she watched as Katie cautiously approached the car.

"This is yours?" Mark's wife asked, staring at the THERE IS NO PLANET B bumper sticker affixed to the back window.

"It is." Willow pulled up the back liftgate. "A hundred and ninety thousand miles and counting. I drove this bad girl to Alaska, if you can believe that." She grinned and reached inside, tugging on the handle of a storage container and bringing it to the edge. When she was married to Mark, she had a twelve-piece custom luggage set from Goyard, each adorned with a monogrammed brass nameplate. She'd taken three of the pieces with her, and they'd all died various deaths over the years. Now she was schlepping clear plastic storage containers through the country. They worked well when she moved into the hosted houses, but now she felt a moment of embarrassment in front of Katie. She pushed the emotion away and glanced toward the house, making sure that Mark hadn't followed them out.

"Look," she began. "Straight shit, okay?"

Katie raised one perfectly shaped brow. This bitch probably waxed her entire body.

"This is going to be weird for you: Mark and I had an unhealthy relationship. We got things from each other—things that maybe you two get from each other and maybe you don't." Willow shrugged like she didn't care, like her entire soul didn't rise and fall wondering what Mark's new marriage was like. "I just want you to know that I'm here for a few weeks, and then I'm gone and you'll have everything back, just the way you had it. So don't stress. Mark will be stressed enough for the three of us, trust me." She smiled.

Katie didn't return the gesture. She didn't do anything other than stare at Willow as if she was trying to process the idea.

That was okay. Katie would have plenty of time to get used to this. Willow picked up the container and held it out to the skinny blonde. "Here. Carry this."

CHAPTER 38

ANDREA KENDAL

"At least with Roxanne, you knew what she was. Someone from the rough fringe of society, who had made something better from her life. She didn't pretend to be part of the Crestmore crowd—and besides, everyone knew she had a family full of skeletons, and we all kind of liked it, to be honest. It brought a little texture to a group that was really cookie cutter and boring. Andrea . . . she made out like she was cut from the same upper-class mold as the rest of us, but I never trusted her. I bet if you scraped a layer past all that plastic surgery and dug into her past, you'd find a single-wide trailer and a lot of dirt."

1442 Kingsmere Drive
Hole 6, Stone Hollow

Eric's absence was like the amputation of a limb. Without it, Andrea didn't know how to move, how to sit, how to think about anything else.

She stared at the room where he was being questioned. There was a reception area and desk between them. Through the frosted glass window in the door, she could only see fuzzy shapes. One Walter. One Eric. The detectives. Movement. Nodding. Talking. About what?

Her hands started to tremble, and she clasped one over the other and squeezed the fist. She thought of the glove box of her car, where, hidden in the leather portfolio of the owner's manual, there were two Virginia Slim cigarettes. A lighter was in the rear trunk, in the cavity by the jack.

No one would know if she stepped outside to smoke. The scent would be gone by the time she got home, and she could change her shirt as soon as she walked in the front door.

If any occasion deserved a cigarette, it was this one. Reckoning day for a five-year-old crime.

Her stomach cramped and she tried to clear her throat, to catch a bigger breath, but it felt like something was sitting on her chest. What did they have on them? Would they arrest them here? Would she have to spend the night in jail? She needed to call the nanny, see if she could stay the night, just in case. She should have made something other than that stupid soup. She'd had five hours—could have made a week's worth of precooked meals and stocked the fridge, and instead she had labored over a broth that would likely be thrown out in the morning.

Andrea checked her watch. Eric had only been in there for eight minutes. Eight minutes and it felt like her psyche was going to explode. She should get the cigarettes. This wasn't a *want*, this was a *need*, and if she didn't get them, if she didn't have that glorious moment of silence when the nicotine pushed through her lungs and out through her fingertips and nose—she might just die.

She stood and approached the desk. "I have to go out to my car for something. It's right there." She pointed to the window on the left side of the room, the one that overlooked the small visitors' lot. "You'll be able to see me."

"Oh, go ahead, honey." The woman stapled two small stacks of papers together. "You aren't under arrest. You can come and go as you please."

"Oh. Okay." Andrea hitched the strap of her purse higher on her shoulder. "I'm sorry. First time in a police station."

A lie, but even if she hadn't been hiding her past, the prior times hadn't been like this. For one, they had all been in Lincoln Park, the station packed with people, all angry and indignant over their right to justice, or a spot in line, or the removal of the parking boot on their car. Here, there was elevator music piped in over the speakers. There was a bowl of mints on the table. There was her husband, less than a hundred feet away, and their thousand-dollar-an-hour attorney.

"It's fine." The woman waved away her apology with an armful of bright gold bangles. "Everyone's nervous when they come in here. It's just part of the vibe."

Part of the vibe. Right. Andrea nodded and tried to walk as normally as possible toward the double doors. They opened smoothly, and she made it through the second set without breaking into a run. Out in the open sunshine, she inhaled deeply and seriously considered just getting in her car and taking off. How far could she get before they came after her? Maybe it would take days. Maybe months. Maybe they would never catch her and she could settle in a new town, get a new identity, and start over.

Without Ryder.

Without Cameron.

Without Eric.

The fantasy died, and that was the problem with loving someone. It meant that you were tied to them for life. Their crimes became your crimes. Yours became theirs. You fought with the ship even if it meant your certain death.

She pulled out the two cigarettes with trembling fingers, same with the lighter. Leaning back against the SUV's front bumper, she lit the first cigarette and took a long, greedy inhale.

It didn't help.

CHAPTER 39

SARA BATCHER

"Our office prepared the prenup for David and Sara back when they were wed. It was pretty standard for California. All assets prior to the marriage stayed the property of that respective spouse. Any assets generated or acquired during the marriage would be divided equally at the time of dissolution. And it was during our setup of the prenup that the life insurance policies were purchased. Five million dollars each. I know she's got money, but still. No one's turning down a five-million-dollar opportunity."

16 Branwyn Hill
Hole 18, Silverwood Preserve

In the attic were all of David's things. Sara pulled the chain, illuminating the space, and stared at the neat rows of cardboard boxes. Each one was labeled and had a printed list of the contents taped to the side of it. The beauty of money. It made everything easy, including the organization of a dead man's life.

Sara slowly walked down the aisle between the boxes, her bright-white sneakers quiet on the padded rubber floor. She had showered after the police station, and used a pomegranate body scrub until her skin felt raw. It hadn't removed the feel of the place.

She shivered, her hair still wet from the shower, twisted up and in a clip, exposing her neck to the frigid blast from the attic's air-conditioning, which had its own system for the five-thousand-square-foot space. She tucked her hands into the sleeves of her sweatshirt and crossed her arms tightly over her chest, trying to stay warm.

Now that she knew for sure that David wasn't coming back, she should get rid of this stuff. There were companies for this, estate-management firms that would know what to do with his baseball card collection and his vintage espresso machine. They could come up here and, within a matter of hours, get rid of all of it.

And maybe one day she would be ready for that. But right now, she wasn't. She got to the end of the row and crouched down, looking for the box that she wanted. It had been a few years since she had put it up here, but to the best of her recollection it was—there. She spotted the box without the printed list on the outside, the one that was simply labeled Research—David in permanent marker. She opened the lid, and there, beside his computer and his address book, was her notepad. It was a black Moleskine journal–style pad, with a band that kept it closed. She moved it to one side and pulled out a hunter-green cashmere sweater. Holding it to her nose, she inhaled, desperate for a bit of David's scent.

It was gone. She tried again, in a different place in the fabric, but there was nothing there, and that's where heartache hid—in the absence. The lonely void. "I miss you," she whispered quietly, into the sweater. "I miss you so much."

This time, when the tears came, she didn't wipe them away. She let them fall, the salty drops running down the curve of her jaw, a few droplets hitting the interior of the box as she sifted through the few remaining items. A few bottles of pills. His favorite coffee cup. One of his watches. She made a note to ask the police if they'd found a watch and his wedding ring. Would they turn those over to her? She hoped so. She looked down at her own hand and rubbed her thumb over the platinum band. It was a thin strip of diamonds, and something she should have stopped wearing years ago. She had considered taking it off when the insurance company issued their payout. Having a third party agree that he was dead, that had felt like a monumental moment that she should recognize, formal permission to stop being a wife—but she had decided to leave it on a little longer. A little longer that had turned into three more years.

Now it was probably the right time. She studied the ring and left it on. Maybe tonight, when she went to bed. Maybe.

She would need to buy a casket. Get a headstone. Did people hold funerals in this situation? Probably not, though she felt like she should. Maybe she would do something small, just here at the house. A celebration of life—that was what they'd done at the company when Stanford in HR died last June.

She picked up David's address book and thumbed through it. Some of the names she recognized and could invite to a memorial. Most she didn't. She and David had, in many ways, been two separate silos, connected by sex and meals. Roommates who ate and slept together and fought the remainder of the time. In the last few years, they had avoided each other except for a few nights and a few dinners each week. Were most marriages that way? She didn't know. She had no basis for comparison.

Her last memory of him was a fight. He'd been getting dressed in the morning and she was in bed, and he asked her to get his razor, which was just a few bathroom drawers away. And she had snapped at him to get it himself, and he said that she didn't need to sleep any later, and it snowballed into him saying that he would stay at the condo that night and her telling him to just stay there the rest of the month.

He'd always threatened to stay at the condo, yet he rarely did. Only on nights when he went out for a big dinner or drinks with clients. He'd liked to come home, liked his bed and the steam shower and the way she tucked her feet under his body at night to keep them warm.

He'd liked the smoothies she kept stocked in the fridge and the way that, when he left his clothes on the floor, they were picked up when he returned, and that he didn't need to know where anything was because he could just ask his wife to get it for him, and she would bitch and complain, but she would do it, even if she was warm and in bed and he was already up and about.

In seventeen years of marriage, she couldn't think of a single time that he'd gotten something for her. She had never thought to ask him to. That just wasn't the way their relationship worked, and maybe that was why it had broken.

CHAPTER 40

KATIE MORROW

"You know, Katie's favorite movie growing up was Pretty Woman. I think that's why she was so gaga over Mark, from day one. She wanted that knight-in-shining-business-suit to whisk her away to his mansion and feed her bonbons. And apparently, she didn't care if he might have murdered his first wife. I told her it was a mistake, but she's naive and thinks the best of everyone. Gets that from her father."

28 Blackberry Summit Road
Hole 1, Stone Hollow

"I don't understand why she's here. I don't understand why you called her. And I really don't understand why you had her cell phone number *this entire time* and you never once told me." Katie's words ran together, her voice hiccuping on the last sentence, and she pressed her fingers to both eyes, trying to stop the flow of tears. Whirling away from Mark, she moved to the settee at the end of their bed and sank down on the expensive linen.

Mark stood by the set of double doors to their suite as if he was about to leave. He'd been hovering there ever since she'd said they needed to talk. Now he held up both hands in innocence and gave her an annoyed look. "Katie, you're making this into something it's not. I need you to calm down."

"Don't tell me to calm down!" she spat. "You don't know what it was like, having her waltz around our house like she owns the place. She's obnoxious, Mark. She looks at me as if she's laughing at me. And she can't resist dropping all of these stupid comments to point out what she knows or what you and her have done. I swear, I will kill her if I have to spend a week with her in this house."

"You're not going to kill her," Mark said reasonably, stepping closer. "Let's face it, you don't have the strength or capacity for that."

She dropped her hands and glared at him. "You think you're funny? You think any of this is funny?"

And he seemed to. From the moment he'd gotten back home, he'd been in a good mood. Lighter. Happier.

It was fucking infuriating. And it scared the life out of her.

"Look." He crouched in front of her and gripped her shoulders. "Don't be threatened by Willow, babe. You're my wife. Our marriage . . . her visit doesn't change anything about that." He smiled, but his eyes flicked to the door, and she could feel his itch to get downstairs and talk to her.

"Why is she here?" Katie whispered. "She said you called her. Why did you call her?"

He stared in her eyes. He wasn't as attractive from this angle. "I called her because I didn't like the questions the cops were asking me. I can tell everyone till I'm blue in the face that Willow's fine, but no one believed me then, and it was looking like it might turn into a big thing all over again. So I asked her to come here for a short visit. Just so everyone can see that I didn't murder her and dump her into one of the golf course lakes." He grimaced at the thought. "You don't . . . you don't know what it was like, when she left. How people treat you when they think that you've done something terrible."

No, she didn't know what that was like, but she had experienced the peripheral effects. She'd been left out of book clubs, snubbed at social events, and heard the snide comments—and that was all two years after Willow had disappeared. She couldn't imagine what it had been like right after the fact.

There had been moments when even she had considered the fact that Willow was dead. Not because she hadn't believed in Mark's innocence, but there had always been the possibility that Willow had met with some kind of foul play. Maybe she had been driving away from their life, headed to a new one, and broken down on the side of the highway. Gotten picked up by a stranger and ended up dead in a dumpster, her body never found.

Katie had listened to enough true crime podcasts to know that it wasn't just a possibility—it was a probability. Women didn't ever walk out of a situation and break all ties, without any trail. They didn't stop using their credit cards, cut off their friends, and leave no forwarding address.

Not unless you were hiding. And that was what Katie had never been able to figure out. Who or what had Willow been hiding from?

Katie stared into Mark's eyes and wondered whether he knew.

CHAPTER 41

WILLOW MORROW

"Let's see, Willow was in Fort Myers two summers ago. She house-sat for the Goldbergs, who have the condo next to mine. We were the only two people in the whole building under seventy, so we became fast friends. But Willow never talked about her past. She was full of stories about her travels and such, but I never once heard her mention an ex-husband or San Francisco. Honestly, I thought she might be a lesbian. We got drunk one night and made out a little, and I am not like that at all, but Willow has this sort of relaxed energy that made it seem like it wasn't a big deal."

28 Blackberry Summit Road
Hole 1, Stone Hollow

Willow had missed this view. She stood on the back porch and stared out at the hills and valleys of the golf course. The sun was low in the sky, bathing the greens in a golden glow, and the ponds shimmered like they were topped with diamonds.

The view was better from the second floor, best from the large terrace off their bedroom, but she didn't think that Katie would appreciate her going up there. For now, she settled into one of the large padded chairs around the firepit and twisted off the cap on a beer.

They had chosen this house because of its lot. It was at the end of the street, surrounded on three sides by the course. They had a large lake that separated them from the tee box and giant live oaks with branches that arched over and around the house like protective arms.

Mark had been obsessed with golf, and she had loved to ride in the cart, read a book, and get sloppy drunk. Twice, the course marshal had picked her up on the back nine and given her a ride home because she had been too distracting. They had received a letter reminding them of proper course conduct, and warning them that their Stone Hollow memberships would be suspended if they did not adhere.

Mark had been traumatized at the thought of losing his standing at the club, and forbade Willow from coming along anymore, which led to a fight. She had been drinking too much, and didn't back down when she should have, and now, looking back, she could recognize that she'd been a brat about it. Most of their fights, now that Willow thought about it, had been both created and escalated by her.

That particular fight had been pretty bad, and it had ended in the basement. There had been a dinner they were supposed to go to a few days later, one she'd had to cancel and make excuses for. Mark always made an effort to keep injuries in places that could be hidden by clothes, but it was hard to sit comfortably, to smile and carry on a conversation, when you had welts across your backside.

"Hey." Mark walked through the open French doors and lifted his own beer to his lips. He wore a casual dress shirt, the top buttons undone, the sleeves rolled up to his elbows, revealing tan forearms and his Patek Philippe watch, the one she'd given him on their fifth wedding anniversary.

"Hey." She sipped her beer and watched as he took the seat beside her. "Where's Katie?"

"Oh, she's changing upstairs. She'll be down in a bit." He studied her for a moment, then lowered his voice. "They found the body. ID'd it as male, so no one's thinking it might be you."

She nodded, absorbing the information. "Do they know who it is?" If they didn't, it shouldn't take them long to figure it out. Hell, anyone could solve that mystery instantly. Three people had disappeared that summer. Her, David Batcher, and Roxanne Kendal. Only one man on that list.

"I haven't heard anything about that, but maybe you should go by Sara's house. Check in with her." Mark adjusted his khaki shorts.

She considered the suggestion. It wasn't like she'd ever been close with Sara Batcher, but their husbands *had* played golf together and they had all been members of the country club, which had put them in the same spaces often enough that a friendship of sorts had formed. She tried to consider how she'd feel if Mark's body were found five years after his disappearance. Sad? Unsurprised? Confused?

Mark was right. She should go by Sara's. Worst-case scenario, the woman would tell her to fuck off, but much more likely, she'd invite her in. Hell, maybe she'd be glad to see her. Willow was kind of a celebrity, one who hadn't received much of a homecoming since returning to town. It would be nice to have someone other than Katie gape at her in surprise.

She stood up. "You're right. I'll head over there now. See what I can find out."

"Right now?" Mark tried to grab hold of her hand and missed it as she headed toward the house. "I thought maybe we'd talk a little. Catch up."

Catch up. That was the last thing she wanted to do with Mark. Just this brief interaction and she could already feel the pull of regret and longing. They had been dysfunctional and toxic, but there had been love there. In the past five years, she'd spent too many lonely nights missing a man who was now married to someone else.

"We can catch up later." She downed the remainder of her beer and tossed the bottle toward the trash can by the door. It made it in with a loud crash, and she stepped into the house.

Her purse and keys were still in the kitchen, but she ignored both, taking the short flight of steps down into the garage and flipping on the switch. Opening the key cabinet, she surveyed the options, smiling when she saw the Maserati key still in its rightful place, as if it had been waiting, this whole time, for her return. Pressing the button for the fourth bay, she turned to see the door roll up, the evening sun streaming in and putting a spotlight on the glossy red convertible.

Oh, heartbreak and skeletons aside, it was good to be home.

CHAPTER 42

ANDREA KENDAL

"My son is best friends with Cameron, so I've spent a fair amount of time with both Eric and Andrea, all focused on the kids. You'd never know that Eric wasn't Cam's father. Andrea yields to him on all major decisions. It would really piss me off if I was Cam's real father. I asked Andrea once about him, but she said he was dead. Lucky woman. My ex-husband is a bitch in terms of our son."

1442 Kingsmere Drive
Hole 6, Stone Hollow

It was almost seven o'clock when the detectives finally released Eric and called Andrea back for questioning. They passed each other in the hall, an audience of uniforms looking on, and shared a quick kiss.

"I have to go back to the hospital to tie up some things," Eric said.

"Okay, I'll meet you at home." Andrea squeezed his arm and watched as he headed to the doors and tried to read his gait, the expression he'd had on his face. Had that been relief on his features? Possibly. It was hard to tell through the deep lines of exhaustion. This was taking its toll on both of them. Maybe they could leave town for a bit.

Finally take the kids to LEGOLAND, a trip they'd been promising Cameron for ages.

Except what was that they always said in the movies? *Don't leave town.* Such a melodramatic cliché, except that maybe LEGOLAND wouldn't happen, all because of *this*.

"Mrs. Kendal?" The same detective who'd taken Eric away was now standing in the entry to a private room, holding the door. "We won't keep you too long, I promise."

How could they promise that? How, when they had no idea of what she'd done?

She followed him into the room and took the chair beside Walter. Across the table was the same female with the severe bun and no-nonsense expression. "Hi," Andrea said awkwardly. "I'm Andrea. I didn't get a chance to introduce myself earlier."

She nodded without smiling. "Detective Hanner. And you already know Detective Palentick?"

"Yes, we met before." She set her purse on the ground and crossed her legs at the ankle, cupping her hands together in her lap. She glanced at Walter, and he gave her a reassuring smile.

"This won't take long," he said, and hope entered her chest. Just what the detective had said, only Walter knew her level of involvement. He wouldn't say that if this were about Roxanne, which meant that maybe all this *would* be quick. Maybe LEGOLAND was on their horizon after all.

"You were already told about the remains that we found in your neighborhood," the woman started. "We called you in because the body was located directly behind your home, in the pond that is part of the sixth hole."

Every ounce of stress in Andrea's body flooded out of her. "You're kidding," she breathed and tried not to smile. *This* was nothing. This would be cleared up. "Okay. Do you know who it is?"

Walter tapped her arm. "Andrea, they have a few questions to ask you. Let them go through those so that we can get you back home to the kids. I can update you on the details."

In other words, *shut up*. She nodded and pinned her lips together, looking to the detectives for their questions.

"We can't share the identity of the victim yet, but it is a male, in case you were concerned about the Roxanne Kendal case."

"Oh," she said softly. "Okay." There. Walter couldn't be upset over that. *Oh. Okay.* Just two words that didn't give them anything.

A male. So David Batcher, probably. Missing persons weren't a dime a dozen in this area, and access to the neighborhood and courses was strictly monitored and controlled. She thought of Sara and sent a silent prayer of support over to the woman, who was probably dealing with her own questions from police, all while navigating such devastating news.

Detective Palentick cleared his throat and began. "We're trying to establish a timeline of events here. While we don't know the exact date that the death occurred—"

"Yet," the female detective interjected.

"Yet," he added, "we're guessing that it was in May of 2021, based on outstanding missing persons from this area."

David Batcher. Definitely.

"So I just want to make sure that you weren't involved with Eric Kendal at that time."

"'Involved'?" Andrea let out a nervous laugh. "I didn't know Eric then. I wasn't even living in this area then."

"Yes, this says that you were in Florida at that time, is that correct?"

Dots appeared in Andrea's vision, and she began to feel lightheaded. "Yes?" she said faintly. This was bad. If they dug . . . if they looked into her past . . . she couldn't afford what they might find.

"So you didn't know Eric or Roxanne Kendal in 2021?" Detective Hanner asked.

She couldn't look to Walter for help, not on such a simple and obvious question. "No."

"Was it your understanding that Eric and Roxanne were living together at the time of her disappearance?" Hanner wrote something down on her pad as she asked the question.

Suspect seems nervous. Must be guilty. Andrea could just picture the words, her blue felt-tip underlining the final word.

"Mrs. Kendal?" the man prodded.

Andrea flinched. "Sorry. Yeah, they lived together up until . . ." She faltered. "I'm sorry, I don't know the dates of when she was attacked."

"Oh, we have that here." Hanner smiled like a cat watching her prey. "February second. Three months, almost to the day, before David Batcher disappeared."

"Oh, okay. So yeah, they were living there during that time." She looked to Walter. "Is that all?"

"Not quite." Detective Palentick stepped back in. "Did Eric ever mention the Batchers to you? Either Sara or David?"

"I mean, I know the history—that he ran off on Sara or whatever. There are a lot of rumors going around the neighborhood, depending on who you talk to. I asked Eric about it when I heard about it. That was years ago. I really don't know when it was. I feel like that was one of the first things I heard about when I moved into the neighborhood. That and Willow."

"Yeah, between those two and Roxanne, there could be a serial killer in the neighborhood." Hanner widened her eyes, almost in glee, and Andrea frowned at the thought.

"I mean, probably not. I feel like they are all three very different. At least, Roxanne is. Maybe Willow and David ran off together—that's what some people say, though I think that's probably not right, given how far apart they were . . ." She trailed off at the feel of Walter's knee, hard against hers. Talking too much again. As her mother loved to say, she did not raise a quiet daughter.

"So what did Eric tell you?" Palentick asked.

She wrinkled her nose and tried to honestly think of what Eric's take on the Batcher disappearance had been. "Ummm . . . I can't really remember what he said. He wasn't interested in it. You have to realize, Eric is not exactly into neighborhood drama or gossip. I think he said they split and people were turning it into something it probably wasn't." She paused, aware that she had been about to misspeak, and chose her next words very carefully. "I don't think he had an opinion. Eric is very based in and focused on facts. He doesn't buy into theories. So if he doesn't know about something, he doesn't speculate."

The two detectives looked at each other, and she tried to decipher the silent communication they shared.

"So you don't think that Eric killed David Batcher?" Detective Hanner asked abruptly.

The question was so absurd that Andrea laughed. "No. Absolutely, unequivocally not."

"What about Roxanne?" The man leaned forward over the table toward her.

"No," she said immediately. "He loved Roxanne." *More than me.* The words screamed silently in her head but never made it past her lips.

"He wouldn't kill her? Crime of passion, maybe?"

"No," she said firmly and looked between them, making sure they saw the resolution in her statement. "Never."

They looked at each other again and seemed to believe the lie. From beside her, even Walter smiled in approval.

CHAPTER 43

SARA BATCHER

"When Sara sold InkRose, every employee in the company got a check for ten thousand dollars, on top of any stock options or bonuses. Even the ladies who came in twice a week and watered the plants got one. That was all Sara's doing, and someone generous like that—they wouldn't kill somebody. And trust me, she didn't need any insurance money."

16 Branwyn Hill
Hole 18, Silverwood Preserve

If there was any life left in Sara Batcher, it was scared out by Maggie's dramatic burst into the study. Her house manager stumbled in, knocking over a lamp in her haste and clutching her chest as if to keep her heart contained. "You'll never guess who is here."

"Keanu Reeves," Sara said dryly, putting a notecard in her journal and closing it.

"No, but let's continue to root for that." Maggie set the lamp back in place and pushed her hair away from her face.

"David's mother." Sara capped her pen and added it to the cup on her desk.

Maggie grimaced at the thought of the overbearing woman, who had once given her a self-help book on weight loss. "God, no. Willow Morrow."

Sara looked up, genuinely surprised. "Are you sure?"

"Saw her myself on the gate cam. Definitely her."

"Willow Morrow is here, at the gate?"

"Well, no, I let her in, so she's probably walking up the front steps, but yes, she's here."

Sara sat back in her seat and stared blankly at Maggie. "Holy shit. I really thought she was dead."

"You and everyone else." Maggie grinned. "When I saw her, my first thought was *Oh my God, watch David show up next.* How morbid is that?"

"Morbid." Sara shook her head in disapproval and stood up, walking to the window and peering out of the blinds, trying to see down to the driveway. "I don't get it. Why is she here?"

The doorbell rang, and both women turned toward the sound. "I guess we'll find out," Maggie said.

Sara invited Willow onto the back veranda, where they settled in at the seating cluster that overlooked the koi pond. Dusk had fallen, and as they took their seats, the automatic landscape lighting glowed to life, casting dramatic uplights on the trees and foliage. Maggie hustled toward them, a lighter in hand, and lit the candles on the table, then fired up the two fire towers on either side of them, turning the flames to low. They were shielded from the wind by a stone wall that dribbled water in rivulets down its granite surface, but Sara was still appreciative of the heaters, especially with nightfall coming.

"Can I get you anything to drink?" Maggie paused beside them, the lighter gripped in both hands as if she were an acolyte.

"Clase Azul, if you've got it. Otherwise . . . surprise me." Willow ran a hand through her hair and looked around. "Damn, Sara. This is beautiful. Last time I was here, the pool was different, right?"

"Ah, yeah. I redid it a couple of years ago." Sara nodded to the guesthouse, where Maggie lived. "I removed the rose garden and put in the guesthouse. Maggie uses it."

"Oh, that's right; I remember all the blooms." Willow nodded, almost manic in her energy, and Sara tried to pair this woman with the sleek trophy wife who had disappeared. Willow Morrow had always been one of the more beautiful women in the neighborhood, a standard that she had taken seriously. Sara had never seen her look anything other than perfectly put together. This version of Willow was wildly different. She was wearing cut-off shorts and a baggy T-shirt with a blinged-out dinosaur on the front, a long knit cardigan over the top, and Converse sneakers. With big sunglasses perched on top of her head and her hair long and wavy, she looked like one of those bohemian hipsters who hung around all day at the coffee shop.

"Have you been by your old house?" Sara said cautiously, not sure how to bring up the fact that Willow had left all of them hanging when she'd disappeared. It wasn't that they had been close—more acquaintances. But she'd been friendly enough to all their social circle that if she planned to leave, she should have said something to *someone*. The abrupt disappearance without any warning—that was what had fueled the rumors.

"Yeah, I went there first. Met Katie." Willow grinned. "Very different, I gotta say. At least from me. Seems like a sweet girl, though."

"I haven't met her," Sara replied. "So I wouldn't know."

"You haven't met her?" Willow crinkled her brow. Had there not been any Botox wherever she'd gone? She was overdue for a round in the 11's and an appointment with some tweezers.

Sara tried not to stare at the woman's overgrown brows. "Ah, no. They don't entertain. Not like you guys did. I'm not exactly at the top of invitation lists when parties do happen, but I haven't missed any at your place, far as I'm aware."

"Oh my God, Mark must be going stir crazy." Willow looked pleased at the possibility, and her smile widened at the sight of Maggie returning, a tray with their drinks in hand. "But all that aside, Sara, I really stopped by to pay my respects to David."

Sara's back stiffened. *Pay my respects.* She hated the sound of that, hated the interruption of her evening, hated the way that the woman's voice just dropped to almost a whisper. Was this what was ahead for her? Hours of stilted and polite conversation with people she barely knew?

"I'm surprised you heard." She forced a smile. "You've been in town, what? Just a few hours? And yet somehow you're the first in line."

Willow tilted her head and studied her. "You don't have to make it sound predatory, Sara. I found out an old friend died, and I stopped in to console his widow. You know, there aren't a lot of people in these gates who will see you as that. Because most of them, right now? Are talking about you as his killer."

Maggie, who had been in the process of moving their drinks off the tray, paused, Willow's glass in hand. The tumbler was heavy, and she shot Sara a questioning look, as if asking whether she should throw the contents in Willow's face.

Sara's gaze flicked from Maggie to Willow, and it took every ounce of her self-control to smile. "That's an interesting assumption from a woman who hasn't been here in quite some time."

"David went missing a few months before I left," she said bluntly, taking the glass from Maggie's fingers and downing the tequila in one quick sip. "I know what everyone was saying, Sara. What everyone thought. And trust me, it was your closest friends who were saying it loudest."

"I know what people thought," Sara said quietly. "But people also thought you were dead, and you're not. People are wrong more frequently than they are right."

"You're taking this the wrong way." Willow leaned forward, and the candles' reflections glowed in her irises. "I believe you. I just wanted to say that I'm sorry and that he was a great guy."

He had been a great guy, at least when he wasn't in withdrawal. Tears pricked the corners of Sara's eyes. "You know, he was really funny. That's why I fell in love with him. He kept me laughing."

And he had. David's humor had been what had both attracted Sara and sealed the deal with her. But a marriage couldn't survive on laughter alone.

Especially since there were some things you couldn't laugh off.

CHAPTER 44

KATIE MORROW

"Mark and Katie got married at the courthouse. I always thought it was odd. I mean, the man could give her a wedding at the Hearst Castle if he wanted to, but they just had a quiet ceremony at the courthouse, followed by a reception at his agency's beach house. Katie seemed fine with it all, but personally, I would have been pissed. But Katie is very go-with-the-flow about things."

28 Blackberry Summit Road
Hole 1, Stone Hollow

"Okay, so Willow's here. People can see her. She can talk to the police. She doesn't have to stay at our house, Mark. That's weird. Very weird." Katie chopped an onion into halves, then quarters, lining up the pieces and hacking the blade through the tender white chunks.

"It's not weird. Willow was my best friend, Katie. For almost a decade. When your cousin comes to visit, she stays here."

"Michelle?" Katie whirled around and pointed the knife at him. "Don't even try to put Michelle in the same category as your ex-wife. I never slept with Michelle, Mark. I didn't drop to my knees and burst into tears at the sight of *Michelle*, Mark." She jabbed the knife with each mention of his name, and the aggression felt good. Maybe this was why people went to those rage rooms and threw plates and smashed windows. Right now, driving a sledgehammer through a microwave seemed cathartic in a way that the fajita prep was not.

"But Michelle *did* stay with us for a month," Mark countered, and he was not this stupid of an individual. There was no way he was this dense.

"Say *Michelle* one more time," Katie threatened. "Say her name one more time and I'll jab this knife into you."

He laughed and held up his hands in surrender. "You will not, and you know it."

She sagged against the counter and turned back to the cutting board. Her eyes were tearing up from the onions, and she wiped them with the back of her knife-holding hand. "Just . . . put her in a hotel."

It wasn't a difficult request. It was reasonable, one that any wife would make. One that any husband would yield to. *Okay, honey. Sure. No problem. I'll call and let her know.*

But he didn't say any of those things. Instead, he walked to the beverage fridge and opened the door, withdrawing a seltzer beer for her and a Heineken for him. Putting hers on the island, he popped the cap on his and took a swig.

"I'm not drinking." She pushed the can back and waited for him to ask why. Not that she would tell him the news—not right now. And not because of the timeline, but because of her. Willow wouldn't taint this for Katie. If she had to wait to share the news until she pushed that woman and her luggage out the door and locked it behind her, she would.

Mark didn't notice, didn't even think about the possible reasoning; he just picked up her beer and returned it to the fridge.

Willow was my best friend. For almost a decade. She thought of the lace thong tucked in his suit pocket. How could she compete with that? If Katie left him, right now, and walked out the door—in five years, would he say the same thing about her? Would he welcome her into his home? Break down in tears at the sight of her?

No. No way. The father of her future child, and she wasn't sure she would get much more than a bewildered *What are you doing here?* from him.

She chopped faster, the blade blurring through the tears.

CHAPTER 45

WILLOW MORROW

"I've been Sara's house manager for eight years, so I'd heard of Willow, and of course, we'd gossiped over her leaving. One of the theories going around the neighborhood was that David and Willow had run off together, but that was less likely than a cat volunteering for bath time. I mean, Willow did seem a little like the free-love, cheat-on-your-husband kind of woman, but David . . . David wasn't romantic enough, or organized enough, to run off with someone. He needed Sara to function. I honestly think, if he'd been ready to leave, that he would have needed her help to pack the bag and book the flights."

28 Blackberry Summit Road
Hole 1, Stone Hollow

After two hours of drinking, the outdoor cabana was beginning to spin. It was a new phenomenon for Willow, who had been the queen of drinking everyone in Bottleburr, Montana, under the table. The bar there had engraved a stool with her name—not that she'd ever make it back to that sleepy town or that delicious bartender with the dimples and the hick accent.

She looked across the table at Sara, who was currently leaning in to Maggie's shoulder and laughing. Sara wasn't conventionally pretty, but there was something attractive about her. It was like a bunch of broken pieces that fit together to make a mosaic. To be honest, it was refreshing, in a neighborhood full of plastic faces, to see a woman with a nose that was crooked and a narrow gap in between her two front teeth.

"Okay, new discussion point," Willow said, lifting the tequila and pouring them each a shot. They'd finished off the first bottle and moved on to Don Julio, which was already half gone. "Biggest regret romantically."

Silence fell. Sara blew out a breath and stared at the grooved ceiling. Maggie made a face, started to say something, then stopped. Willow held her tongue, waiting to see what the other two women would say.

Sara sighed. "I would say . . . marrying David. That's horrible to say, isn't it? I mean, given the timing."

"Who would you have married instead?" Willow leaned forward and selected a cracker from the platter Maggie had prepared, then dug it through the fish dip. The tray had three dips in total, but so far only the pimento and brie had been destroyed. No one had touched the artichoke.

"Oh my God, Jackson Bloom. Gorgeous man, with . . ." She held her palms an impressive distance apart from each other, and they all giggled like they were in high school.

"Jackson Bloom . . ." Willow intoned. "Sounds like a cowboy."

"Oh my God, no. He was a lifeguard from Santa Monica. You know what, take that back. I couldn't have married him. My parents would have disowned me."

"Why was David a mistake?" Maggie asked, turning to Sara. "You guys always seemed like the golden couple."

The golden couple. Willow had a sudden memory of David, looking down at her, his eyes gleaming, the smell of alcohol heavy on his breath. *"Your husband told me you like it rough."*

They hadn't been a golden couple. David had been a train wreck, one who never missed an opportunity to share his attraction to Willow. Mark had always blown off his behavior, blamed it on alcohol, but Willow . . . she knew. She'd had a father like David, and men like him didn't make great husbands. She watched Sara's face, curious how she would respond.

"He started to resent me, I think. For my company's success. He was okay with my family's money, but when InkRose started to blow up, he got . . ." She shook her head and pinched her lips together. "Nasty. Bitter. Started going out after work and staying at the condo more. For all I know, he started sleeping around."

That had been the one thing Willow had never had to worry about with Mark. He had the opposite of a wandering eye. Rather, he had been fixated on her.

Dangerously so.

Had that faded with time? She cradled her drink and thought of tonight, him reaching for her as she had passed by, the look in his eyes. *I thought maybe we'd talk a little. Catch up.*

She was both afraid and exhilarated by the idea that his obsession—his need—was still there.

CHAPTER 46

ANDREA KENDAL

"The park where Roxanne was attacked? I used to run on that same trail. But I never ran that late in the day. It was just too dangerous, too empty in the late afternoon. All it would take is one psychopath hiding in the bushes, and I could have ended up like her."

1442 Kingsmere Drive
Hole 6, Stone Hollow

Andrea pulled into the driveway and stopped, taking a moment to look at the beauty that was their home. The brick Tudor had ivy that covered the east wall, the greenery creeping across the red brick like a blanket pulled up to someone's chin. The oil lanterns on either side of the front door were lit, casting a warm light across the entry. Most of the interior lights on the first level were on, and through the open curtains, she could see the beautiful rich interiors.

So different from the home she had grown up in. While it had been the biggest house on the block, it was also the darkest. Kids didn't come over to play, not at her house. Every window of the home had an electronic reader that would send out a notification if opened, but the notifications were never needed. As a child, she'd known her place. Her room had been both her prison and her sanctuary, and she had never looked out the windows and rarely ventured outside the door.

As a teenager, while her friends were sneaking out to meet boys or planning trips to the mall or going to Malibu, she had been curled up in the soft chair in the corner of her room, reading Agatha Christie and Tom Clancy. No boy had been stupid enough to ask her on a date. Her first date wasn't until college, when she'd finally been far enough from home for no one to know what her last name meant.

In contrast, her home with Eric looked like every magazine she had dog-eared as a child and fantasized about as an adult. And it was hers. This beautiful life was hers. Had it been worth it all to get it?

Yes. Even though it had risked putting them in jail, even despite all the pain, the lies, the blood . . . yes. Because now they were a family, one that deeply loved each other. Cameron was safe and Ryder would never know fear. So, yes. It had all been worth it.

She took her foot off the brake and the vehicle rolled forward. Following the driveway's curve, she pressed the button on her visor and opened up the first bay. Pulling in, she parked beside Eric's Mercedes and killed the engine. She checked the time.

Too late to tell Cameron and Ryder good night. By now, they'd both be sound asleep.

The doors were open to the back veranda, and she found Eric on his phone, his reading glasses on top of his head, leaning against one of the porch columns, looking out on the view. He turned at her approach. "She just got home," he said into the phone. "Let's talk tomorrow."

He hung up. "That was Walter. He said we did well."

Andrea sighed. "I'm exhausted. Can we not ever do that again?"

He pulled her into his arms and rested his chin on top of her head, squeezing her into his chest. "I think the worst is over."

She pulled away and looked up at him. "So . . . we're safe? They don't suspect anything?"

"A dead body was found less than a football field away from our back porch." Eric tilted his head in the direction of the lake. "We'll be of interest until they figure out the truth. But yes, as far as Roxanne is concerned, they don't suspect anything."

She followed his lead, trying to see the area in the dark. It was hard, with plenty of trees and bushes between them. "I can't believe that David Batcher's been out there this whole time."

"They asked if I saw anything back then, and I told them that I didn't even notice the apparent circus that's happened in the last forty-eight hours of them discovering and excavating the body. Have you?"

She shook her head. "No. But I wasn't paying attention. Especially not back here." Their yard was thickly landscaped, with a manicured lawn surrounding the flagstone paths, the stone pavers, the pale-turquoise pool. You couldn't see past the border of mature olive trees, their silvery leaves a thick barrier to the golf course hole behind it. The only glimpse out of the yard was an arched opening built for their golf cart and framed in bright-pink bougainvillea blooms. Occasionally, if the moon was bright enough, you'd see a reflection off the pond through it, but nothing in the dark woods near the water.

No wonder someone had thought to dump a body out there. It was doubling down on the concept of hiding it in plain sight while still having protection. Andrea used to run on the course at night and had never seen so much as a dog-walker out there on the links. It was like a thousand-acre private park that became a secret world at night, one that only a few had the key to.

"You know, I knew David Batcher," Eric said. "He pitched me medical equipment a few times. Supplied us with the artificial valves we used to use."

Andrea closed her eyes. "You're kidding me. That isn't good."

"One in ten people in this neighborhood are in the medical field. If they start suspecting his client list, they're going to have a lot of suspects. The only thing that they did bring up . . ."

The reluctance in his voice caused her alarm to spike. "What?"

"His company's valve was part of the Brody Pitt surgery. Formatic was the company. They were one of the major parties listed on the wrongful death lawsuit."

Brody Pitt. The lawsuit had occurred just a few months after Roxanne's disappearance. Andrea hadn't been privy to the details, but she had seen the stacks of files that Eric had collected as evidence, and known that there was a risk to Eric's professional reputation and malpractice insurance. Patients shouldn't die three weeks after surgery, but even the most skilled surgeon couldn't fight the inevitability of certain medical outcomes, especially when faulty equipment was involved.

"So David died before he could testify?"

"No, he testified. He didn't say much that helped or hurt the case, best I can remember."

"Did you meet with him? Around the time that he disappeared?"

"No. My only experiences with him were a few isolated sales calls. I barely remember him; not sure I could have picked him out of a lineup."

"Yeah, but between that connection and . . ." She gestured to the lake. "Our proximity to the scene."

"We're innocent. Don't worry about it." He tugged at a lock of her hair and grabbed his sweatshirt off the closest chair, preparing to go inside.

We're innocent. Don't worry about it.

They were innocent of this. And maybe he was right and there was nothing for her to be worried about. But it wasn't the David Batcher murder that was stressing her out.

It was the scrutiny. She wasn't sure they'd hold up under that.

CHAPTER 47

SARA BATCHER

"The victim's body appears to have been submersed in fresh water for approximately five years, which accelerated decomposition, leaving us with very little soft tissue to examine. We didn't find any obvious signs of perimortem trauma—no fractures, no bullet entry or exit points, no blade marks—but that doesn't rule out foul play. Drowning, for example, leaves no trace on bone. Same with poisoning. I sent samples for diatom testing and toxicology, but realistically, the cause of death may remain undetermined."

16 Branwyn Hill
Hole 18, Silverwood Preserve

Sara leaned over the bathroom sink and splashed water on her face, rubbing her palms vigorously over the skin in lieu of her normal four-part evening regimen. Turning off the faucet, she straightened and looked in the mirror. Her mascara had run, giving her a raccoon-like appearance, and she opened the center drawer and withdrew a cotton ball. She went for the pale-blue bottle of eye makeup remover and misjudged the distance, knocking it over. The room swayed. Maybe Sara should have stopped when they'd finished off the second bottle of tequila.

Maggie had done a better job of keeping up with Willow. They had been the bad influences, the two of them pushing Sara for one more, then one more. She got the cap off the eye makeup remover and wet the cotton ball. God, when was the last time she had been this drunk? Probably the Jahtunicks' wedding. At least this time she hadn't gotten up on a stage and kissed the DJ. At the time, she had heard the crowd chanting their support of the action. Later, Maggie had told her that the chant had been for her to "sit down" and that the DJ was only seventeen. His mother had sent Sara a letter, chastising her for molesting a minor and threatening to report her to the authorities. The letter had included a sponsorship form for the DJ's soccer team, which was raising funds for a trip to London.

Against Ian's advice, Sara had completed the form and enclosed a check for $15,000. That had seemed like an inexpensive way to avoid prosecution. It had worked.

She did a hack job on the mascara cleanup but managed to get the majority of it off, leaving a small mess of dirty cotton balls on the counter, then turned off the light and headed for bed, pulling off items of clothing as she went.

Her crocheted sweater hit the tile just past the steam-shower door. Her jeweled belt, she hung on the towel hook. Her cream linen pants, on the Egyptian leather rug. She undid her bra and tossed it in the direction of the closet and left on her socks and underwear. Willow hadn't been wearing a bra. The points of her nipples poked through the baggy shirt she'd worn, and she'd shed her long cardigan sweater around the time they'd decided to order a few pizzas from Rotania's and eat them on the floor in the den.

Sara couldn't imagine not wearing a bra. It felt like something hippies did, and while she wouldn't have pegged Willow Morrow as a hippie before, after spending the evening with her, she was . . . Sara frowned as she wormed underneath the covers. Chill. Like how Sara had always wanted to be, except that she didn't seem to be built that way, and it was impossible to be chill when there was always important work to be done, a company to run, and an unending to-do list to finish.

At least, there had been when she owned InkRose. Now that she no longer owned it, now that she was just another member of the board and called on quarterly for a meeting and otherwise ignored . . . she could be chill.

There was a soft knock on the door, and the right side eased open. Maggie peeked around the edge of the door. "May I come in?"

Sara nodded and sat up in the bed. "Think she suspects anything?"

Maggie shook her head. "I don't think she has a clue."

CHAPTER 48

KATIE MORROW

"I remember when Mark called to tell us Katie was pregnant. It was about two months after the wedding, and my mom thought that was probably why he married her. And it tracked, since I remember him saying that he'd never remarry after Willow left. So, why marry Katie? It had to be because of a baby. But joke's on him, because she lost the baby, like, two weeks after he told us. He should have waited until she was further along. Or even better, should have just let her have the baby out of wedlock. This isn't the fifties. It's not like her honor is at stake."

28 Blackberry Summit Road
Hole 1, Stone Hollow

Katie spat in the sink, then opened the door to the toothbrush caddy, put in her brush, and closed the cover. Pressing the button on the front, she started the clean-and-sanitization cycle. Closing her eyes, she inhaled deeply, counted to three, then exhaled. 10:42 p.m. 10:42 p.m. and Willow wasn't back.

This was ridiculous. What if she came back at 2:00 a.m.? What if she brought a man back? "So we're just supposed to wait up for her?"

She called out the question as she returned the toothpaste and floss to their places, then grabbed the counter disinfectant and got to work, blanketing the white stone surfaces in the orchid-scented spray.

"She has a key and the alarm code. There's nothing we have to do," Mark said from inside the toilet room, his voice muffled through the door.

"It's rude. You don't stay at someone's house and then come back late. She didn't even tell us that she was missing dinner." Katie used a soft cleaning pad to rub the disinfectant in, flipping over the pad to wipe up the excess. The smell, which normally soothed her, didn't touch her mood. If anything, it irritated her.

The toilet flushed and the door swung open. Mark moved past her, heading to his sink. "You didn't want her to eat dinner with us. I think you made that pretty clear to her."

"I've been extremely nice to her," Katie objected, tossing the pads in the trash, then using the glass spray on the mirror. "You can't say that I haven't been nice to her."

"You've been a bit stiff." He squirted some hand soap into his palm, and Katie wanted to point out that Willow would have never hunted down the black currant blend from their Maui honeymoon. Mark had commented twice during that stay that he had liked the smell, and Katie had spent a solid three days contacting the hotel's corporate headquarters, then the soap manufacturer, then four different private distributors before finding one that would sell direct to her. She'd had to buy eight cases of it in order for them to agree to the purchase. Mark had glanced at the bottle and said, "Neat," before asking her what they were doing for dinner.

You've been a bit stiff. Well, Willow had been a bit of a bitch, but to point that out would only make Katie sound like a scorned wife, so she swallowed the retort. "She said that you two *got* things from each other. What does that mean?"

"What?" Mark turned to her as he dried his hands with a monogrammed towel. "What are you talking about?"

"She said that you two had an unhealthy relationship, and that you 'got' things from each other." She wiped down the glass and surveyed the counter area, making sure that everything was in line and place. It was a quirk, her need for everything to be in perfect order at the end of each day, but it was a quirk that worked for her and gave her a sense of calm that typically carried her through to sleep.

Typically. Tonight, she had a feeling she could clean the grout with the electric scrubber and she'd still crawl into bed with a belly full of knots.

"I don't know what she was talking about. But yeah, it was unhealthy in ways. We were both young. We fought a lot. She's probably talking about the chaos. We both liked chaos, her more than me."

We both liked chaos? Chaos was the opposite of their household. If anything, Katie bent over backward to make sure their home was a sanctuary of calm and serenity. Mark had enough stress at work; she didn't want him to worry about anything here at home. "So, you like chaos?"

He hung the towel on the ring and pulled her into his arms. "I did, back when I was young and too stupid to know better. Now what I need is what you give me. Only you."

The towel was crooked. It was all front loaded, with barely enough on the back. He pulled her tighter, squashing her against his chest, and she tried not to let it bother her. "I love you," he said gruffly.

The entire bathroom was pristine, except for the water droplets by his sink and the sloppy towel. She squirmed in his grip and he released her. She opened the cabinet under his sink and removed a replacement towel from the rolls there. Grabbing the spray, she quickly spritzed the entire area, then used his dirty hand towel to clean the sink, faucet hardware, and counter. She ran the new towel through the bar and proportioned it correctly, then stepped back, examining the area.

"Katie." He sighed. "Come to bed. It's almost eleven. I want to finish before it gets too late."

She turned off the bank of lights on the wall and considered telling him that she didn't want to have sex tonight. He would understand, given the fight they'd had earlier about Willow. There would be some light complaining, but then he would get on his phone and she would read her book, and they would go to bed.

But she didn't say anything. She removed her silk night set, folding the top and the pants and placing them on the bench by her side of the bed. Then she climbed onto the California King and lay on her back, spreading her legs and waiting as he climbed up on the mattress and lowered himself on top of her.

As usual, it took a few minutes of quiet movement, and when he was done, she redressed and lay in the dark next to him. Their sex had been, at the beginning, a little more exciting. He had been a big dirty-talker at the beginning, but Katie never seemed to say the right things, and he'd done it less and less as time went on, until their sessions became a quiet and quick event that satisfied his needs but never hers. Beside her, his breath changed tempo and got slower and deeper as he fell asleep.

It wasn't fair, for him to fall asleep so easily. How was he not concerned about her feelings, about her reactions and concerns about his ex-wife? Ten hours ago, she had all but assumed that Willow was dead or, at minimum, someone she would never see or have to deal with. Now she was their houseguest, one who had a much closer relationship and bond with Katie's husband than she had ever anticipated.

She stared up at the ceiling, which had an elaborate print covering of a jungle. It was all hand drawn, from the point of view of the jungle floor, looking up into the trees. It was a piece you could study for hours and still not see everything. It was Katie's favorite part of the room, and one of the reasons why she had three night-lights scattered over the large space. In the dim light, she could study it, and examining the details gave her overcrowded mind a chance to relax.

Willow had picked out this ceiling—had found this print, brought it to a wallpaper shop, had them print it out at one hundred times the size, then mounted it on the thirteen-foot-high ceilings. How could a woman with the insight and passion to do all *that* be the same horrible drunk who had just bulldozed her way into their home?

She couldn't. Or maybe she could and then she'd changed.

Or maybe good interior design tastes had nothing to do with being a good person.

Yes, that was it. It was just funny that, for the past three years, every time Katie looked up at this ceiling at night, she had felt a sort of kinship with Willow. They both liked the same man. The same art. The same books. Katie had gone through Willow's junk room and discovered a box of CDs from the nineties and flipped through the titles, smiling at the familiar covers. LFO. Sublime. Matchbox Twenty.

While she had assumed that she would never meet Willow, she'd also thought that, if she did, she would like the woman. And Mark had always been kind in his references to Willow, which was such a refreshing change from so many men who were venomous about their exes, especially if the women left them.

But maybe that was a bad thing. Who wanted a husband who was still hung up on their ex? Maybe it wasn't fond memories—maybe it was love that was still fierce and strong.

She heard a sound. A door. She pushed herself upright and reached for her phone. Pulling up the alarm app, she checked the log.

Disarmed at 11:29 p.m. Armed at 11:30 p.m. Willow was here.

"Willow's back," she announced into the dark.

Mark rolled onto his side. "Go to sleep," he murmured. "She'll be fine."

Sure, stumbling around the house. Looking at things. Touching things. It would be impossible to know how many items she would have infected, if not tonight, tomorrow. Or the next day.

Maybe Katie should go downstairs to see what she was doing. Find out where she'd been all night. Mark had said she went to Sara's house, but she couldn't have been there this entire time. It had been almost six hours. No guest stayed at someone's house for six hours.

She returned the phone and lay back down. Maybe Willow would just go straight to sleep. If the time at their house was any indication, she was probably trashed and would collapse in bed.

Mark rolled over and wrapped his arms around her body, pulling her into him. He smelled slightly of sweat, and she hugged his forearm, and the thought of going downstairs died, at least for the moment.

She kissed his arm and closed her eyes, ordering herself to relax and go to sleep. There was no better feeling than being held by Mark, and she refused to let Willow ruin that for her.

CHAPTER 49

WILLOW MORROW

"I did some work for Mark Morrow, after Willow left. Trash removal, mostly. He was cleaning out their basement and had dozens of trash bags filled with stuff. Normally, I just take stuff to the dump, but he actually followed me there and watched as I threw each bag into the incinerator. It was weird. Made me wonder what he was hiding in those bags."

28 Blackberry Summit Road
Hole 1, Stone Hollow

Willow woke up to the smell of coffee. She lay there for a long nostalgic moment, savoring what it used to be like, living in this house. The mornings had always been the best, their time together before he had gone off to work and she had gone back to bed.

She rolled onto her back and listened, trying to hear whether any voices were coming from the kitchen. Not hearing any, she sat up and swung her legs over the side of the guest bed.

She pulled on a baggy Kurt Cobain shirt and cut-off jean shorts. She'd forgotten to charge her cell phone last night, so she plugged it in, then wandered down the hall to the kitchen. Mark was sitting at the island, reading glasses on, in a suit, the newspaper in hand.

She stopped just before the doorway and took a secret moment to watch him. The reading glasses, they were new. Her love for him swelled at the outward sign of imperfection.

"Morning," she said quietly, stepping into the room.

He looked up at her greeting, a warm smile stretching over his face. Moving his glasses up to the top of his head, he stood and gestured to the stool next to him. "Come and sit. I'll get you a cup of coffee."

She took the seat, watching as he hurried around the island toward the espresso machine. "Remember how I like it?"

He scoffed. "Come on, now. I'm older, not dead. And we even have almond milk."

"Nice." She hooked her heels on the rungs of the stool and looked around the kitchen. From this spot, it was easy to pretend that nothing had changed and that it was a half decade earlier. Even the familiar twinges of a hangover headache . . . it was all there. "Put a shot of Baileys in there."

He raised his brows but didn't comment, and he wouldn't. She could swig Baileys from the bottle until she fell off the stool, and he'd just pick her back up and ask if she wanted anything else. That was Mark for you. He'd enable you right into a coma.

"Where's Katie?" she asked, her voice dropping in volume.

"Asleep." He glanced at his watch, then fit the espresso portafilter into place. "Her alarm goes off at seven."

Thank God for Willow's internal alarm clock. She crossed her arms and rested her elbows on the counter. "I had a nice chat with Sara last night. The police don't have a cause of death for David. He was all bones, so it's hard to do a majority of the tests, but they can look for things like blunt force trauma, broken bones, stuff like that."

He opened the cabinet and shifted through the cups. "Makes sense. But I guess that means that they can't really know much, then? About what happened?"

"Right. Oh, you still have that mug." Her heart tripped at the elephant cup in his hand. It was all hand painted and thrown, the handle made from the animal's trunk. They'd gotten it in Africa, on a safari they'd taken for their eight-year anniversary.

"Of course." He set it on the counter before her, and she picked it up, turning it over in her hands. "You can take it with you if you want."

She studied the designs on the large mug. It was crazy how such a small item could hold so many memories. "No, but thank you." She set it down.

"You didn't take anything with you when you left," he said quietly, pulling out a bottle of Baileys from the cabinet and breaking the seal on the lid. Twisting off the cap, he poured a generous amount into the cup. "I looked, but I could never find anything that you took. It was like you just walked out of here one day and didn't come back."

"I took a few bags. We just had so much stuff that it was hard to miss any of it." She stopped him before he returned the bottle to the cabinet. "You can leave that out."

He paused, then set it down. "You're drinking too much."

"I thought you liked it when I drank," she flirted.

He looked at her, and her heart tripped at the concern in his eyes. No one had looked at her like that in . . . well, in five years. She had forgotten what it felt like to be in the grip of Mark's love. She'd found it suffocating, but now her throat yearned for it.

We got things from each other. Unhealthy things.

Mark liked to antagonize her and she liked to push back. A pushback that often turned the situation violent. It was why she'd had to leave. If she hadn't, Mark would have taken it too far. Neither of them had the self-control to stop the fight from progressing. She had to leave, otherwise one of them would have ended up dead, the other in jail.

"Willow . . ." he pleaded.

"Stop." She shook her head. "Don't. Don't remind me why I left."

"I miss you. I need you. You know I do." He put his palms on the counter and looked at her as if he could pull her into his soul with his stare, and in a weak moment, he could have.

She picked up the cup and chugged the Baileys, then slammed the mug on the counter so hard the ceramic cracked.

Dammit. She pushed herself up off the stool. "I'm going back to bed."

He didn't say anything, didn't stop her, didn't block her path, or grab her arm so tightly that he left bruises.

And she didn't react, didn't whip around, scream at him, or lunge for his throat.

Still, the possibility hung in the air, and she walked quickly back to the room and avoided looking toward the basement door.

CHAPTER 50

ANDREA KENDAL

"The fact that the body wasn't Roxanne's doesn't matter. Eric Kendal thinks he's going to get away with killing my niece, and he's not. I'll find out the truth, and if he killed her, there's nothing to say that he didn't kill David Batcher as well. Maybe Roxanne and David were having an affair. I mean, my niece was a good woman, but she was a woman. They don't always make the best decisions in life."

1442 Kingsmere Drive
Hole 6, Stone Hollow

Andrea woke on Saturday morning with a new mission in life, which was to move on with their lives and ignore the fact that a dead body had been unearthed a hundred yards south of their home.

It didn't have anything to do with them. The cops had seemed satisfied with their line of questioning. They could put it behind them and focus on the future. She showered and used the blow-dryer until her long locks were shiny and straight. Moving into the giant walk-in closet, she disrobed and selected a matching cotton bra and panty set from the center island drawers. After pulling those on, she chose a pair of cropped white jeans and a red off-the-shoulder blouse. Lacing up a pair of designer sneakers, she hummed along to a '90s Spice Girls hit that played over the house speakers. Kaitlyn must have been working today. The young housekeeper loved anything vintage, which to her meant '90s and 2000s. She was likely rocking a Hanson T-shirt and would feed a Tamagotchi on her lunch break.

Cameron's room was quiet, the door still closed, and Andrea passed it without knocking, content to let the four-year-old sleep late. She took the stairs down to the main level, unsurprised to hear Ryder's babbles coming from the playroom. Sticking her head in, she smiled at the nanny who was kneeling beside the toddler, entertaining him with a large block puzzle. "Morning, Anna."

"Good morning," she chirped. "Oh, you got a couple of phone calls. I left the messages in the kitchen."

That was probably the pharmacy. Cameron's inhaler needed a refill. Eric had called it in last week, and they still hadn't had a chance to go by and pick it up. That was okay, she could do that today. "Cam has a birthday party this afternoon . . . I was thinking I'd take Ryder along, if you want to do a deep clean of the toys and their rooms while we're gone? A sanitizing sweep."

"You got it." The older woman smiled. They had hit the jackpot with the retired teacher. She'd been an overnight nanny for both Cameron and Ryder and, God willing, would be for their next one. "Is he still asleep?"

"Yeah. If you haven't heard from him in the next hour, wake him up."

The woman nodded, her attention returning to Ryder. Andrea left the door open and walked through the entry hall and down to the butler's kitchen. By the phone board, there was a note in Anna's neat handwriting.

Call from Detective Palentick. Says to call him back.

Call from Tony. Update on autopsy. Call him back.

Two calls, both from law enforcement. Not a good sign. So much for a zen-filled Saturday. She stared at the small blue Post-it note and felt her anxiety close in on her, a small whine of concern ramping up into a piercing scream.

This will be okay.

This will be okay.

This will be okay.

Andrea felt the same way she had five years ago, when things had gone from bad to worse, every day bringing a new concern, and she had started to spiral down, reaching the point where suicide seemed like the only way out.

She couldn't take that path now. Not with Roxanne already in Eric's past. The cops wouldn't be okay with a second dead wife—and unlike with Roxanne, Andrea's death wouldn't solve anything. It wouldn't make any of these things go away; it would just leave Eric to shoulder it all.

Ryder's happy warble came from the playroom, and Andrea twisted toward the sound. And there it was, one of the lines that stood between her and running away from her problems. Escape was not a consideration with Cameron and Ryder, which meant that Andrea had to face these problems, even if doing so meant jail time.

She needed the detective to stop looking into them.

And just as importantly, she needed Roxanne's uncle to go back to his hole and leave them alone.

Call me back. No, they definitely would not call Tony back. The dead body belonged to David Batcher, whom Tony didn't care about, so there was no need for further discussion on the matter—especially not with her.

Detective Palentick's call was another matter. That one would have to be returned, and she had to assume the worst—that they had found no trace of Andrea in New Jersey and, possibly, no trace of her at all. Another problem, added to the top of the stack.

"Hey."

She jumped at the sound and whirled around to find Eric in the entrance to the secondary kitchen. He had on a faded red Stanford tee and running shorts, his hair damp from his morning shower. "Shit, you scared me."

"Sorry." He stepped forward and pressed a kiss on the side of her head. "What are you doing in here?"

She moved her palm over the note, hiding it. "Just thinking about that party Cameron has this afternoon. I've got to get a gift, wrap it."

"Okay." He glanced at his watch. "I'm going to run an errand, and there's a golf tournament on in a couple of hours that I want to watch."

"I'll make a juice for you," she promised. "It'll be in the fridge when you get back."

"You're the best." He moved past her, heading toward the back door, then stopped right before it and turned back. "Oh, the detective called me just now."

Her fingers curled around the paper, crushing it. "Yeah?"

"He asked about Brody Pitt."

Andrea closed her eyes, half grateful that the call hadn't been about her, half alarmed that they were focusing on this point of connection. "So they made that connection. What'd you say?"

He shrugged. "I told them the gist of the case. I'm sure they have the court transcripts."

"Are you worried about it?"

"No." He shook his head and opened the back door. "I told you, there's nothing there for us to worry about."

There's nothing there for us to worry about. He had said that. He'd also said something very similar to that on the night of Roxanne's attack. Andrea hadn't believed him, had been certain that they had forgotten some detail, overlooked some piece of evidence—but he had been right. A surgeon's attention to detail superseded that of a normal human. Even Tony, in his dogged pursuit of his niece's killer, hadn't turned up a thing.

So she should trust Eric now. If he said there was nothing there for them to find, then there was nothing there.

CHAPTER 51

SARA BATCHER

16 Branwyn Hill
Hole 18, Silverwood Preserve

On Saturday mornings, David had watched cartoons. Sara lay in bed and stared at the TV, flipping through the channels. She had a moment of pain at the understanding that David would never again be in his pajama pants, a bowl of Cocoa Puffs in hand, sprawled across their sectional. *I'm sorry,* she sent up to him, wherever he was, whatever he was doing. *I'm sorry.*

It had been a cute habit when she met him. He was such a high-powered guy, always going a mile a minute, so to find him at ten thirty on a Saturday morning, lying on his side on the couch, *The Ren & Stimpy Show* on the television . . . it had been endearing. Even more so when he had pulled her down on the couch beside him and wrapped his leg around her body, cradling her against him. It had turned into a weekend tradition—staying in their pajamas until noon, ordering breakfast in, and being lazy until early afternoon, when they would finally get dressed and head out the door.

It had stopped being cute when he was forty and still continuing the tradition. By then, his toned six-pack abs had turned into pale fat that hung over the top of his pajama pants. He'd snored loudly through most of the cartoons, jerking awake at odd moments to ask what had happened, then starting the episodes over. Her list of to-do items hadn't stopped when Saturday morning started, and the long stretch of unproductivity only brought more stress, not enjoyment. An afternoon round of pills would be the only thing to get David up, and then he would be wired and overly happy for the rest of the day, which only inflamed Sara's irritation.

It must be nice, she'd often thought, to work a few hours each day and take off every weekend. To have a job that involved wining and dining doctors and little else. No one woke up each morning dependent on David's performance. No one was power-calling his phone or asking for raises or threatening to quit and hold the company's progress hostage.

There was a rap of knuckles on her bedroom door, then it swung open. Maggie entered, a tray in hand with a glass of orange juice and a bottle of Advil. "Good morning," she sang out. If she had a hangover herself, she was hiding it well.

Sara grunted, shaking out two pills and taking the glass of juice. "Thank you," she croaked, wincing as her phone shrilled from the bedside table. "Shit." She twisted and grabbed it, making a face at the name on the display. "Hello?"

"Good morning, Mrs. Batcher." Detective Palentick sounded chipper as hell. "I just wanted to give you a few updates on the case."

"Great." She watched as Maggie straightened the items on her dresser. "Anything new?"

"Well, to start with, I wanted to see what you know about Brody Pitt."

CHAPTER 52

KATIE MORROW

"I was one of the contractors on the Morrows' basement-remodel job. We had to redo the theater lighting three times, thanks to Mark's wife. Katie drove us nuts with change orders. But she was sweet about it, and paid us on time. And she invited me and my wife over for dinner. We went, mainly because I was dying to hear some stories from Mark. Did you know he reps Tyford Henry?"

28 Blackberry Summit Road
Hole 1, Stone Hollow

Willow hadn't left her room all day. Katie paused outside her door and listened closely, trying to hear what she was doing in there. She couldn't still be asleep, could she?

Maybe so. Katie's sister had been an alcoholic in college, and she used to sleep till noon each day. It was . . . one thirty, so maybe so. She considered knocking on the door, but it was ridiculous to check up on Willow. She was a grown woman. If she wanted to spend the entire day holed up in the guest room, then she could. If anything, that made Katie's life easier.

She returned to the main living room and sat on the couch, turning the television to a home-renovation show. It was a competition episode, where one team tried to outdo a different team, and Katie watched it for fifteen minutes before realizing that she had no idea what was going on in the show and didn't care.

No one slept until two o'clock, not unless they were recovering from a major surgery. Willow had come home last night before midnight. That was early, by party-girl standards. And she had made it home, so she couldn't have been too inebriated. Katie had gone over every inch of the Maserati and hadn't found a scratch. Which was great, except that Katie had half hoped for a dent, something on Mark's precious baby, something that would give her ammunition to support the eviction of Mark's ex-wife, pronto.

She turned off the television and stood up, doing a slow spin in the room and looking for something to clean. The room was, as always, in perfect order. She could steam clean the baseboards or get the ladder out and dust the crown molding rails near the ceiling, but she had done that in the last month.

She decided to check the expiration dates on the pantry items, and headed in that direction, stopping short when she saw movement out of the corner of her eye. Stepping backward, she spotted Willow, standing stick straight in the middle of the hall, staring at the basement door.

"Oh. Hello. I didn't know that you were up." And better yet, she was already dressed, in a baggy T-shirt and cut-off shorts. Maybe she was going somewhere. Maybe she was all packed up and leaving! Katie's optimism cheered at the thought.

"It's two in the afternoon," Willow said dryly, as if it were obvious that she was up, and what kind of a person was Katie to sleep that late?

"Well, yes. I know. I just wasn't sure how late you were out last night. Can I get you anything to eat, or do you need help with something . . . ?" She glanced from Willow to the basement door. "Did you want to go watch something on TV? I can show you the theater setup."

"Theater?" Willow tilted her head. "Is it in the basement?"

"Oh, yeah. We put it in a year or so ago. Come on, I'll show it to you." She opened the door and flipped the light switch. "It's a bit much, but—" Jogging down the steps, she paused and looked over her shoulder.

Willow hadn't moved, and if Katie didn't know better, she'd say that the look on her face was one of fear.

"You coming?" she asked. "We fixed the broken step, if that's what you're worried about."

Willow took one slow step forward, then another, until she was on the landing. She bent forward and looked down the stairs, then gave a tentative smile. "I'm sorry. I'm . . . claustrophobic. The basement always freaked me out."

"Well, yeah, it was like a tomb before." Katie kept moving down the stairwell. "But you'll love it now. Come on and see. It's my favorite part of the house."

Mainly because this was the one area that Willow hadn't had a hand in. While her mark had been on the other rooms in the house, this level had been an empty shell. And Katie had to say, she'd done a damn good job with it.

She stepped into the basement lounge. "This is Mark's area, which, I admit, is a bit much." Spreading her arms, she gestured to the luxurious space, which Mark used as a man cave. It had a pool table, a full bar, a poker table, and a gaming setup with a theater-size screen and giant U-shaped couch. Mark had told the designer to give it a cigar bar feel, and they had delivered, with dark wood walls, soft leather furnishings, and gold accents.

Willow's gaze darted around the room. "What happened to the rest of the space?"

Not the reaction Katie was hoping for, but she let it slide. "Well, I have holiday storage there, and the bigger house pantry next to that." She pointed to the doors as she went. "And on this side, the theater and an apartment, which isn't being used right now but was designed for a nanny or maybe Mark's mother."

"That's a mistake," Willow murmured and reached for the doorknob of the house pantry. Twisting it slowly, she eased open the door, then swung it fully open. "Holy shit," she breathed.

It *was* quite impressive. Katie's pride swelled at the room, which had eight rows of shelving organized with clear bins, all color coded and labeled. There was everything from extra light bulbs to sunscreen to six months of food backup, all in the climate-controlled room that contained its own inventory system and database.

"Did you see what was here before?" Willow asked, her hand still on the knob, her body blocking Katie's entrance to the room.

"It was just a big open basement when I moved in. I had plans drawn up and had the contractors construct the rooms."

"So he got rid of everything."

Katie shrugged. "The demo guys cleared some stuff out. What did you guys use it for when you lived here? More storage, like the junk room off the garage?"

"It was more of Mark's area," Willow said. "He spent a lot of time down here."

"Yeah, I know there was some stuff left from the original owner. He had big dogs, right? Monica next door told me they threw out a large cage."

Willow stepped back and closed the pantry door. "I'm going to go upstairs and lie down."

"Did you want to see the theater? It's got really comfortable couches, if you want to take a nap."

"No." Willow headed for the stairs, then stopped, backpedaling a few paces until she was beside the bar. Reaching over the counter, she grabbed a bottle of liquor. Hugging it against her chest, she headed up the stairs.

Definitely an alcoholic. And rude, not even looking into the theater room. Katie reached out and tapped the light's control panel, and the floor went dark.

CHAPTER 53

WILLOW MORROW

"I saw Willow that night, the night that David disappeared. She was at the bar at the Onyx, dressed to the nines and taking shots as if they were candy."

28 Blackberry Summit Road
Hole 1, Stone Hollow

Willow stumbled away from Katie, bumping into the wall in her rush to the guest room, clutching the bottle of vodka to her chest. Just before she reached the door, she cast one last look over her shoulder.

Katie stood in the doorway to the basement, gaping after her. Mark's new wife wouldn't understand why Willow was traumatized by the tour of what used to be a torture chamber. And she never would, but that didn't mean Willow couldn't warn her, in a dozen little ways, of what her country-club-loving husband was really into.

One day, Katie might put all the pieces together. One day, Mark might tell her. Or one day, she might skip a yoga class and decide to surprise Mark while he was on a "business trip," or she'd look up his internet search history, and then all the pieces of her perfect world would crack and crumble and die.

As soon as Willow stepped into the guest room, she shut and locked the door. Her world pieces had cracked early on, before they were even married. She had no excuse for why she had stayed or why she had let it go on for so long, or why it had gotten so dark.

It was her fault. That was what Mark had said, over and over again, and he was right.

It was her fault. She could have behaved. She could have kept her mouth shut or her hands to herself or stopped drinking once she hit her buzz. She certainly could have walked away from the bar before someone ended up dead.

CHAPTER 54

ANDREA KENDAL

"The whole timeline with Andrea and Eric is super sketchy. They met at a charity event, dated for a couple of months, and then were suddenly married and living together. Ask me, they were having an affair way back when he was married to Roxanne."

1442 Kingsmere Drive
Hole 6, Stone Hollow

Andrea stood in the guest room closet, a sweater stuffed against the bottom of the door, and returned Detective Palentick's call.

He didn't answer, so she left a voicemail, her tone light and breezy, like a housewife without a care in the world. Ending the call, she turned her phone off. The last thing she needed was for the detective to call her back when she was with Eric. He would be mad enough when he found out that Tony had called her directly. It would only add more stress for him to find out that they'd been digging into Andrea's past.

Her backstory was supposed to be ironclad. That was what they had paid for, from a private investigator who seemed to know his shit. They had specifically mentioned that law enforcement might dig into it, and he had assured them, over and over again, that it would be fine. Andrea Fountain had a medical history, a high school transcript, even a Social Security number. The only thing they wouldn't find for her was a marriage license, and that was explainable. Eric hadn't wanted to officially marry Andrea, not with Roxanne's crime still unsolved. Technically, there was still the possibility that she might show back up. How would it look for Eric to divorce his ex, or file a petition to have her legally considered dead? It wasn't necessary, not when a wedding was for everyone else.

Eric and Andrea knew the truth—that they were bonded in soul and heart in ways that defied a conventional marriage.

It didn't matter if Andrea wasn't his wife on paper.

It didn't matter if the world considered her to be his girlfriend and not his wife.

Where it mattered—between the two of them—they were married.

The rest of the world be damned.

CHAPTER 55

SARA BATCHER

"Hair can retain traces of certain substances—drugs, heavy metals, even some poisons—for months, sometimes years, depending on exposure. But it's a delicate process. We have to send it to a specialized lab, and turnaround time can be anywhere from four to eight weeks, assuming the sample's viable and they don't have a backlog."

16 Branwyn Hill
Hole 18, Silverwood Preserve

Sara had forgotten all about Brody Pitt. She answered the detective's questions to the best of her limited recollection and wrote down the name on a pad that she found in the dresser.

Brody Pitt.

She underlined the name three times and doodled an asterisk as the dot in the *i* of his last name. Brody Pitt had been, best she could remember, a negligent-death case that David's company had been involved in. Something about a heart valve that had failed. He'd had to testify in court; that was the only reason she'd even been aware of it. It had been around the time Sara's company was going through acquisition pitches, so she'd been focused on that and not the latest screwup in David's life.

Still, maybe there was a potential suspect there. Brody had been nine years old. Emotions always ran deep with a child's passing. Maybe the parents had gone after the medical device that had failed their son and chosen a vigilante approach with the salesperson responsible for the use of that device.

"And we've sent off the hair for testing, so we'll have those toxicology reports in two weeks. That will help us rule out poison," the detective continued.

Her pen stalled on the pad. "Oh?" she managed. "That's good." Beside her, Maggie twisted toward her in concern, her eyes widening.

David's skeleton had been a dry mess of bones and clothes. Sara tried to remember his skull, turned to one side. Had there been hair on it?

Fucking man and his vanity. Half bald and he'd been so desperate to keep the few hairs he had left. How many times had she told him to shave it all off? She should have just done it herself during one of his drug-induced sleep sessions. He wouldn't have remembered it, and she could have blamed it on him.

"I'll keep you posted," he promised, and the thought filled her with dread.

"Okay, thank you." Sara ended the call and caught Maggie up on the conversation. "Shit."

"'Shit' is right." Maggie rubbed her temples. "We're fucked."

"Maybe not. We don't know what the toxicology reports will show. His hair is, what—five years old? I mean, how intact could it be? He was underground or underwater or whatever. I mean, let's not freak out about this yet."

"I thought we were clear of this." Maggie flopped back on the bed. "I mean, Sara, he was alive when he left here that morning."

"I know. We didn't kill him."

"Are you saying that to convince me or you? Because if you say it like that to the cops, it doesn't sound convincing." Maggie winced.

"Oh my God, this is not good for my hangover. We drank too much last night."

"Agreed." Sara pushed to her feet. "Okay, even if they can prove that we were medicating him—"

"Poisoning him," Maggie corrected. "Whether we meant to or not, that's what it's going to look like."

"Okay, but they still won't be able to prove that's the cause of death, right?" Sara paced, her bare feet creating a path through the thick carpet.

"I'm more worried they won't be able to prove it's not the cause of death," Maggie said quietly, and she was right. No blunt force trauma—that was what the detective had said. No broken neck or other damage. It wasn't like they could check his heart or neck muscles or see if he'd been stabbed in places that missed major bones.

"I need to call Ian," Sara said. "He'll know what to do."

Maggie rolled onto her belly and stood. "I'll go downstairs and fix us something to eat. And take a migraine pill."

"Save one for me." Sara scrolled through the address book, then clicked on Ian's name. Bringing the phone to her ear, she listened to it ring.

Ian would know how to handle this. He knew how to handle everything.

CHAPTER 56

KATIE MORROW

"The problem with rich people is their attorneys. It'll take a case months longer than it should, just because a witness doesn't know how to say good morning without running the wording past one."

28 Blackberry Summit Road
Hole 1, Stone Hollow

Katie was in the linen closet, reorganizing the pillowcases, when the doorbell chimed. Climbing down off the stepladder, she checked the notification on her smartwatch. The camera feed showed a couple on the front porch, and she squinted at them as she headed toward the front door. The bell rang a second time, and she let out an annoyed huff as she hurried through the living room and up the short set of stairs into the foyer. If this was the neighborhood HOA about their new landscaping plan, she swore to God—

She pulled open the front door. "Oh." She paused. "Hello."

"Hello, Mrs. Morrow. Sorry to bother you." The male detective was in a cornflower-blue shirt and a pair of khakis, his badge hanging on a chain around his neck. He was with a woman in a navy pantsuit with the same neck chain.

"No, it's fine. Is everything okay? Do you need to get back in the pond?"

"No, this is about something else. May we come in?"

"Uh—yeah. Sure. Of course." She stepped back, glancing around the entryway to make sure that everything was in place. Willow had left her keys on the side table, and Katie swiped them off the surface, then used the sleeve of her shirt to wipe the spot. She tucked the keys in her back pocket and pointed to the living room. "We can sit in the living room, if you like. May I get you anything to drink? A soda? I have tea, or sparkling water?"

"No, we're fine." The woman took the lead, stepping down into the sunken living room and choosing the mohair armchair that Willow had criticized. The man took the opposite one, and Katie perched between them on the edge of an ottoman.

She felt underdressed for the occasion, but it wasn't like she had known the police would be coming by. She pulled on the sleeves of her pale-pink cashmere lounge set and adjusted the boat neckline. "So, what's up?"

What's up? What was she, thirteen? Still, they didn't seem to notice.

"We've identified the body as David Batcher's," the woman started.

"Okay." Katie nodded. "Did you know that Willow's here? My husband's ex-wife? I just wanted you to know, because I think that maybe someone had thought that the body was hers, but obviously, if you've identified it, it's not, but I just thought you should know that she's fine, just in case."

"We've known that it was a male for a while, so no, Willow wasn't considered a possibility. But yes, we are aware that she's here. She called us earlier today."

"Oh," Katie said, surprised. "Okay, cool. I know she came back so you could see she's okay. She's here, if you need to talk to her."

"We will, in a moment, but we'd like to speak to you first."

Katie smiled, confused. "Okay. Sure. What—" She stopped herself before she repeated the juvenile phrase. "What can I help with?"

"We have been working on a tighter timeline for David Batcher's last whereabouts. That last night he was seen, he was at the Onyx, which is a bar downtown. It's in the same building where he owned a condo."

"Yeah, I know the bar." Katie pinned her palms together, in between her knees.

"Ever been there?" the woman asked.

"Ah, no. But I've heard people talk about it."

"Ever heard your husband talk about it?" he asked.

Katie's nerves pinged in alarm. "Um, I don't know. I think we've talked about going there for a drink before." She let out a nervous laugh. "To be honest, I don't know if he's ever been there or if we've ever talked about it. I might have seen it online or heard about it at the club. But I'm sure Mark's aware of it."

"The last time David was at the Onyx, he charged four drinks to his condo account." The woman leaned forward and rested her weight on her thighs. "That night, just an hour after he put those drinks on his account, Mark's credit card was charged for more drinks."

They both looked at her.

"Okay," Katie said, shifting to a new position on the ottoman. "I'm sorry. I'm missing something. Is that a big deal?" The Onyx was a popular spot. Why did it matter if Mark went there the same night as David? He'd known David. In these circles, all the rich knew each other. Hell, he'd probably bought David a drink.

"It could be a very big deal," she said.

"What's going on?" Willow stood by the arched opening that led to the kitchen. For a woman who had likely spent the last three hours getting trashed in her room, she looked good.

"Willow Morrow?" Detective Palentick stood up, and the female followed suit. "We'd like to talk to you about David Batcher."

"What about him?" Willow didn't move, and her tone was a little harsher than Katie would have used.

“Maybe you’d prefer if we asked you these questions at the station.” The female detective smiled, and Katie hadn’t been the only one to sense the hostility in Willow’s words.

“Maybe you’d prefer if I called my attorney,” Willow snapped.

“We can play it any way you want,” she responded, and Katie stepped in to intercept.

“Look, why don’t I call Mark and we can just—”

“Shut up, Katie.” Willow stepped into the room. “I’ll say this once, and I’m not saying anything else without an attorney present. David and Sara ran in the same circles as us, so we were acquainted but not friends. The last time I saw David was at a bar downtown. I don’t remember when it was or how close it was to his disappearance. We ran into him, we chatted some, and then we moved on to our next conversation with someone else. I remember it because I thought it was odd that Sara wasn’t there and I didn’t like how David was acting.”

“In what way?” Detective Palentick asked.

Willow lifted her chin. Katie still wasn’t over the fact that she had told her to shut up. “Like he was single. Hitting on women. Drinking too much. It wasn’t appropriate, considering he was married.”

“Did you say anything to Sara about it?” The female detective crossed her arms over her chest.

“No. I’m not the judge and jury over her marriage. For all I knew, they had an open relationship. To tell the truth, I didn’t think too hard about it.”

The two detectives looked at each other, and Katie could feel their mental gears churning.

“Okay,” Detective Palentick said. “Katie, has Mark ever mentioned the name David—”

“She’s not answering any questions without an attorney present,” Willow cut in. “Come on, guys. You’re not playing these games with us.” She nodded toward the door. “Come back with charges or don’t bother.”

“Well, ummm . . .” Katie faltered, not sure what to say, but it didn’t seem right to refuse to help.

The two detectives turned to her, waiting, and she swallowed, suddenly afraid to say anything. "Thank you for coming by?" she said weakly, hurrying ahead of them to open the front door. She held it open as they approached.

"Mrs. Morrow, just to confirm . . ." The man stopped in place and twisted back to face Willow. "The last time you saw David was at the Onyx? Is that correct?"

Willow was already heading back to her room, and she wiggled her fingers in the air in a parting way. "Lock that door behind them, Katie," she called out.

I'm sorry, Katie mouthed, and carefully, making sure not to slam it into the frame, shut the door in the man's face.

She should add a backbone, she decided, to this week's shopping list. In the meantime, Willow was probably right. They shouldn't talk to the cops or answer any of their questions. Even if they were innocent.

CHAPTER 57

WILLOW MORROW

"According to the statistics, the most dangerous place for a woman is her home."

28 Blackberry Summit Road
Hole 1, Stone Hollow

David had been wearing a soft gray V-neck T-shirt. Willow had kissed his neck, then gently bitten the skin.

Charcoal-gray slacks with a black belt. She had pulled the belt off, then looped it through its clasp and pulled it over his head and tightened it around his neck like a noose.

Willow watched as Katie practically kissed the detectives' asses as they lumbered out. Such a Goody Two-shoes. How the fuck had Mark lasted this long with her?

The blonde literally waved through the glass windows at the two cops, as if she were holding an open house. When she finally flipped the lock closed, Willow was already back in the kitchen.

"Willow!" Katie's quiet little steps pattered after her, and Willow stopped to see what the woman wanted.

"Yes?" She raised her eyebrows.

"I made some soup and potato salad, if you want some."

Both sounded good to Willow's empty stomach, but she made a face in an attempt to preserve her pride. "No thanks."

"Is there anything I should know about . . ." Her voice dropped off, and if she thought Willow was going to hold her hand with this, she was sorely mistaken.

"About what?" Willow asked.

"About the David thing, or about . . . I don't know. Whatever. It just seems so odd, the way you left so suddenly."

"Have you ever tried to leave Mark?" Willow asked.

She blanched. "No! Never."

"He doesn't take it well." Willow paused, then amended the statement. "He didn't take it well. I left suddenly because I had to leave when he wasn't here. And I didn't leave—I ran away. It was the only way to get the divorce. I left and I hid where he couldn't find me. And I stayed hidden until he signed the papers, and then I hid longer, until I thought he had gotten over me."

Her gaze drifted over to where Mark had been standing when he first saw her, and she stared at that place, hoping that Katie would get the reference. "Maybe I should have stayed away longer. Maybe he isn't quite over it."

Katie flinched. Bull's-eye.

In this marriage, there were so many easy targets to hit.

CHAPTER 58

ANDREA KENDAL

1442 Kingsmere Drive
Hole 6, Stone Hollow

BODY FOUND IN PRESTIGIOUS NEIGHBORHOOD

The body of David Batcher has been found on the Stone Hollow golf course in Crestmore Estates. This gated community, which contains three golf courses and over four hundred homes, is known for its multimillion-dollar estate lots. You're more likely to cross paths with a Fortune 500 CEO than a dead body. However, that's exactly what was unearthed in a lake adjacent to hole six of the Pete Dye–designed course.

David Batcher, a medical sales executive, was reported missing by his wife, Sara, more than five years ago. The case went cold, with little evidence pointing to foul play. Now the file is being dusted off and treated as a homicide. Anyone with information on David Batcher's whereabouts or situation on or around

> May 5, 2021, should call Detective Palentick, San Francisco Homicide Division.

The newspaper was in the center of the kitchen counter, right beside the thermos with Andrea's coffee. Eric had left a rose from their garden beside the paper. She picked up the delicate pink bloom and smelled it. The scent was faint. She buried her nose deeper into its soft folds and inhaled again, then lowered it toward Ryder. He was strapped into the carrier on her front and grabbed at the flower and shook it. "Careful," she cautioned, taking it back and checking it for thorns.

Eric was such a good husband. Always had been. Very few men were as thoughtful as he was, especially when they had as many things to think about as he did. She withdrew a small vase from the cabinet and filled it with water, then threaded the rose through the thin stem, placing it beside the prep-sink faucet.

Settling onto one of the stools that hugged the counter, she pulled the paper toward her and popped open the top of the thermos. She opened up the paper and there, below the fold, was a story on David.

At the bottom of the article was a phone number. Detective Palentick's, who had yet to call her back. Rather than be comforted by this omission, Andrea was concerned by it. Maybe they were digging deeper. Building more of a case. Getting curious about what else she might be hiding. She rubbed her hand over Ryder's leg, squeezing his ankle and humming to him.

The lack of new information in the article was disappointing. Tony probably knew all the nitty-gritty details, but he was the last person they'd call to get a scoop. She took a long sip of coffee, which was especially strong this morning. Good, she needed all the caffeine she could get. Last night, she'd tossed and turned the entire time. Around three, Ryder had started to cry, and she'd moved into his room and rocked him until around five, when they had both fallen asleep in the giant double recliner. She had woken up with a line of drool down her cheek and a crick in her neck.

May 5, 2021. So that was the date he'd been killed. She stood up and went around the bar, carrying her thermos with her as she walked down the hall and to her office. *Office* was a strong word for the space, which was mostly used to hold mail and packages. Once a month, she paid bills at the desk, and used the desktop computer on rare occasions when she had to return emails or complete school registrations.

Roxanne had been attacked on February 2, three months before David was killed. She logged onto the computer and pulled up Eric's work calendar, which was synced with her cloud account. Scrolling back five years, she got to May and slowed down. His calendar was a grid of meetings, an alibi, but exhausting if you wanted to chase down your husband for a romantic evening.

The date in question stood out, as did the entire week around it, every single cell empty. She stared at the block of uninterrupted time and then leaned back in her chair, trying to think back.

May 2021. An entire week where Eric had been gone.

There was only one possibility, and she didn't have to pull up her personal calendar to double-check the time frame.

It was when he'd come to see her in Los Angeles. The week they had buried Roxanne.

CHAPTER 59

SARA BATCHER

"When a patient mixes a depressant with another depressant, they're not doubling down—they're risking death and playing Russian roulette with a full chamber."

16 Branwyn Hill
Hole 18, Silverwood Preserve

Sara dressed in the same black pantsuit she had worn for the closing of InkRose. She straightened her hair with a hot iron and put on makeup, taking extra care with the eyeliner, and grabbed the keys to the Aston Martin. The end result was that of a confident woman, one who could take on anything that was thrown at her.

Inside, she felt as if she was on the verge of breaking. What she wanted to do, more than anything, was retreat upstairs to her bedroom, order in Thai food, and gorge herself until she passed out dead asleep. But that plan, according to Ian, was the wrong one. His stance was that the toxicology report wasn't going to go away. They needed to get ahead of it, and there was only one way to do that.

Tell the truth, or at least some of it. Share his abuse of lorazepam and Vicodin and admit her part in the former.

She parked in a spot on the far end of the lot, away from the other cars. The Aston had been a stupid decision, and she considered returning home and borrowing Maggie's Nissan hybrid. Then again, it wasn't like the detectives would see what she drove here, and it wasn't as if the detectives didn't know she was rich. If the worst outcome of her transportation choice was some scratches or a theft attempt, so be it. At this point, the distraction would be welcome.

She engaged the emergency brake and unbuckled her belt. She watched through the front windshield as a squirrel ran along the top of the security fence. She checked her watch, then her phone. Ian had texted her eight minutes ago.

TEN MINUTES OUT.

She dropped her head back against the headrest. Ian had to get her out of this. What was the point in paying an attorney's exorbitant rates if he couldn't make things like this go away?

Things like this. She hated herself for saying that. David hadn't been a thing, his death wasn't a thing . . . but if she thought of him as a person, she'd fall apart before she even made it through the station doors. Already, she could feel her composure cracking, and Ian had told her to be strong. *Just tell them what happened. The good, the bad, and the ugly.* There was no way she could tell all the *ugly*, but she'd do her best with the *bad*. The ugly was between her, David, and God.

She closed her eyes and remembered that last morning. She hadn't known that it would be the last time she'd ever see him. She had just known that it was Saturday and she had things to do, and he was just sitting at the dining room table in his underwear, staring blankly at the wall before him. "I'm leaving you," he'd announced, as if she cared. As if that were a bad thing.

She'd ignored the statement and jabbed the scoop into the protein powder, taking an extra-generous amount and pouring it into the blender, on top of the ice.

She would have loved for David to leave her, but as much as he hated her in the mornings, he clung to her just as fiercely in the evenings. His love and hatred were on a regular cycle that was 100 percent based on his level of medication or withdrawal.

The problem was that she didn't have an ebb and flow. She only had the ebb, an ebb of affection that was retreating further and further from him with each new day.

She'd watched as he reached for his pills and dumped the bottle on the table, then arranged the pills in a long line in front of him, treating each white tablet as if it was precious.

"Do you know why I'm leaving you, Sara?" he'd asked in a singsong voice, and she could anticipate the next three hours. Cruelness. Mocking. Then anger. Maybe a few rage-outs. He'd try to wait as long as he could before he took the pills, savoring the anticipation of the high and making sure that it would last well into the night. Then euphoria. He'd apologize. Love-bomb her. Talk a mile a minute about the stupidest things. Call everyone in his phone. Eat. Drink. Laugh. Then the downward spiral, until around dinnertime, when he would re-dose and repeat.

She couldn't deal with it. Not on that day, when she had her own things to do and didn't feel like dealing with a roller coaster of hell. She'd eyed the clock and stuck her hand in her bathrobe pocket, pulling out two lorazepams and dropping them into the blender. She'd unscrewed the top to the macadamia milk and poured it in, then capped the lid and pressed the button.

The lorazepams had been guaranteed to put him in a coma until early afternoon and get him through his bitchy spell. She hadn't cared if that kept him up all night, because she could always just hit him with another dose then if she needed to.

Would the police understand her drugging her husband? Probably not, not unless they had their own addict for a spouse, or a child, or a parent. But if Ian had said that she should tell it, she would. She could keep the ugly part of it to herself. The ugly was that every time she dosed him, she prayed that he'd alter his schedule and take a pill early and that the combination would trigger a reaction and he'd die.

The ugly was that for the last two years of their marriage, she'd been rooting for that outcome.

The ugly was, when he disappeared, she'd taken a moment to celebrate that it might have actually happened.

The ugly was that maybe it had.

CHAPTER 60

KATIE MORROW

"I always told Katie, if she ever wanted to leave him, she could come home. A woman should always have a place to go."

28 Blackberry Summit Road
Hole 1, Stone Hollow

Katie retrieved a small suitcase and wheeled it into the closet, setting it on the couch. From his spot at the sink, a string of floss in hand, Mark watched.

She flipped through the hangers, pulling off a red blouse and a belted jumpsuit. She pulled out two folded cashmere sweaters and a few pairs of jeans. Overkill for one night, but maybe she'd stay mad and extend the trip a few more nights. After dropping the items into the suitcase, she crouched down, looking at her flats.

"Katie, you don't have to do this." The objection had less starch than one of his suits. It was as if he wanted her to leave, and that was the most infuriating part of all this. Honestly, when she'd first announced that she was going to spend the night at her parents', it was really just a ploy for attention. Only her husband hadn't reacted in any of the ways she had hoped for and expected. According to Willow, Mark had freaked out and practically imprisoned her in an attempt to keep her in the marriage. *I left in a hurry because I had to. I left and I hid where he couldn't find me.*

"I don't like feeling like the third wheel in my own marriage, Mark." Katie grabbed a red suede pair of ballet flats and a shoe bag, zipping it around them and adding it to the suitcase.

He worked the piece of floss through his teeth, and it felt like an easy way to avoid responding. He was going to do it. He was going to let her leave without really trying to stop her.

She brushed past him and into her side of the bathroom. If he knew that she was pregnant, would that make a difference? The problem was, it didn't matter. She wasn't about to use that as a card to push her husband into fighting for her—for them.

"Do you know what she told me?" She yanked open the second drawer and withdrew one of the travel bags. "She thinks you aren't over her."

He managed to remove his hands from his mouth. "Katie. Come on. You don't think that."

"I'm not sure." She threw her hands up in the air. "I mean, you guys are having silent conversations with your eyes every time I'm in the room."

He snorted out a laugh. "That's ridiculous. You're paranoid. Look—Willow and I are old news. You know that. I don't even know why we're discussing that. If you want some time away, I get that. A lot is happening right now, with the cops and the questioning . . . I don't blame you for not wanting to deal with it."

She spun around to look at him. "Oh my God. You're trying to talk me into leaving!"

"So now you're going to be mad at me for sympathizing with you?" He shook his head in disbelief. "You're ridiculous, Katie. I swear, I can't win with you."

Here it was, the switch to blaming her. Next he would start to get pissed, and she already knew how this would end. Her apologizing as he stewed and punished her with stony silence. Well, screw that. Not tonight.

He may want her to leave right now, but he would regret this later. She shoved items into the bag and hurried past him, stuffing it into the suitcase and zipping it closed.

She hoisted the suitcase off the sofa and onto the floor, raising the arm and wheeling it toward the door. She exited the suite, and he followed without saying anything, and if there was ever a time to hold his tongue, this wasn't it.

She paused at the long bank of stairs, and he materialized beside her and picked up the suitcase.

"Here, I'll get that for you."

She swallowed the lump in her throat and followed him down the stairs. At the bottom, Willow waited, her shrewd gaze immediately understanding the situation. Katie met her eyes, and she didn't have Mark's mind-reading ability. She didn't understand what the look on Willow's face meant, only that it didn't look happy but it didn't look upset either.

Mark carried the suitcase all the way to her Porsche, where he put it in the back seat. When she got behind the wheel, he blocked her from closing the door with his body.

"Mark, stop," she said, but there was no fight in the words.

"Meet me for breakfast. At Soleman's. We'll talk. I'll tell you everything."

Everything. She hadn't known that there was an *everything*. "Tell me everything now," she demanded.

He pinned his lips together and glanced back to the house. "I can't. I have to take care of a few things. But tomorrow morning, okay? Nine o'clock. Or ten. Whatever. You tell me. I'll be there."

She clenched her jaw and reached up, hitting the garage door opener. "Move out of the way."

He stepped back and allowed her to close the door. She put the SUV into reverse and backed out, refusing to look at him as she swung the back end around and then accelerated down the drive.

Was it a mistake, leaving them alone together for a night?

Maybe.

Probably.

But she wasn't sure you could lose something you didn't have to begin with. And she was beginning to realize she had been borrowing another woman's husband this entire time.

CHAPTER 61

WILLOW MORROW

"I never believed that Willow was some abused wife, on the run. It just didn't fit."

28 Blackberry Summit Road
Hole 1, Stone Hollow

Mark came back from the garage and closed the door, then looked at Willow. "She's gone for the night. I'm not sure if she'll be back tomorrow or not."

He didn't sound upset or concerned, and maybe that was what a normal marriage was like. An environment where fights happened and it didn't lead to violence or a cage; it just led to one person storming out and another person watching.

"You guys fight often?" Willow crossed her arms in front of her chest.

"No."

"So you aren't like us."

He shook his head with a wry grin. "Babe, I don't think anyone's like us."

Babe. The term used to fill her with joy. Now it was like pressing on a bruise. A painful reminder of what had happened. "Don't call me *babe*."

"Or else what?" His voice turned husky and he stepped closer.

She moved a step back and held up her palm, warning him. "Mark, stop. She just pulled out, for Christ's sake. Have some self-control."

"I've never had self-control with you." He advanced farther, and she retreated, then winced when her elbow jammed into the wall. Out of room to run. She could shut down. Disengage. Do what the shrinks had all advised. Choke out the fire with a lack of oxygen. If she didn't give him rope, he wouldn't hang himself. All she had to do was remain calm and not take the bait.

But the truth of the matter was, she needed this too. And that was the problem with their entire relationship. Their marriage. And what had happened on May 5.

She pushed off the wall and met his eyes. Then she reached out and grabbed hold of his throat.

FIVE YEARS AGO

The First Missing Person: David Batcher

CHAPTER 62

May 5, 2021

Willow had kept her husband in the cage for over eight hours. When she finally released Mark, the heel marks across his chest had bruised and there were blisters in the corners of his mouth from the gag. He crawled to the shower in the corner of the basement and turned on the lower faucet, gulping water from the spout before slowly pushing himself to standing. She stepped into the space and nodded to the handles. "Turn it on for me and get it hot."

She undressed, and when she stepped in beside him, her touch was light and kind. He sank into it. She squeezed a pineapple-scented body wash into the loofah and passed it to him, then turned, letting him wash her back, the curve of her spine, the generous roundness of her butt. She rotated to face him and leaned back against the tile, exposing her body to him, and he took his time, half washing, half worshipping the front of her body.

"Good boy," she murmured, lowering her hand to touch him. "You are such a good boy."

And he was. While Mark was a ruthless alpha male in his line of work, in their household, he surrendered everything to her. And the more she took advantage of that, the more he needed. They had started with blindfolds, then handcuffs during sex. Then the play got rougher. In year three of their marriage, she started making him sit on the floor next to her while she ate. When he irritated her, she made him sit in the closet, facing the corner. When that wasn't enough, they ordered a cage.

She pretended that it annoyed her, that she was disgusted by it, but the more she scorned him, the more grateful and aroused he became. The level of worship was addictive, and the power . . . the knowledge that she could do anything to him and he would beg for more . . . it was exactly what a bored housewife with narcissistic inclinations needed. As her therapists later said, it was kerosene to her fire. And every time the flame burned low, she poured more kerosene on it.

He leaned in to her touch, his breath growing ragged as she stroked him, slowly at first, then faster.

"I want you to do something for me," she said into his ear. "Tonight, I want you to bring me a pet. Just for the night. Can you do that for me?" Her hand tightened around him and he nodded, gasping as his pleasure mounted.

"I'll go with you and we'll pick him out. And you can watch him please me. Would you like that?" She bit his earlobe and he twitched in her hand. "Tell me," she ordered.

"I want that," he said, his voice straining with need.

She smiled wider, then released him in the moment before he came, and he whimpered in disappointment. Turning off the shower, she stepped out and pointed to the stack of towels. "Not yet. Tonight."

He hurried to get a towel, and from down the basement hall, his phone rang, the device announcing the caller's name. It was his newest client, an MLB rookie who had a $100 million deal on the table. His gaze flicked to the sound, then returned back to her.

"You want to answer that?" she asked, lifting one foot onto the toilet lid so that he could dry the leg off.

"No," he said hoarsely, and the flame in her burned brighter.

They ended up at the Onyx, and there was no sign of subservience in her husband, who held open the door for her. His sharp gaze swept the bar and he took a seat with his back to the wall. She swept her high ponytail over one shoulder and took the chair across from him.

The band was playing a catchy song from the '80s, and she sang along with the chorus, enjoying the vibe of the crowd as he flagged down a waiter and ordered them drinks. She sipped hers and laughed at a story he was recounting from the firm when her gaze caught a man at the bar. Leaning forward, she set her vodka on the table and lowered her voice. "Look who's at the bar, by the blonde in the blue dress."

He turned his head, disguising the peek behind a move to rest his arm on the back of the booth. After giving the man a long look, he turned back to her. "A little close to home."

"What, don't think you could get him to do it?" She picked up her drink and took a sip.

"He's been wanting to fuck my wife since he first met her, so yeah, I could get him to do it." He reached under the table and brushed his fingers over her knee.

"I'm not sure you could," she challenged, enjoying the way his gaze darkened at the words. His fingers closed over her bare knee.

"Is my wife attracted to him?" he asked huskily.

"Your wife wants to punish him for every time he's flirted with me when Sara was on the other side of the room." Willow licked the liquor off her lips, enjoying the game.

He glanced over at the pharmaceutical sales executive. "Looks like he's out without her now."

She sat back and moved her knee away from his hand. "Go talk to him. See where she is and if he wants to come to the house for a nightcap."

He tilted his head to one side. "If his wife finds out, it could be messy."

"Are you questioning me?" she asked, her voice sharpening.

"Maybe," he dared. He was always brave in public.

She grinned at the challenge. “Don’t worry.” She leaned forward and gave him a long kiss on the mouth before pulling off. “He won’t talk. They never do, do they?”

And they didn’t. Mostly because they didn’t remember it.

They agreed to meet out front of the Onyx, and Willow and Mark found David on his phone, his voice loud and brash. Willow took the moment to push Mark against the building’s brick facade. He fell easily, always a pawn in her hands, and looked down at her with a glazed look of appreciation.

With his negotiation in the works, his rookie leaning on him heavily to maximize his payout, Mark’s stress was at an all-time high. This, a day in the cage, a night of kinky punishment, and jealousy . . . it was exactly what he needed. Right now, the last thing he was thinking about was questionable drug tests or trade deadlines. This was about clearing out the cobwebs in his brain, pushing aside the stress and the obligations of work, and having a moment of base pleasure.

The first domination had been a fluke, like wandering into the wrong bar by accident and then liking the vibe and staying. They had been in a fight and she had lost her temper. Willow had tried to leave in a huff, and he had chased her to her car. When she had dressed him down and spat at him to crawl back to his pathetic life without her, his eyes had grown dark with arousal, and it had been a switch that both of them suddenly, instinctually understood. When she had slapped him across his face, he groaned.

That night, she had tied him down to the bed and sexually teased him until he begged for completion.

The orgasm denial had unlocked the door. The pain . . . it came later. Years later, after a slow deterioration of their boundaries.

It wasn’t that Mark liked pain. He didn’t. But he liked the desperation he felt at the thought of losing her. He craved the fear of her being displeased with and uninterested in him. It was chaos that somehow shuttered all the other pieces of his psyche back into place.

“Hey,” he said softly and leaned forward to kiss her.

She stepped back, out of reach, and turned to David. "Get off the phone. We're ready."

The man paused, his gaze going to Mark as if to question her tone. He ended the call, and Willow smiled. He wasn't going to get any sympathy from Mark, and David would listen to her, at least for now. The possibility of sex always made a man more pliable. He'd come with them to the house, where he'd learn how this game was played. He'd bend to her or he wouldn't.

Sometimes they didn't. She looked into his eyes and there was a defiance there, an edge of something that told her that he might not.

The possibility didn't worry her. If anything, she appreciated the challenge. After all, this was a game. And sometimes, rarely, she lost.

But typically, even the most dominant of men would yield to the call of sex.

She looped her arm through David's and pulled him toward their car.

They started in the living room, because everything was easier there. Willow took off her sweater, exposing the clingy camisole top, and David's gaze dropped to the twin peaks of her nipples. She fixed them a round of drinks and carried a handful of pills into the room. Passing David his glass, she held out a pill. "Want to play?"

He took it without asking what it was, and she watched as he downed it with half of the glass. She passed Mark's to him and then straddled David on the couch. "Tell me," she whispered in his ear. "Tell me your darkest fantasy."

And just like that, it began.

CHAPTER 63

May 5, 2021

The pill was a benzo, something they often used to relax a third wheel but also to help cloud their memories of what would happen. Mark took one also, the drug softening any possessive tendencies that could turn the vibe dark.

While darkness often was the tone for Mark and Willow's role-plays, any threesomes were designed as more of a worship session of Willow. Four hands instead of two. Two mouths on her body. An interaction designed to bring her pleasure and torture Mark with jealousy instead of pain.

On these evenings, she was in charge of two men instead of one, and she enjoyed using the power to push the limits of her husband and any guests who were along for the ride.

David, as it turned out, was all about the ride.

The man produced two Viagras from his pocket, guzzled them down with a swig of whiskey, and all but flung himself down the basement stairs at Willow's invitation. He spotted the room's bed, then the Saint Andrew's cross, then the cage. His grin widened and he rubbed his hands together, then looked to Mark. "Who spanks who?" he asked, but it wasn't cruel. It was *interested*, and Willow shrugged, then gestured to the room. "Go ahead. Explore. Let me know if there's anything you want to try."

It was the shock clamps that he chose—an interesting option, and one that Willow had never cared to take out of the box or use. Mark had purchased the pair, and she had deemed them too extreme, preferring to stick to her wheelhouse of verbal domination, denial, and mild forms of abuse. Mark was loud enough as it was. Run an electric current through him and he might have a heart attack from the exhilaration.

David didn't seem to be concerned over the risks, and when Willow made it clear that the device was for him and not her, his enthusiasm grew even greater. Within minutes, he was spread-eagle on the bed, handcuffed by his wrists and ankles, his hairy thighs stretched open, his smooth shaft as erect as a flagpole as she attached the clamps to each of his nipples.

She turned the dial on the control to 5, halfway up in intensity, and turned to Mark. "Go face the corner," she ordered. "You don't get to see this."

Later, she would question why she had made Mark turn away.

Why she hadn't started at a lower intensity.

Why she hadn't read the directions on the kit.

She pressed the button, and David surged off the bed. A spark came from both nipples, and he let out a yelp of pain. Mark turned to see and she barked at him to stay put. Horrified by the scent of burning flesh, she leaned forward, looked at the clamps, and let out an involuntary gag.

David twitched and grunted, his face turning red, and she touched his cheek, soothing him. "Shhh. It's okay. Let me take them off." His eyes bulged in panic and he reached up, trying to yank at the cords, but the handcuffs were too tight.

"Wait, wait." She looked at the shock device, double-checking that it was off. He was twisting against the bed, and she tried to pin him down long enough to unclip each clamp.

"Mark," she said, and he was immediately by her side. "I think something's wrong. Get his handcuffs off. David, are you hurt?"

Mark freed his right hand and David groaned and clutched at his chest, his eyes wide open and darting around the room. He wheezed again and her alarm spiked. "This is bad, Mark. What if he's having a heart attack?"

There were dots of sweat along his forehead, and she wiped them, her heart sinking at the cold, clammy feel of his skin. His gaze stilled, his body losing all strength, and she reached forward, shaking him. "David!" she yelled but he didn't respond. Leaning forward, she put her ear to his mouth, but there was no air movement.

"Mark, feel for a pulse. Do CPR." She fled the room and pushed through the basement door, pounding up the stairs and to her phone. She grabbed her purse off the couch and dug through it, then dumped the bag upside down and shook the contents out onto the coffee table. Lipstick. Brush. Mints. Wallet. Receipts. Hairbands. Charger. Where the f— She shot to her feet and ran through the butler's kitchen and into the garage. Mark's sedan was unlocked, and she jerked open the driver's-side door and leaned in, spotting her cell phone in the magnetic holder on the dash. She grabbed it.

A heart attack. Maybe a stroke. Either way, Mark should be doing CPR. He had been a lifeguard in college, spent seven years on the swim team—CPR should be second nature. She burst into the basement and down the steps and into the makeshift room they were using. Mark was on his knees beside the bed, pumping David's chest. He looked over at Willow, his eyes glazed from the benzo. "He's dead."

She paused, her finger mid-swipe on her phone, bringing up the call app. "What?"

"He's dead." He stopped his efforts and looked at her. "I'm not even sure he had a heart attack. What did you give us?"

"What do you mean? Keep going!" She pointed to the man, who was staring straight up, his eyes open. Mark might have been right. He looked dead. Horror seeped through her, and she circled around to the other side of Mark and fell to her knees. Dropping her phone, she touched his chest tentatively, then felt for his pulse.

He didn't react, didn't blink, didn't breathe, and she let out a low sob. "Mark," she whispered. "Keep going."

He started CPR again, pumping his chest, then breathing into his mouth, then pumping his chest. She found her phone on the floor and picked it back up. "I was going to call 9-1-1," she said and waited for him to respond. That was the right thing to do, wasn't it?

"What did you give us?" Mark repeated, lifting his mouth free.

"Um, benzos. The two-milligram ones. Same thing you've taken a dozen times." Same thing she'd taken a dozen times. They were safe. "There was no way they would have caused this."

"We drugged him and electrocuted him, Willow. You can't call the cops. How are we going to explain this?" He held up David's wrist, and there were cuts from where he'd struggled against the handcuffs.

She looked at the man's face, and his eyes were still open, staring up at the ceiling. They could explain this. Tell the truth. It was an accident. *Manslaughter,* her sister's voice whispered in her head. *An accidental death is manslaughter. Up to eleven years in prison.* "Do it more," she said desperately. "Just try it for another two minutes. Just in case."

It would take an ambulance ten minutes to get there, at least. Her mind ticked through the realities of the situation. They wouldn't be able to restart his heart, even if she had immediately called them. The CPR wasn't working, and Mark was right.

David was dead.

She was suddenly aware that she was completely naked, her teeth chattering from the chill in the room, and she rubbed her hands over her arms, trying to warm up. "Please, Mark."

He was already resuming his efforts and she stood. "I'll be right back."

"Get me a water," he rasped, and his cheeks puffed out as he blew into David's mouth.

Willow walked slowly up the stairs onto the main floor, then up to the second. Her feet felt heavy, like she had done an hour of squats and lunges. Like her legs might give out. The detachment that came with a copious amount of alcohol was there, but the buzz was suddenly gone, and she felt like a balloon that had lost its air.

David was dead. Downstairs, in their basement, naked.

What had they done? Had they done something? It was a heart attack, surely. She had seen one before, in a restaurant she had worked at in Burbank, a customer in the first booth by the door had clutched his chest in the same manner. Gone gray in the same manner. The ambulance had shown up within a few minutes and taken him away, but she had called later, once her shift had ended, and they told her that he had died.

Maybe even if they had called the ambulance right away, as soon as he had started to act strange—maybe he still would have died. All that was so fast. Before she even found her phone. It had been, what? Two minutes? Three? It would have taken an ambulance at least ten to get into Crestmore and way back into their portion of the gated neighborhood.

In their closet, she dressed in a pair of black sweatpants and a long-sleeve T-shirt. She worked her arms into a zip-up hoodie and put her hair up into a ponytail. She went into the bathroom, pulled down the sweatpants, and sat on the toilet.

The bathroom was so hot, and she felt clammy. Maybe this was shock, this detached emotion that was somewhere between hysteria and numbness. She should get in the shower. Spray herself with cold water.

"We drugged him and electrocuted him, Willow. You can't call the cops. How are we going to explain this?"

Mark was right. Even drunk and high, he was thinking clearly when it came to covering their asses. They couldn't call the police. What would they say? Confess to giving David drugs and alcohol and handcuffing him down to the bed and putting shock clamps on his nipples?

The timetable calculations on the ambulance didn't matter. Their actions had triggered the heart attack, and those actions might not even fall under manslaughter. They might fall under murder.

She finished peeing and flushed the toilet, taking her time in cleaning up and washing her hands. She looked into the mirror. Her eyes were hollow. Dead. Her lipstick was smeared. With trembling fingers, she used a cotton pad to wipe at the red stain. David had kissed her, on their way into the house from the car. He'd tasted like liquor.

From downstairs, Mark yelled her name.

She inhaled deeply and dropped the pad onto the counter. The man had a job and a wife and a life, one that had just been extinguished with one stupid night. Willow had fucked up a lot of things in her life, but this was unforgivable.

For the first time in a long time, she had no idea what to do.

CHAPTER 64

May 6, 2021

They left David in the basement. It seemed insane, to leave his body on the mattress, his eyes still open, staring at the ceiling, his mouth slightly open, his body naked. She had covered him with a blanket and hesitated, then covered his face with a towel.

They needed to think and to plan. Mark needed to come off the benzo and back down to earth. She started the shower and they both stepped into the large double space. Silently, they stood at opposite ends and washed. Willow used her strongest exfoliant and scrubbed her skin until it was red, then shampooed her hair before following Mark out of the stall. They dried off and dressed for bed, then got into the large California King. Mark rolled onto his side and faced Willow. "I'm hard."

"Jesus, Mark." She lay on her back, on the verge of an anxiety attack. She was still freezing, her teeth chattering whenever her jaw relaxed. It was possible she was going into shock.

"It's the Viagra. I took two of the one-hundred-milligram."

"Well, fucking deal with it or ignore it," she snapped. "I can't think about your dick's problems right now."

"I'm just saying that it's hard to go to sleep like this."

"Say one more word about it and you can sleep in the guest room."

He sighed, and she rolled away from him. She stared at the double set of doors that led to their balcony and thought about David's wife.

She had met Sara a few times. She was nice. Very smart. She'd asked about her tonight, and David had told them that they had separated. Was it true? Willow hadn't really cared, and maybe this was karma for her act as an accomplice to infidelity.

What the fuck had happened tonight? How had one night of relatively innocent play ended up with a dead man in their basement? And how culpable was she for this crime?

Pretty fucking culpable, it felt. If she hadn't entertained Mark's proclivities, if she hadn't brought up the idea of bringing home someone tonight, if she had thrown away the shock kit when Mark had ordered it, or not given David the benzo, or just been an ordinary good little wife like every other house in this neighborhood . . .

David would still be alive.

This was 100 percent her fault, and if they got caught for this, she'd have to take the fall. Mark had a reputation and a business to protect. She had an exceptionally high record on *Candy Crush* and little else. No one would notice if she went to prison for a few decades. No one, aside from Mark and maybe her sister, would likely care.

But maybe they wouldn't get caught. She ticked through everything that had happened at the bar. It had been crowded, so much so that it was likely no one had noticed them talking to him. And if they had, it wouldn't have stuck out as strange. They had left separately, and his car was still somewhere downtown. He had ridden in the back seat of their car, which meant that he wouldn't show up on the neighborhood's security cams at the entrance and exit gates. His cell phone was here, and that was a problem. She rolled out of bed.

"Where are you going?" Mark asked.

"I'll be right back."

She found David's phone downstairs, in the pocket of his pants. She touched the screen, and it lit up with a photo of a football player Mark had represented a few years back. She used a hammer from the utility room and smashed the screen until it splintered, chunks of it falling away as she hit it harder and harder, until it was as broken up as her life. She dumped the shards into the garbage compactor and ran a cycle.

She returned to their bedroom, and Mark was already asleep, softly snoring in the dark, the blanket slightly tented at his hips.

CHAPTER 65

May 7, 2021

At 2:00 a.m. the following night, they used a sharp knife to pierce David's abdomen and lungs, to prevent any bloat that might bring him to the surface, then dressed him in the clothes he had come in. They used two pairs of handcuffs to attach a twenty-pound kettlebell from their home gym to each of his ankles, then put a hat and glasses on him.

Mark grunted as he hefted each of the kettlebells onto the seat, next to David. His body was stiff, but not the rigor mortis brick she had expected. It had been easy to bend him into a seated position, easy to redress him into his clothes, easy to loop his hands over each of their shoulders, and half carry, half drag him into the back seat of the GEM golf cart and strap the seat belt across his lap and torso.

Once David was secured, Mark started up the silent electric ATV and opened the garage door, and the three of them drove through the backyard gate and down the course until they reached the big lake on hole six. They kept the headlights off, their white paved golf cart path standing out easily in the dark, against the dark-green turf. Normally, when they went for night drives, they played the radio—not too loudly where it would disturb the neighbors—but not tonight. Tonight, they were silent. Willow held her breath for most of the drive, terrified with each corner they took that there would be the headlights of another cart, or the glow of a runner's flashlight or late-night bicyclist's headlamp.

They had rarely ever passed someone on the course, especially not at two thirty in the morning—but still, her chest was tight, her nerves raw.

Mark had once been told the lake at hole six was twelve feet deep in the center, so they parked in the trees on its border and looped David's arms around their shoulders, each carrying a kettlebell, and waded David out until the water was at Willow's neck and their feet were at the edge; then they swam another ten feet out. It was an awkward journey, with more splashing than Willow liked, but it was a struggle to pull David with one hand and hold the kettlebell with the other. As soon as they got above the deep drop-off, Mark counted to three and they let go.

David sank, as they say, like a stone. Like two kettlebells into pitch-dark water. Willow treaded in place for a moment, staring down into the water, certain that he would suddenly bob back up.

He didn't and she rotated, a bit of lake water getting into her mouth, and she thought of all the warnings she'd ever gotten as a kid about amoebas and ponds. More karma. An infection, bacteria growing in her ear that would make her deathly ill, and she would have to go to the emergency room and lie when they asked her if she had swum in any algae-filled ponds, and then she would die and David would be waiting for her in hell, that cocky little smirk on his face. *Shouldn't have hidden my body. Should have just called the cops.*

"Willow!" Mark shout-whispered from the shore. "Come on!"

She swam to him, kicking as quietly as possible, until she reached the point that she could touch the bottom, then waded out and alongside him, her teeth chattering, as her wet clothes were exposed to the night wind.

She was going to hell. This right here was past the point of no return, and she had taken it. She had hidden a body. Never mind how it had happened. She had had the option and had covered up the crime.

"Here." Mark passed her a dry sweatsuit, and she stripped in the cover of the trees and pulled it on, suddenly frantic over the time. She squeezed the water out of her clothes and stuffed the garments into a trash bag. Getting back into the cart next to Mark, she held the bag on her lap and hurriedly shoved her feet back into her flip-flops.

Now to get home undetected.

"That was easy," Mark said as they rounded the curve on number five.

"We haven't made it back yet," she said. Maybe the kettlebells wouldn't hold. Maybe the skin would rot off his bones and he would float back to the top, and in three days he'd be bobbing like a top, right in the fairway's sight. "Don't jinx us."

They drove down five, then four, then three, and she finally allowed herself a full breath at the sight of their home, the second floor visible above the trees, peeks of their pool and their own pond coming into view. When they were back in the garage, the door closed behind them, she let out a sob and leaned in to Mark's body, clutching him as if he were a life raft and she were drowning.

It was, in their seven years of marriage, the first time she'd ever cried in front of him. He was typically, out of the two of them, the more emotional one. But he gripped her, and he didn't cry. He didn't do anything more than hold her, and that was fine. She needed him to be strong, and like always, he was what she wanted and needed him to be.

Back inside, she went straight to the shower and stared at the wall of tiles, the rainhead on its strongest setting, drilling her back with thin needles of heat. It shouldn't have been that easy to get rid of a body. She had spent the entire ride expecting a problem, her nerves as tight as a guillotine wire as she waited for the moment that it would all fall apart. Now her body was exhausted and her mind was nonstop, the silver ball in a pinball machine, ricocheting from one potential alarm to another.

The crime seemed foolproof but it wasn't. There was a hole, a gap, a something they'd forgotten, a something that would trip them up and flag them as guilty, a smoking gun that would land them both behind bars. She had to find it, to figure it out, to tie up whatever loose end was hanging, and it was likely that there was more than one. Maybe two. Three. Five. The entire basement was a crime scene. Evidence everywhere. He'd ridden in their car. More DNA. More fingerprints. His phone, the pieces in her garbage disposal. The call to 9-1-1 that she had started to place and stopped. Had she pressed send? Had she cleared out the numbers before she locked the device?

So many witnesses at the bar. What had they heard? What had they seen?

She turned off the water and stepped out into the bathroom. The heated floors were on, and she grabbed a towel off the warming rack and pulled it on. So far, everything seemed pretty airtight. Which didn't mean there wasn't a potential problem, only that she hadn't thought of it yet.

She twisted her hair up in a towel and pulled on her robe, avoiding a peek at the small gold clock that sat at the edge of her perfume bottles. She'd never realized how many clocks there were in this house. Every room had one, the hands ticking by, the time chasing her. One above the mantel in the living room. One on the microwave display. The small one that looked like a seashell by her bed. No matter what room she was in, her gaze was drawn to the clocks, her madness in tune with the ticks.

It had been twenty-three hours. Almost twenty-four. Had he been reported missing? Were the police already on the case?

David had leaned in and told her, his loafers hooked onto the rung of the barstool, that he and Sara were estranged. Said that they hadn't shared a bed in months. Was it true? He'd lifted his gaze to the ceiling and remarked that his condo was on the ninth floor, and suggested they come up for a drink. If he did live alone, his wife might not even know that he was missing. Did his office? Maybe he had a girlfriend. Maybe he had a dog. Her gut wrenched at the thought of a pet, locked in the condo, with no one coming. By now, their bowels would have given up. Their water dish would be empty.

The idea was somehow even more horrifying than the thought of Sara. A woman could fend for herself, could pick up the pieces of her life and build a new one. A dog . . . it wouldn't understand. It would know only that David left for drinks and never came back. It would know only that it was hungry and there was no one there to feed it.

She slid under the covers next to Mark, whose attention was fixed on the television. The channel was on a sports commentary where two men argued over a prediction, and he stared at the screen as if the outcome mattered. She rolled onto her side, away from him, and her stomach flipped in disgust. Was this how their life would continue? As if nothing were wrong, like nothing had happened? Tomorrow morning, would they go to brunch at Mariposa's and drink Bloody Marys and mimosas and order eggs Benedict and bitch about the service before overtipping the waitress? She plugged in her phone and pulled up social media, searching for David's name and scrolling down his profile.

For an hour, she read his posts, going back almost six years. She joined two local groups he was a part of and searched for and read all his comments. She read until her eyes ached and Mark snored, and she finally dropped the phone onto the bed and closed her eyes.

Willow went to sleep and woke up and waited with increasing anxiety for someone to sound the alarm about David.

Finally, three days after they'd dropped him into the water, word hit Crestmore that a husband was missing.

FIVE YEARS AGO

The Second Missing Person: Roxanne Kendal

CHAPTER 66

December 25, 2020
Thirty-Nine Days Before Roxanne Disappeared

They all took their seats for the meal, every insert added to the tables, thirty-four bodies in the ballroom, which was on the top floor of her father's house. Roxanne had eaten Christmas dinner in this room her entire life, and it had never changed, for as far back as she could remember. Same brown terrazzo floor. Same long white curtains over the windows. Same wooden tables. Same overhead fluorescent lights. The two men by the door were strangers, but had the same look of every one of her father's security detail, down to the blank expressions on their faces and the guns on their hips.

To her left was Eric, to her right was her cousin Michael, and Tori, her sister, was across the table, her new husband next to her. He had the alarmed look of a new addition, but that would fade over time. Take Eric. His first family meal, he'd been on the offensive the entire time. Today, her uncle Tony had tossed a football with him, even gave him a hug.

"What're ya, not drinking?" Michael poked her with his elbow and gestured to her tea.

"No, I am," Roxanne said quickly. "Assuming that a bottle ever makes it this far down the table."

Michael laughed loudly, someone belched from farther down the row, her mother gave a sharp reprimand, and the attention was off Roxanne, at least for the moment. Under the table, Eric's hand closed on her knee in a warning.

She didn't need it. They had discussed, ad nauseum, keeping her pregnancy hidden for as long as possible. At three months in, her ass had already started to balloon, and the comments from her family had been brutal. No one had yet made the connection, but there were still hours left in the meal. From the far end of the table, her favorite cousin waggled her fingers at her in a hello.

She smiled in greeting, but the nurse's eyes sharpened, sensing that something was wrong. She tilted her head toward the kitchen, suggesting a sidebar, but Roxanne shook her head minutely. *Not here.*

The prayer came just before the turkey was served, and as always, the first mention was of Joey. Roxanne inhaled deeply and thought of her brother.

"I'll always protect you, you know that, right?" The little boy had looked up at her with a fierce look on his eleven-year-old face, his hands balled into fists, as if he was ready to leave the hardware store right then and kick someone's ass.

He had still been relatively innocent then. That was before he'd started working at the distribution center. Before their dad had given him his first gun. Before he'd had his sixteenth birthday at the strip club. Before he'd killed his first man.

"Keep him in heaven with your angels until the time that we join him, Heavenly Father . . ."

Roxanne wasn't sure that Joey was in heaven. Her brother had killed at least a dozen men, and those were just the ones she knew about. There was only one way to rise to the top of a family, and that was by earning the respect and the reputation through blood.

Joey had been the future of the family, the son, the only proper heir in the hierarchy, until that night in October when he wasn't. His body was dismembered and mailed in eight different packages to different family members as a message. She had gotten hers at the hotel where she and Eric were honeymooning. It had been wrapped in expensive ivory paper, with a white satin bow, and was on the dresser of the suite's bedroom. As the waters of Saint Lucia sparkled out the window, Roxanne opened the package and stared at Joey's right hand.

The message was clear, and one she had felt her entire life. They—the forces who opposed her family—could get her anytime. There was no safe place, no weekend retreat, no moment of relaxation or celebration that was without risk.

When Joey had died, it was a sudden weight of pressure on her and Tori. Not the pressure of grief, but that of expectation. Her father was in his late sixties, her uncles and cousins doing their part to carry the business, but a new son was needed. A new future heir to the Accardi throne.

"I have an announcement." Tori spoke as soon as the prayer ended, and everyone paused, their silverware in midair, their attention snapping to Roxanne's younger sister.

Roxanne's stomach clenched because there were few good announcements to be made. Tori's decision to marry Richard had been the latest bad announcement, one that their father had taken hard, almost as hard as Roxanne's decision to marry Eric.

Eric's job, his money—it was all an issue with her family. Not because it was there, but because it hadn't been earned through the family, and therefore was assumed to have been earned in disdain of the family.

Eric didn't understand that. He didn't understand how their lifestyle was a threat or an insult to her relatives, and she didn't have the energy or the inclination to continue to try to explain something that didn't make sense. There was no rational justification for why her family hated him, except that he was different from them, and he had made her both different and independent of them, and that was unacceptable.

To add insult to injury, there were alliances that could have been formed with a marriage, and both Tori and Roxanne had failed in that strategic positioning.

"I'm pregnant," Tori said, and Roxanne inhaled sharply, her hand involuntary pressing on her own stomach in a defensive move of the baby that was growing there. Hopefully not a boy. God, she prayed that it wasn't a boy.

There was a pause, a moment where the announcement sank in, and then a round of spontaneous cheers. A baby was always a celebration, and Roxanne forced a smile with her applause.

"Fantastic." Her father beamed, lifting his glass in a toast as he half rose from his seat. "Let us drink to a boy. We are in dire need of a future head of the Accardi family."

Everyone cheered, and Roxanne lifted her glass and joined in on the toast. Her eyes met Tori's, and she could see the desperation hidden behind the tight smile on her face.

"Tori, you've been to Salvatore?" Her father retook his seat and everyone quieted. "All is healthy?"

"I'll go this week. I didn't want it to ruin the surprise." And it would have. Salvatore was their family doctor, one who was paid handsomely to handle injuries at all hours of the day and without asking questions. If an Accardi daughter came to him with a pregnancy, he would have tripped on the way to the phone to call their father.

"Do that tomorrow. And of course, you'll move into the house," her father instructed. "As soon as you confirm his gender." He set down his glass and picked up a steak knife. "Your mother will help you with it, but we need to keep it safe and make sure it's raised right."

Tori's husband's mouth opened as if he might argue, then closed, like a fish gaping for air. "It might not be a boy," he said meekly. "We don't know yet."

"Oh, I can feel that it is," her father crowed. "I was just telling Patrizia yesterday, wasn't I?" He twisted in his chair to face his wife.

"He did," she said smugly. "He said, right as we were going to bed, that we would have a grandson born this year. Tori and Roxy, I texted you both when it happened."

Yes, Roxanne had gotten the text. She had vomited after reading it, and it was anyone's guess if it was pregnancy nausea or a reaction to her mother's words, but it had felt like the woman was spying on them, like she knew of the secret they were keeping, and Roxanne had had Eric check the house for cameras and bugs, just in case.

"It might not be a boy," Tori cautioned, repeating Richard's statement, but her father wasn't listening.

Roxanne glanced at Eric, and from the somber look on his face, she could tell that maybe it was finally starting to sink in, what they were up against.

Her husband thought they could raise this baby on their own, insulate it from her father. But in this family, a boy was an asset, one that would be owned and controlled and groomed until the day he was put into service.

A son would never be theirs. He would always be her father's.

CHAPTER 67

January 19, 2021
Two Weeks Before Roxanne Disappeared

The news was delivered like the thrust of a blade, the doctor beaming as she waved the wand over Roxanne's belly and pointed out the small nub that was her baby's penis.

A boy. Roxanne reached out and gripped Eric's arm, her eyes welling with tears. She had known. She had felt this, in the same way that her mother had felt that a grandson was on the horizon; the fact had been in her gut this entire time. A baby boy.

She walked numbly out of the small clinic two hours north of San Francisco, a facility run by a med-school colleague of Eric's. They had promised the exam would be kept off the books, and made the appointment under a false name, and accepted the payment in cash.

"It's okay," Eric said, for the fourth or fifth time, as he opened her car door and helped her into the passenger seat. Her anguish swelled and she wished he would stop saying that. It was *not* okay. If he thought her family was an overbearing presence in their marriage now, he had no idea of what was to come. Tori's baby had been a girl, so now everything in their family's future was shouldered on this little fetus and his tiny little infant feet.

They were out of time. Roxy was starting to fill out in the face, the pregnancy weight causing her own feet to swell and her small breasts to balloon. Her mother's birthday party was in three weeks, and not attending wasn't an option. The last time Roxanne had missed a family event had been four years earlier, when she had gotten into a car accident on the way to the event and her aunt had sent a driver to the hospital to collect her. When the emergency room doctor had refused to release her, both of her parents had shown up four hours later, then visited her at home every day for the next two weeks. Eric had joked that he wasn't so sure that they cared about her well-being as much as confirming that the car accident was legitimate and not just an excuse to miss her cousin's retirement party.

"Don't worry." He fastened his seat belt and looked at her with a fierceness that both scared and comforted her. "We'll figure this out. We'll protect him."

She dropped her head back against the headrest and stayed silent. Eric's passion was great, but it didn't really matter how determined he was to succeed. When Nico Accardi set out to do something, he did it—and he'd never let his only grandson have a normal life. Her son would be raised and groomed to be the head of their criminal organization. Roxanne could either get on board with that or be cut out of her son's life. It didn't matter if it was legal or right. Her father played dirty, and she'd spent her life watching him ruin his opponents. He would think nothing of killing or destroying either of them if it meant getting the heir he needed.

"I love you." Eric put the car into drive and reached for her hand. "It'll be okay, Roxy. I promise you, we'll figure it out."

She nodded but didn't believe him. Unless they killed her father, it would never be okay.

CHAPTER 68

January 20, 2021

The next morning, she found Eric sitting on the back porch, cup of coffee in hand. He looked up with a smile, one that immediately dropped at the sight of her face. "What is it? Cramps? Pain?"

"This isn't going to work." She fell into the chair next to him and gestured to her face. "Look at me."

He didn't argue with her, and as much as she would have liked an innocent and sweet assertion that she didn't look like she was puffing up like a marshmallow, she appreciated the honest assessment when he sighed and nodded. "I know." He set down his coffee cup. "Roxy, I was up all night thinking, and I have an idea." He tented his fingers together. "It's crazy, but I think it's a solution."

She resisted the urge to roll her eyes; Eric had never had a crazy thought in his life. But then he began to outline the details of a plan that was, in fact, crazy.

She loved it from the minute she heard it.

As Eric talked his vision out, hope blossomed in her chest and spread throughout her entire body. Even her baby seemed to agree, kicking against her inner walls.

Peace.

Separation from the curse that she had lived with for her entire life, one that hung like a dark cloud over her marriage, her decisions, and her friendships.

Safety for her baby.

A normal life for her son.

And all that had to happen was Roxy needed to die.

CHAPTER 69

January 26, 2021
One Week Before the Disappearance

Eric had thought out the execution, and it seemed simple. Almost too simple. They just needed blood and a crime scene. She could donate the blood and stage the crime scene. And it could happen quickly, in the next forty-eight hours. Her heart skipped at the thought that freedom could be that soon.

No mother's birthday.

No interactions with her father—ever again.

Her problems, all of them—gone.

Eric had the blood bags and draw equipment. She would drive her Audi out to a secluded spot while Eric was out of town and around plenty of witnesses. She would stage the scene, then leave on foot and hike to an adjacent road, where she'd catch a ride that would take her far away from the scene. She'd stay out of town and out of sight during the investigation.

Her departure from the scene and to a safe location could be handled without an accomplice, but they agreed that a trusted individual would reduce the likelihood of a cab driver or public-transport employee identifying or recognizing her if the media ran the story, looking for leads.

The second part of Eric's plan was a little more concerning, but required if she wanted to keep her life. She'd have to drastically change her appearance in order to protect her identity and allow her to reunite with Eric. He had the medical connections and assured her that they could handle all the physical alterations with private surgeries that would be kept confidential, even from police investigations.

She would have to spend six months in seclusion until the baby came to term. Then the work would begin. A C-section that would include a breast augmentation, liposuction, and tummy tuck. One month later, the first round of facial reconstruction, including a brow lift, chin and cheek implants, and a facelift. Six weeks after that, a second round of facial refinements and a dye job, one that would make her a blonde. She would work with a speech therapist to remove the Italian lilt from her voice and have laser surgery on her eyesight.

She would emerge a completely new version of herself, one that nobody would ever recognize or associate with Roxanne Kendal. Not even her mother.

"And what about you?" she asked, studying her husband. "Will you love me if I look completely different?"

He looked at her as if she were mad. "It'll still be you, Roxy. I'm in love with your soul, not your face."

She had been afraid of the change, but also a little excited at what sounded like a supermodel makeover. For the first time in her life, she would be beautiful. Not just pretty or cute. Stunning. That was what the plastic surgeon had said after studying her X-rays and using his computer to forecast what her face would look like after the seventeen proposed procedures.

She looked at the woman staring back at her from the computer, and suddenly, the pain and the unknowns around the surgeries didn't seem so daunting. She loved the beauty of that woman and, even more, the freedom that woman would have. She could love her child out in the open. She could live with her husband without being tied to her family. She could have more children without worrying about whether they would ever be threatened by organized crime.

She spent a day thinking on it, making sure that she was okay with the plan and all that it entailed. It wasn't just the dangers to her and her health; it was also a huge risk to Eric. Staging a crime was a felony, a risk that was mild compared to the threat from her family, if they ever discovered the truth. Eric would face their scrutiny and suspicion, and the more believable Roxy's death, the more they would investigate and harass him. It would be bad for a long time, and their reaction to her death was likely to be explosive.

The next day they sat down at the dining room table and discussed everything. Eric was on board, and so was she. They talked through every single step and point, then stared at each other for a long uncertain moment.

"You'll need a new name," Eric said.

"I've thought of that. I think I'll go with your grandmother's name. I've always liked it, and it'll be a good way to honor her memory."

"Andrea?" Eric thought it over, then nodded. "I like it."

Andrea. Andrea Kendal.

It had a nice ring and seemed fitting for a fresh start.

CHAPTER 70

February 2, 2021

Roxanne dressed carefully on what would be her last day of life. She talked to her parents on the phone and ended the call with a promise to see them at the birthday party on Friday. She went grocery shopping and stocked the kitchen with all of Eric's favorite snacks, drinks, and ingredients. She wrote down his favorite meals and the recipes for each of them, though she doubted he would ever pick up a pot. They had gone over the timeline carefully. Eric would join her in Los Angeles for the birth and her major surgeries, but otherwise she would have to fend for herself. He needed to play the part of the grieving husband and would have to suffer as one until his path crossed with the new version of Roxanne and he "fell in love" with Andrea.

They weren't sure how long the timeline would be between Cameron's birth and Andrea's coming-out party to Eric's social circle. It would have to be after all evidence of her surgeries had healed, and there was no way to know if there would be complications from those. They had to mentally prepare for a separation as long as two years, though Eric hoped it to be closer to one. They also had to gauge public perception and not rush the introduction of a new wife too soon after Roxanne's disappearance.

The urge to pack a bag was maddening, but she resisted. Kisi would have a bag for her with a week's worth of clothes. Roxy wasn't on any medications, and would buy anything she needed in Los Angeles. There, in her new apartment, a two-bedroom townhome that was leased in Kisi's name, she'd finally be able to purchase a crib. Baby clothes. A breast pump and birthing books and diapers. She would be able to celebrate her pregnancy instead of hiding it.

And she would do it all alone. The thought hit her hard, and she paused, looking into the mirror and cupping her hands over her stomach. She and Eric had planned to get pregnant when his workload eased up, but not for a few years. This wasn't ideal, especially in how it had come about, but a baby was still a blessing. And this plan, as crazy and extreme as it was . . .

It would give her freedom. She was almost breathless at the thought.

She laced up her running shoes and rolled her socks over the bottom of her black leggings. She used athletic tape to carefully tape the blood bags to her stomach and sternum. Eric had drawn a pint and a half, an amount that he promised would make a mess. She pulled a thin T-shirt over the bags and topped it with a pullover sweatshirt. She left her hair down but put a hair tie on her wrist. The smartwatch, she left on the charger. The last thing they needed was for it to track her heartbeat long after her time of death.

As a final item, she went to the safe in the closet and opened it using the six-digit combination. In it were their passports, wills, the deed to their house, and a few stacks of emergency cash. She counted out $2,000 and put it in the zippered pocket of her sweatshirt. Before closing the safe, she hesitated and removed her passport, flipping it open.

Roxanne Accardi

She had never updated it after the wedding, and she ran her fingers over her maiden name. Being an Accardi had, in many ways, made her life easier. Doors had been opened for her—forced open, in some circumstances. Money had, her entire life, never been an issue. She had attended private schools and had her own driver. A driver who, as she grew older, she understood was a bodyguard. There had never been an attempt to shield her from witnessing the violence, but there had always been safeguards in place to protect her, Tori, and her mother. Even more so after her brother was killed.

The adage that the children were off limits was bullshit, at least in the circles that Nico Accardi operated in. He killed women and children as easily as he killed men. His competitors were more than happy to return the favor, which was why fear had become an accepted part of her life.

Would she know how to live without it?

She flipped through the pages. There were so many stamps. So many memories. Traveling was something that she and Eric loved to do. Together, they had explored Venice. Hiked Kilimanjaro. Swum in the Dead Sea and ridden elephants in South Africa.

Andrea would not be able to have a passport. They would have to limit their travels to spots within driving distance, but that was okay. World travel didn't work as well with a child in tow.

She returned the passport and closed the safe. Then she grabbed her purse, and Roxanne Kendal left her home for the last time ever.

She parked in the lot on the north end of the Fox Trail. Most runners and hikers parked and started on the south end, so she was unsurprised to see it empty. She took a spot on the end and called Eric's hotel in Austin. The operator transferred her to his room, and he answered on the second ring.

They went over the plan for a final time, then said their goodbyes. She ended the call and took a deep breath, steeling herself for the act. She would need to be quick and fast. No mistakes. No witnesses. If it took more than a minute, she was doing something wrong.

She opened her purse and removed her gloves and sweatshirt and double-checked the blood packets under her shirt. She took the large Ziploc bag out of her purse, then made a quick survey of the car. She tucked her purse into the passenger floorboard, out of a thief's sight. She opened the door and stepped out.

It was late afternoon, and the sun was already to the tree line, the long shadows casting the Audi into the shade. It was chilly, and she moved quickly, dropping the sweatshirt and gloves by the front of the car; then, reaching back into the vehicle and opening the center console, she removed the short paring knife. She closed the door and turned slowly, checking the entire lot—deserted—and the woods—quiet. The trail, which curved to the left after a long stretch, was empty.

Now or never. Quickly, before someone came. She took a deep breath, then lifted her shirt and pierced the bag with the paring knife. She yanked, tearing the bag open, and then dropped the knife and squeezed a quarter-size amount into her palms and rubbed them together. She shuffled back, then forward, making a mess of the mulch. Some blood dripped from her hands, and she went to grab for the door handle, intentionally missing it. She swiped at it again and grabbed the handle, yanking it open. Blood dripped from the gash in the bag, and she went to step in the SUV, using the steering wheel to pull herself in, then fell back. She left bloody palm and finger smears on the inner doorframe and seats, then shuffled back a dozen steps, gently punching her stomach repeatedly to encourage more blood to leak onto the mulch.

She heard a sound and paused, whipping her head around to see if anyone had appeared down the trail. No one was there, and she hurried back toward the SUV, using the same path and disturbing the mulch as she went. When she was back at the car, she slammed her side into the side mirror, bending it back, and grabbed it with her bloody hand for good measure.

Now to escape. She quickly stripped off the shirt and blood bag, shoving them into the Ziploc and sealing it shut. She grabbed the gloves and pulled them on, then the sweatshirt. After getting the air out of the Ziploc bag, she stuffed it into the top of her yoga pants and pulled the sweatshirt down over the bulge. She used her glove to shut the car door, then double-checked the scene.

It looked horrible. Blood everywhere, with clear signs of a struggle. Someone would be by here and see it and immediately call the police. She spotted the knife still on the ground, and grabbed it, leaving the car key in its place. Then she carefully stepped around the front of the car, making sure not to disturb the mulch, and moved into the woods, out of sight and in the opposite direction of the trail.

The woods were thinned out, and according to the map, there was a road a quarter mile to the north. She started to run, her breaths short, her panic starting to mount.

It was too late now. The crime scene was set. Her phone and wallet were in the car. She checked her watch, then remembered she didn't have it. She picked her way down the hill, moving as quickly and carefully as possible. The last thing she needed was a twisted ankle.

She cupped her stomach as she moved, rubbing the small swell of her belly. "Getting you to safety," she whispered. "I promise I'll take care of you."

Five minutes later, she broke through the trees and hit the two-lane road. She looked left, then right. A hundred yards down the road, Kisi flashed the lights of her Honda sedan.

FIVE YEARS AGO

The Third Missing Person: Willow Morrow

CHAPTER 71

When David Batcher's absence was finally noticed, the news swept over Crestmore like a fever. It was all everyone talked about, the speculations as varied as the emotions around it. Some were giddy at the idea, some cynical, some sad. Sara Batcher, who Willow watched as closely as possible, was blank. She walked into events with a mask on, her features quiet, her voice scratchy, her head still high, despite what everyone was saying about her.

There was a prevalent opinion that she and her yoga instructor had conspired to kill the man. Willow had fed the rumor mill, telling Chelsea Kuntic that she had seen Sara and the man having drinks at a small martini bar in Marin County and that they'd been all over each other. There were a few threads of conversation about a possible gambling addiction, and one that he'd run off to the Caymans with enough cash to set up a new life.

A month after David died, Mark wanted to mess around. He pushed her buttons in every way he could, but she didn't take the bait. He begged her to tie him down, to punish him for his part, to do something—but she couldn't. Whenever she felt the faintest surge of pleasure, her body shut down at the realization. She became colder and colder, and he grew needier and needier. She moved into the guest room, and Mark started to sleep on the couch. The more she withdrew, the more he clung to her.

She started to run each night on the course, pushing her body harder and harder in an attempt to make herself miserable. With each run, she stopped at the lake on the sixth hole and stared out at the smooth water, at the ripples exposed by the moonlight, certain that David would bob to the surface.

She did a juice fast for eleven days. Started to meditate. Stopped showering and let her armpit hair grow out. Her husband started to work from home and was checking on her constantly. He was a weighted blanket of suffocation, and the crueler she got, the more he wanted.

She met with a divorce attorney and had him structure a simple settlement, one that gave her enough funds to live comfortably while letting Mark retain the house and the bulk of their assets. She presented it to him after dinner, on a night when he was in an especially amiable mood. That night, he took enough pills to kill himself. He clung to her as he vomited and dry heaved onto the granite kitchen floors. Her psychiatrist told her that it was a call for attention and that as long as she was present, he would act out until she reacted.

The next night, on her run, she considered continuing on. Pulling a Forrest Gump and running until the road gave out. She could find a bus station. Convince someone to buy her a ticket. Make it all the way to the East Coast, somewhere Mark would never find her. Key West—she'd heard that it was nice.

Her watch pinged and she looked down at it to see a text from him.

COMING BACK SOON?

The following week, she had the attorney revise the divorce settlement into a one-page agreement that didn't require any follow-up transactions or transfers. It had him retaining all their assets and giving the attorney power-of-attorney to transfer any of her ownership to Mark. It divested her of the marriage and their communal property and waived any right to spousal support. She purchased a car with cash from their safe and parked it in the neighborhood's visitor lot.

She signed the settlement in front of a notary and, that night, slipped three lorazepams into Mark's drink. Once he passed out, she packed two bags, emptied the rest of the cash out of their safe, and left the paperwork and her cell phone on the dining room table with a note telling him that she was done and for him to sign the papers and return them to her attorney's office. She walked to the visitors' parking lot and left. She drove all night and stopped the following day in Oklahoma, where she pawned her four-carat wedding ring, one of her watches, and a pair of diamond earrings.

And just like that, Willow Morrow was gone.

CHAPTER 72

SARA BATCHER

16 Branwyn Hill
Hole 18, Silverwood Preserve
Present day

The interview room of the San Francisco substation was beginning to feel like a second home. Sara stood against the wall, her arms crossed over her chest, and watched Detective Palentick unwrap a cheesesteak sandwich like he had all the time in the world.

Beside him, the female detective wrote something on her notepad. She'd been doing that a lot, so much so that Sara was pretty sure it was just an elaborate doodle at this point. She paused and glanced at Sara. "So . . . you don't think David had a girlfriend? Or maybe a boyfriend?"

"I don't think so."

The woman smirked. "Come on, Sara. He had a condo downtown, which he stayed at frequently. He wined and dined customers. Traveled at least once a month. Every wife has suspicions at times. Did you ever dig? Go through his phone? Hire a PI to follow him?"

Ian spoke up from his spot at the table. "Sara, you don't have to answer that. Speculation."

Sara considered the questions and any potential land mines behind them if she told the truth. The truth was that she had always assumed that David was cheating on her in some way, even if it was only emotional. She had assumed that, and discovered, when she dug deep into her feelings on the subject, that she didn't care. Her therapist had said this lack of caring was indicative of Sara's own emotional distance from David.

In other words, she hadn't cared enough about him to care if he was faithful. And she hadn't exactly been faithful herself.

"I didn't dig," she said. "I swear I didn't. David was an adult, and what he did on his own, I didn't have time to babysit. I was really busy back then. My company was in a precarious position, and I needed to pay attention to it. I didn't have time or interest in scrolling through David's text messages or making sure he wasn't screwing his assistant." That, he was definitely doing. Even with eighty-hour weeks and the pressure of keeping InkRose afloat, Sara had sniffed that one out.

"He was likely sleeping with Keely. His assistant," Sara added, just in case they had forgotten her name.

"Yes, Keely Plett did confirm that they had a sexual relationship," the woman said, as casually as when she'd asked Detective Palentick for a pencil.

"Shocking," Sara drawled.

"I gotta say, cheating husband, life insurance payout, plus the divorce split of your assets . . . it's a lot of motive stacked up on your side," Palentick said through a mouthful of his sandwich.

"I didn't need the life insurance, I didn't care if he had a recreational sex buddy on the side, and David would have never divorced me." Sara shrugged.

"But you *were* poisoning him." He wiped his mouth with a paper napkin.

"She wasn't poisoning him—she was medicating him," Ian interjected. "And she shared that with you willingly. Sara has been your biggest resource in this investigation."

It was true. She'd had to harass them into even looking into David's disappearance. When everyone else had said that he had run off or was on a bender somewhere, she'd been the only one consistently saying that something was wrong, that something had happened.

And now look. A murder investigation, five years too late, with a skeleton that was useless in telling them what had happened. Go figure that poison was the only thing they could test for while also being the only thing they could use to implicate her.

She wasn't entirely sure that admitting to dosing David with lorazepam on a regular basis had been the right move. The police had been unsympathetic, and the line between Ian's eyebrows had grown more pronounced with each additional question they asked.

But he had told her to trust the process, so she was. He wanted her to be able to hold her head up high and know that she had shared everything. To not have a mini heart attack every time her phone rang and the detective's number flashed on the display. There was some peace, he promised her, in confession, and he believed that this confession might bring on some judgment but would not lead to an arrest.

She uncrossed her arms. "What about Brody Pitt? Did you find out more with that?"

"It's a dead end." Detective Palentick chewed, then swallowed. "We've talked to his family. Maybe you remember this, but five years ago, we questioned them as well. I don't want to speak in absolutes, but it's highly likely that they have nothing to do with this. David was just an extension of Formatic Medical. If they were going to go vigilante on Formatic, David wouldn't have been a likely target. You read his court testimony."

Yes, anyone who read or had listened to David's court testimony would have realized that her husband barely knew anything about the heart valves he had peddled. If anything, he could have been killed or sued for his incompetence, but certainly not for intentional malice.

"You're certain that it has nothing to do with that?" Sara pushed off the wall and returned to her seat, which she had abandoned twenty minutes ago, when her back had started to complain.

"We're certain," the woman chimed in.

"So then what was the reason?" Sara pulled the chair closer to the table and looked at both of them expectantly. "Who kidnapped him and dumped him in a lake?"

"You mean, who had motive other than you?" Palentick looked at her steadily, and it was in that moment that she realized they weren't looking for anyone else. They thought they had the killer and were just looking for the nails to hammer the conviction closed.

She turned to Ian for help, and he gave her a comforting look.

It didn't help.

CHAPTER 73

ANDREA KENDAL

1442 Kingsmere Drive
Hole 6, Stone Hollow

Andrea laced up her running shoes and double-knotted them. Rising to her feet, she smoothed over the top of her ponytail and grabbed her house keys, tucking them into the hidden zipper pocket of her leggings.

The first night at the new apartment, she'd stripped off her leggings and thrown them into the fireplace, along with the bloody shirt and blood bag. In a baggy tee and pajama pants, she'd started the fire and closed the grate, then moved into the small kitchen and put a bag of popcorn in the microwave.

As the kernels popped, San Francisco police had swept into her Crestmore home, questioning Eric in the dining room as detectives searched every nook and cranny of the seven-thousand-square-foot home. She'd watched the evening news and gotten a glimpse of Tony, his face stiff and angry, marching across their front lawn. Later, Eric had told her that Tony came to the house every day for the first couple of weeks, always with a new excuse or different question to ask.

They'd sent dogs into the state park to try to follow her scent. They'd pulled camera footage from intersections and security cameras in an attempt to see if her car was followed. They'd done a deep dive on her cell phone and cataloged every text and voicemail, call patterns, and location pings. They'd done the same with Eric's, certain that it would show an affair or a hit, something that implicated him in Roxanne's attack.

Now Andrea closed the back slider behind her and walked out the rear patio and down the stepping stones between the pool and the hot tub. At the far end of the yard, she re-latched the iron gate behind her and walked out onto the golf course.

For her first six weeks in the apartment, she and Eric never spoke. She'd gone to her obstetrician appointments alone and saved the ultrasound photos in a folder in a drawer in the kitchen. She'd done yoga each day, counted her calories, and switched to an all-organic and high-protein diet. She'd shopped online and listened to audiobooks and never left her apartment unless she had to. She'd watched the news coverage of Roxanne's disappearance and read online speculations and theories, and obsessed over how her family and father were handling the event.

She had expected, and was unsurprised, when he went nuclear. His first suspicion had been a competitor, and Kisi reported a lockdown of the entire family, which was followed by a spike in retaliatory actions. Unsatisfied by the bloodshed, her father had shoved his way into the investigation and the possibility of Eric's involvement in the crime. He'd sent goons to intimidate her husband and roughed up anyone thought to have a lead. Tony had questioned Kisi, but never as an accomplice, only a potential source of information that might help them find the culprit.

Dusk had fallen over the course by the time she made it to the sixth hole. She crossed the green and approached the woods, studying the pond, which glittered with the moonlight.

It was hard to imagine someone dumping a body there. She thought of David Batcher, whom she had met only once, at a charity event for multiple sclerosis. He had been friendly and funny, and told Roxanne a joke about two doctors at a boxing match.

David had never met Andrea. By the time she'd arrived, his flesh was likely already eaten off the bones by the lake's bacteria.

Andrea glanced up and down the hole. It was quiet and still. In the next ten minutes, a security cart would come by, double-checking that everyone was off the course for the evening. After that, no one until morning. Andrea had jogged the course on very rare occasions, but the course's dramatic rises and falls were too treacherous for a runner in the dark.

It had been smart, dumping the body here. In plain sight, but hidden. She stood on the edge of the water and imagined putting a body into it. You'd have to weigh down the body to keep it from floating up. And while you might be able to do it solo, two people would make the job a lot easier and quicker.

She looked over her shoulder, gauging the distance to their home. The police were right: It was a hundred yards, maybe less. It would have been easy for them to move David's body from their garage to the water, especially if they used their golf cart.

She and Eric had done away with Roxanne to protect her from her father, and then she'd brought Cameron, and now Ryder, to a home with a new killer, albeit one five years silent. She stood in the encroaching dark and lifted her head to the breeze, trying to sense if there was any evil in the air.

Instead, she felt only a sense of calm. David Batcher's death was a bump on their road, that was it. A moment of elevated scrutiny, which so far they had passed.

She turned and headed back to their home, breaking into a jog. Ahead, the three-story house gleamed in the dark, a jeweled box of warm perfection.

It had been worth it. Even if she was a cartoon character of beauty, one that her husband didn't love as much as his first wife.

Her children were safe. Her life was her own. Her marriage, intact.

She ran faster, suddenly desperate to get inside. To her left, the headlights of the security cart swept over the woods as it turned onto the hole.

CHAPTER 74

KATIE MORROW

28 Blackberry Summit Road
Hole 1, Stone Hollow

Katie considered the possibility of not returning home. After all, she had money. She could walk into any bank and access their checking and savings accounts, even their brokerage accounts. She could withdraw $100,000 and Mark wouldn't even blink. She could get an apartment in that cute little neighborhood by the wineshop.

They probably wouldn't even notice if she didn't come back. She'd driven past the house around midnight, and all the lights had still been on. They had probably stayed up all night drinking and laughing and had wild gymnastic sex on their bed with Willow screaming like a whore.

Katie wouldn't even tell Mark about the baby. She'd just let him see her big belly at the divorce proceedings. His stupid mouth would close in a small O of surprise, and her attorney would bring up child support, and he would drop to his knees and beg for her to take him back and she would be stoic and strong and tell him *he* had done this. Him and *her*.

Katie sat in her car, two homes down, and weighed her options. It was almost noon, and Mark hadn't called to see what time, if any, she was coming home. It felt like she would be limping across the finish line in last place if she just walked in, tail between her legs, sullen face on.

A car nosed through the gates of their house, and she winced when the older Jeep Cherokee swung in her direction. She opened the glove box and pawed through it, looking for something—anything—to explain why she was sitting on the shoulder of the road like a pathetic psycho.

Any hope of Willow driving past without noticing her ended when the Jeep pulled over on the opposite shoulder of the road and parked. The door opened and the tall brunette stepped out. She was wearing a long red cardigan and jeans with Birkenstock sandals. She had on a white baseball cap and wrapped the cardigan tighter around her waist as she crossed the street without looking. She rapped on Katie's window and gestured for her to roll it down.

Katie did. "Hi, Willow," she snapped.

"Let's go for a walk." Willow stepped toward the front of Katie's Porsche and waved at her. "Come on."

A walk. Katie considered, for the briefest of moments, rejecting the order, but her curiosity was stronger than her spite. She glanced in the side mirror, double-checking that no one was coming, then put on her hazard lights and turned off the engine.

The breeze was stiff and she paused in the cold blow, then opened the back door and grabbed the windbreaker she kept for emergencies. Shrugging it on, she met Willow at the hood.

Her husband's ex was rubbing her hands in an attempt to get warm, and blew into them, then nodded toward the sidewalk. "Come on."

They walked past the McCormicks', then the Shays'. Katie glanced through the open gates of her home, but there was no sign of Mark or what was happening inside the house. Maybe he was still asleep. Hungover on liquor and sex.

"We didn't fuck, if that's what you're thinking," Willow said, her sandals crunching over a group of dead leaves on the sidewalk.

Katie pinned her lips together in disbelief.

"I'm on my way out. I found a house-sit in Sedona that I'm going to head to. Need to be there in three days."

On her way out. It was both a relief and a letdown. Mark should have been the one to kick her out, to insist that it wasn't appropriate, her staying with them. Instead, it just felt like Willow was running again and likely taking a piece of her husband's heart with her. "So, what, we'll see you again in five years? Or when the next dead body turns up?" Katie said bitterly.

"Look, I haven't been fair to you." Willow stopped walking and turned to her. "But I want to give you a parting gifts, of sorts. About your husband."

Katie squinted up at Willow. She should have grabbed her sunglasses. Right now, the sun was streaming through the overhead trees and right into her eyes. "Forgive me if I don't trust your gifts."

"Sure, I get that. Here, let's move out of that glare." She grabbed Katie's arm and guided her out of the light and beside one of the big live oaks. It blocked the wind, and the chill lessened.

"Just tell me, Willow. Whatever it is."

"I left Mark because our relationship was violent. Abusive. That's why I ran away and didn't give him a way to contact me, and why I stayed off the grid."

"Bullshit," Katie spat. "Mark's not like that."

"You're right, he's not." She paused. "I am. And Mark liked the way I was."

It took a moment to process the double punch the woman had just delivered. "*You* were abusive?"

"Yes. I was rough with him during sex. I tied him up to punish him. I hurt him until he begged me to stop, and I locked him in a cage in the basement when he was bad."

Katie choked out a laugh. Now she understood the issue: The woman was insane. "No, you didn't."

"Yes, I did." Willow didn't act insane. She spoke as if she knew exactly what she was talking about. "And he liked it."

"N-no one would like that," Katie sputtered.

"Mark did. And he still does. Which might be a problem in your marriage, if you don't figure out a way to handle it. He's drowning right now. He needs structure and discipline, or he's going to lose his mind."

Katie felt like her legs were going to give out. She turned away from Willow and covered her mouth with both hands, processing the information. This was bullshit. She was exaggerating. She had to be. "You're lying," she said weakly.

"It's why I left. The more I tried to withdraw, the clingier he got."

Katie took a step away, then another, stumbling back toward the car as she attempted to process the lies. Lies, definitely. Had to be.

"You can pretend it's not true," Willow called out. "But it is."

When Katie made it back to the safety of her car, she pulled her Balenciaga bag into her lap and yanked it open. Then she leaned forward and vomited into it.

CHAPTER 75

WILLOW MORROW

28 Blackberry Summit Road
Hole 1, Stone Hollow

Willow stayed by the tree, giving Katie time to flee, like a little bird into the brush. She leaned against the oak and waited until the blonde drove by, her tires squeaking a little from the acceleration. Katie pulled into their driveway and Willow watched as her bumper disappeared through the gates.

Run along home, little bird. Run into his arms. She gave one last look at the house, at her old life. Then she walked slowly to her car and opened the door.

It was such a shit car. Katie had been in a Porsche SUV, and Willow thought of the Maserati. How it had felt driving it to Sara's. The feel of the heated leather, the smell of the interior. The luxurious cushion of it. Willow had loved driving that car. She'd used it on the weekends, putting down the top to go to Miguel's for lunch or Fillmore Street to shop. She'd driven her G-Wagon during the week, using the luxury German SUV to pick up her groceries and Mark's dry cleaning, to hold her tennis racket and gym bag.

God, she missed this life. The ease of it. The stupid focus on things that didn't matter. The faux stress over dinner party menus and HOA notices.

She could get it back. Pull into the driveway and walk up to Mark and tell him that she would stay. Tell him to get rid of Katie and remarry her.

He'd do it. He'd do it so quickly that poor little Katie's head would spin. And maybe later . . . in her new apartment, reading over the fine print on the divorce settlement . . . maybe then Katie would believe what Willow had just told her.

Willow held the fantasy on her tongue, savoring the taste of it as she turned the key and cranked the Jeep's engine. It chugged and then stopped. She sighed and tried again. This time it caught, and she turned on the defrost and stared through the frosted windshield at the giant gates of her old house.

It had felt good, last night. Standing above Mark, his face tilted up in adoration and longing. She had missed the feeling of power and control. And the worship from him . . . the pure permission to do whatever she wanted, the more horrible, the better . . . that level of trust and freedom was a drug, one that she had proved she couldn't handle.

Yes, she could take him back, make him sacrifice everything for her—but it would end the same way it had five years ago, except that instead of David Batcher dying, it would be Mark, or some other pure thing that their debauchery ruined or killed.

Willow Morrow had been selfish for the majority of her life, but this was one moment that she had to do the right thing. Again.

She shifted the car into gear and, for the second time, drove out of Mark's life and disappeared.

CHAPTER 76

SARA BATCHER

16 Branwyn Hill
Hole 18, Silverwood Preserve

"They're going to arrest me." Sara dropped her head onto the open folder before her.

From the other end of the long dining room table, Maggie closed her eyes as she stretched her neck to one side. "The charges won't stick," she finally said. "They'll release you on bail, and it will go to a jury trial, and they won't convict. There's no evidence."

Sara sat upright and looked over the table, which was a disorganized mess of photos, receipts, phone statements, and more. In it, there was enough to prove that David had been a philandering drug addict with a mountain of problems, all of which unhelpfully stuck more red flags on Sara's back.

There had been a gambling addiction. One she hadn't even been aware of, but that had racked up several hundred thousands of dollars in debt. The problem? David had paid it all, didn't owe his bookie a dollar. More motive for Sara to whack him, though, just to stop that bleed.

Add in his wandering penis. One that had apparently stuck itself in his assistant, his boss, his dental hygienist, a cart girl at the golf course, and their dry cleaner's nineteen-year-old daughter. While it could be argued that his poor bedroom performance might drive anyone to murder, the cops hadn't found it suspicious, and Sara was inclined to agree. Sleep with David and murder wouldn't be the first thing on your mind. A follow-up self-pleasure session to finish the job? Much more likely.

Tack on poor job performance. In addition to the lawsuit over Brody Pitt's wrongful death, David had been on the short list to be fired, largely because of his pain pill addiction, which hadn't been the ironclad secret that Sara had assumed it to be. Turned out, she was less than two weeks away from being David's sugar mama, a promotion she hadn't wanted and wouldn't have stood for. Killing him over that was ridiculous, but apparently plausible, if you listened to the detectives.

The evidence was clear. Sara had been married to a loser. A charming, problematic loser—one who had screwed her over in the worst possible way: by pinning a murder conviction on her.

She looked down the table at Maggie, who was paper-clipping two documents together, and was struck with a sudden wave of gratitude. "Thank you," she said.

"For what?"

"You're the only one who believes me."

"If you had killed David, you would have asked me to help you hide his body," she said simply, as if it was obvious.

"Well, that's an even better reason. You'd help me hide a body."

Maggie moved around the end of the table and approached Sara, wrapping her arms around her shoulders and pulling her in for a hug. "You know I love you, and I'm here for you. No matter what."

Sara sagged. "I'm scared," she whispered.

"I know. I am too. But we'll get through this together." Maggie detangled herself. "Sit tight. I'm going to get us a drink."

Sara watched as Maggie moved toward the kitchen and to the wine chiller. She closed her eyes as a brief memory of David surfaced. The night she'd launched the InkRose website, an amateurish attempt at e-commerce, but one they had celebrated with margaritas and fish tacos at a dive bar two blocks from David's condo.

It was a bittersweet memory, and she blinked back an unexpected surge of tears, her hand quickly brushing at the edges of her eyes.

"Hey," Maggie said quietly, approaching from the kitchen, two wineglasses in hand. "None of that."

"It's just . . ." Sara sniffled. "He was a good guy, you know. Despite all the . . ." She gestured toward the table.

"Meh. Agree to disagree. I will say that you brought out the best in him." Maggie reached out and gripped Sara's forearm. "You were a great wife."

Sara's face crumpled. It was nice of Maggie to say that, but she hadn't been a great wife. She hadn't even been a good one. She had been a good entrepreneur. A good checklist-builder. Excellent at building a brand, a team, and a customer base. Horrible at everything required of a successful marriage.

Truth be told, she had been happier after he'd left. Almost relieved when she'd found out he was dead. The strongest emotions she'd felt since his body turned up were guilt and dread, both selfish emotions that were centered more on the consequences of her actions versus the mourning of a spouse.

And just like that, the final piece of the emotional puzzle clicked into place, and she really realized, for the first moment, that he was gone. Not out of her life, because that aftermath had been a reality for a long time, but out of this world. His heart, which she had listened to in the middle of the night, her ear flush against his warm chest, the sound comforting and calming, a metronome of consistency. It would never beat again. His laugh, which was a belt of pure unrestrained joy, one you could hear across a crowded room, would never sound. He'd never look at her in that way, the one where his skin crinkled at the corners of his mouth, and his mouth twitched into a smile because he was amused by something she'd said or done. He'd never stop at the ice cream shop on the way home to pick her up a pint of cookies-and-cream. He'd never see a Volkswagen on the highway and punch someone's arm.

He would never experience being a father, not even to a dog. He wouldn't ever hit that hole in one or go ice fishing in Alaska or see a Packers game on Lambeau Field.

An overwhelming sense of horror hit at the loss of everything undone in his life, and the thousand ways that he would no longer affect the world and the people in his life.

All because she hadn't been able to deal with his mood swings. All because it had been easier for her to medicate him rather than tolerate him.

"Hey, now . . . shhh." Maggie pulled her into her arms and squeezed her tightly. "Don't cry. Sweetie. Stop."

"I did this," Sara sobbed. "It was me." The possibility, which had always felt rather remote—especially after speaking to the medications expert Ian had brought on in the event this ever reached trial—suddenly felt absolute.

Lorazepam could have triggered a reaction that had killed David. Lorazepam she had administered.

"You don't know that," Maggie said firmly. "Anything might have killed him. Anything and anyone." She squeezed Sara and rocked gently from side to side, shushing her cries.

Anything and anyone. The possibility felt like a cop-out. Sara closed her eyes and sent a silent apology up to David, wherever he might be.

TRAIL COLD IN DAVID BATCHER MURDER

The investigation against Sara Batcher, former InkRose CEO and cofounder, for the murder of her pharmaceutical salesman husband, David Batcher, has closed, according to the San Francisco Police Department. The investigation, performed more than five years after David's disappearance, has been slow, hampered by weak memories and poor recordkeeping by all parties. Chief Joel Stanton stated in a recent interview that "the strong work by our detectives can't overcome a lack of forensic evidence."

Batcher's team of high-priced defense attorneys worked overtime since the discovery of David Batcher's body in Crestmore Estates earlier this year. Sara Batcher was an early suspect, and where most of the investigative efforts have been focused.

With no other strong suspects, the case is likely to return to its cold case status, unless new evidence is introduced.

Anyone with information on the crime is encouraged to call Crime Stoppers at 800-CRIME-CA.

CHAPTER 77

KATIE MORROW

28 Blackberry Summit Road
Hole 1, Stone Hollow

Katie sat on the upper porch of their bedroom balcony and watched the sunset, a glass of wine in hand. Beside her in the soft bassinet swing, Chloe Resin Morrow cooed and gurgled to herself as she played with the hanging mobile above her cocoon.

It really was a beautiful lot. She could understand why Willow and Mark had picked it. The view and privacy were unparalleled, though they couldn't have known that they would be needing to haul a dead body out of the back of it. Still, it had risen to the occasion, and now, with the case closed pending new evidence, it seemed like they had gotten away with it.

Thanks to Katie. Her decision to keep her knowledge to herself and her mouth shut was the only thing that had kept them both out of jail. Sure, they could claim that David's death had been an accident, but with just a skeleton, that would be next to impossible to prove. Three adults had entered their home that night, and one had ended up at the bottom of a lake, weights tied to his limbs. It didn't take a PhD to figure out who was guilty there.

It was the weights that had tipped Katie off. In one of the press conferences, the station had shared a photo of the two kettlebells investigators had found at the bottom of the lake and believed had been used to weigh down David's body.

She knew those weights. She knew those weights because when she'd reorganized the mess that had been Willow and Mark's house, a hodgepodge of expensive workout equipment had been in the junk room, including a set of kettlebells. An incomplete set of kettlebells.

Katie had donated them, along with half of the items in that room, but not after photographing each one, assigning a value, and adding it to a database of donation items that she provided to the local Goodwill and their tax accountant, to ensure that they received a proper deduction.

It had taken less than a minute to pull up the photos and verify that the set was missing two of the powder-coated twenty-pound weights.

Katie printed out the photos and stored them with the memory card of the audio recordings of the night she'd left Willow and Mark alone. She had placed hidden mics in their bedroom, Willow's guest room, the kitchen, living room, and back patio. She had been expecting to catch Mark cheating, but had instead captured hours of walks down memory lane, including a concerned conversation about the ongoing police investigation. At the time that she'd first heard it, she'd found Willow's interest in David's homicide odd, but after making the kettlebell connection, she gave it another listen.

"Can you imagine if we'd had the security system back then?" Mark.

"No. Someone else on the course might have, though. You sold the cart?" Willow.

"Yeah. Just in case. The basement remodel was down to the studs. You think I don't take care of stuff, but I do." Mark.

"You know I came back to make sure you didn't fuck anything up." Willow.

**A laugh* "With what?" Mark.*

"Anything. You were always a shitty liar." Willow.

"You came back because you missed me. Admit it." Mark.

"I'm going to get another drink." Willow.

Of course, the recordings would never be admissible in court, not with California's laws on two-party consent. Still, the tapes were valuable, as was the parting information Willow had shared. Information that, despite Katie's initial disbelief, seemed to be true.

She wasn't going to beat Mark or handcuff him or do any of the ridiculous things that Willow had mentioned, but she had taken the information to her psychiatrist and gotten a master's course worth of education on how she could stimulate and satisfy Mark's desire for domination in ways that didn't gross her out or cause any harm.

Chaos, as it turned out, was what her emotionally absent husband needed. She'd first introduced it unintentionally, by filing for divorce. It was a move that flipped their power dynamic and had Mark suddenly ravenously interested in his now-cold and bitchy wife. She had yielded, staying in the marriage but with a new MO, one where she held the reins and he jumped however high she demanded. A new nursery, one he had finished out himself. She'd had him hang the wallpaper twice, then decided she preferred him to strip it all out and do a venetian-plaster finish instead, a painstaking process that had him applying layers of lime putty and marble dust. In the final months of her pregnancy, she'd demanded he rub her feet and calves while she binge-watched episodes of a trashy reality love competition, then sent him out for her favorite snacks. If he ever balked or refused, she turned ice cold and left. Once, she'd spent a week away, relaxing at a spa resort in Malibu, his number blocked from her cell phone, and returned to find him frantic and apologetic.

It was strange, having power in this relationship, but she didn't dislike it. There was a delicious freedom in having all the attention and respect and the ability to write all the rules.

The easy thing to do would have been to leave. Her prenup agreement was skinny, but it would have given her enough money to get an apartment and tide her over until she found a job.

Not the happy ending she had hoped for, planned for, worked for.

No. Every man had something wrong with him. If she knew the worst in Mark and could use that to her benefit, then she could stay in this life and make it even better, both for her and for their daughter.

And if one day Willow popped back into their lives, or if Mark stopped being a good husband, Katie could always pull out the file, dig deeper into the past, and make sure they both paid for whatever they'd done to David.

Maybe. But not today. Today, as a bird chirped from the nearby live oak tree and the breeze carried in a whiff of honeysuckle, she had everything she wanted. A beautiful baby, a husband who worshipped her, and absolute control over their lives and future. She took a deep sip of wine and closed her eyes, enjoying the warmth of the sun and savoring the moment.

No. Today was definitely not that day.

Acknowledgments

This story began with a simple idea: A woman who vanished years ago returns to her old life. Straightforward enough . . . until the character count started growing, the subplots multiplied, and the twists grew deeper. That's my favorite part of writing fiction. I never quite know where the story is going to head, but I thoroughly enjoy the journey. And this journey was a blast.

To start, I'd like to thank Megha Parekh, who was instrumental in helping me shape the seed of this idea into the layered novel you now hold. Our conversations about characters, motivations, and what-ifs made this book what it is, and I am forever grateful for our creative relationship and the trust and support you give me. Charlotte Herscher, thank you for understanding my style so well and for always pushing me to elevate the story. I love where this novel landed, especially the ending, and I'm grateful for the path you steered us toward to get there. To Rachel Norfleet and your team—thank you for your eagle eyes, excellent catches (so many of them!), and thoughtful insights. You helped to make this book shine.

A big thank-you as well to my agent, Maura Kye-Casella. You've stood by me for more than a decade now, and your faith in me and my work never wavers. I hope to get you down to Key West sometime soon, and buy you a cup of Baby's Coffee and a steak.

And to the rest of the team at Thomas & Mercer—you are the invisible hands that make sure everything shines, from the words on the page to the final book in a reader's hands. I'm so thankful to have you in my corner. A special thank-you to Grace Doyle, Logan Matthews, and Andrew George.

I also want to acknowledge the wives of Sandestin, the gated community I called home for seven years. While no dead bodies ever appeared on its golf courses (thank goodness), the personalities and everyday dramas were more than enough to keep my creative well full. Many of those experiences found their way onto the page in one form or another, and I suspect I'll be drawing on them for years to come.

To the readers and reviewers: This book exists because of you. Every review, every recommendation, every impromptu video, reading list inclusion, late-night message . . . your feedback and reactions are the fuel that keeps me writing. I hope *The Missing Ones* gripped you, surprised you, and kept you awake later than you intended.

With gratitude,
Alessandra (A. R.) Torre

About the Author

Photo © 2022 Jane Ashley Converse

Edgar and ITW Thriller Award nominee A. R. Torre is a pseudonym for *New York Times* bestselling author Alessandra Torre. Torre's bestsellers include *Every Last Secret*, *The Good Lie*, *A Familiar Stranger*, *The Last Party*, *A Happy Marriage*, and more. She lives in Key West, Florida, where she owns a coffee shop and tends to her pet chickens. Learn more at www.artorrebooks.com.